IN THE
BAG

IN THE
BAG

JiM
CARRiNGTON

BLOOMSBURY

LONDON BERLIN NEW YORK SYDNEY

Bloomsbury Publishing, London, Berlin, New York and Sydney

First published in Great Britain in February 2011
by Bloomsbury Publishing Plc
50 Bedford Square, London, WC1B 3DP

A CIP catalogue record for this book is available from the British Library

ISBN 978 1 4088 0270 0

3 5 7 9 10 8 6 4

Typeset by Hewer Text UK Ltd, Edinburgh
Printed in Great Britain by Clays Ltd, St Ives plc, Bungay, Suffolk

MIX
Paper from
responsible sources
FSC® C018072

www.bloomsbury.com

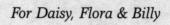

For Daisy, Flora & Billy

FRIDAY

Ash

Friday night is what I'm all about. It's what I live for. If I had my way, I'd sleep through the rest of the week and wake up around four or five on a Friday, then stay awake till Monday morning.

Right now I'm getting ready to go out to the rec. Just like every Friday night. My iPod is docked, music turned up to full, listening to this new American band called the Porn Dwarves. They're amazing. Hardly anyone in this country has heard of them yet. But they soon will.

I grab the deodorant off my desk and give myself a spray all over, even the delicate bits. You never know your luck, do you? Then I strut over to the wardrobe, nodding my head in time to the music. I open the door and have a look for something decent to wear, pull all my jeans down from a shelf and let them fall on the floor. I pick out the black ones that are ripped right across the knees and give them a little inspection. They're a bit dirty. Grass stains from last Friday night, to be precise. But I pull them on anyway. No one's gonna notice at the rec cos it'll be too dark. And everyone will be as wasted as me.

I take a belt off a pair of jeans that are lying on my drum stool and put it on. Look in the mirror. Looking good. I scrub up nicely, even if I say so myself.

I play along to the Porn Dwarves drum solo – give it a bit of air drums – before I look back in my wardrobe and pull out a T-shirt. The black one with a skull on it and silver writing underneath: *Live fast, die young, leave a good-looking corpse*. Too right. That's my philosophy right there. Who wants to die sitting in an old people's home at ninety years old, stinking of piss? Not me. I'd rather be hanging out with Kurt Cobain and Jimi Hendrix and Jim Morrison and Heath Ledger on a cloud with a bottle of whisky, a spliff and my drum kit.

I grab a black zip-up hoodie from the back of my desk chair and a cap that's lying on the floor. Keys, money, fags, mobile. I check my mobile. Fuck it, the battery's nearly run down. I send Joe a text anyway to tell him I'm nearly ready. Undock my iPod, grab my trainers, pull them on and I'm out.

Downstairs, I put my head round the lounge door. Mum's sitting on the sofa, glass of wine in her hand, watching TV. She looks up.

'You off out?'

I nod. I look round the room. 'Dad not home?'

Mum shakes her head. She takes a gulp of wine. 'At work,' she says. She sounds pissed off.

I nod. 'Oh,' I say. 'Right. See you later. Don't wait up.'

Joe

I'm in my room trying to get ready to go out when my phone buzzes in my pocket. It's a text from Ash. **Meet u at the end of ur road in 5 mins**. I put my phone in my pocket and look in the mirror. My hair looks shite, like someone left a pile of straw on my head. I try and sort it out with my hands, pull it over my face, brush it over one side of my head and then the other. I sigh. Useless. I look like a scarecrow that's got birds nesting on its head. Maybe I should get it all cut off. At least that way I wouldn't have to worry about what it looks like.

I go through to the bathroom and fill the basin with water and dunk my head in it. Then I try and plaster my hair down and look in the mirror. Great. Now I look like a drowned scarecrow. I sigh. It'll have to do.

I give my teeth a clean and then go downstairs. Mum and Dad are in the kitchen. Dad's leaning against the kitchen worktop, staring out of the back window and listening to the radio.

Mum's doing the washing up. She looks up as I walk through the hall. 'Hello, Joe.'

Dad turns round. 'Hey, Joe,' he says. It's his joke. It's the name of a Jimi Hendrix song. It's why I'm called Joe apparently, even though Mum and Dad aren't old enough to remember the song when it came out.

'I'm going out now.'

'OK,' Dad says. 'Where are you off to? No, hang on, let me guess . . .'

'The rec,' I say before he has a chance to do his whole routine.

Mum doesn't say anything, but I can tell what she's thinking from the look on her face. Ever since Christmas, when I went down the rec with some friends and got completely wasted, she's been kind of quiet when I say I'm going there.

'The rec?' Dad says sarcastically. 'I never would have guessed that.' He winks at me.

'Who are you going with, love?' Mum says, ignoring Dad.

'Just Ash and Rabbit and that lot.'

Dad nods. 'Well, have fun. Don't do anything I wouldn't.'

'Just make sure you're careful,' Mum says. 'I don't want . . .' She doesn't finish her sentence.

Dad looks at Mum. 'Give him a break,' he says. 'He's learned his lesson, haven't you, Joe?'

I nod. I can feel myself blushing.

Mum smiles at me like I'm a little kid. 'I know. Just me being silly, treating you like you're still my little baby. Have fun,' she says.

I nod my head and then I'm gone.

A little explanation about the Christmas thing. We all arranged to meet up down at the rec on the evening of the last day of term. We were gonna bring some booze and have a party kind of thing. So I had a look around the house and found some whisky – Mum'd already got it in for when Dave (my uncle) came round on Boxing Day. I poured some of it into a water bottle and then refilled the whisky bottle with water. Thought no one'd notice.

When I was down the rec, I started to knock back the whisky neat. It tasted disgusting to begin with, made my throat burn and my stomach twist around. I thought I was gonna vom. But it was all right after a bit. I got used to the taste. It stopped hurting to drink it. Either that or I stopped being able to feel anything. I finished the whole bottle. I think. See, it's all a bit fuzzy. I can remember everything before the rec. And I can remember getting there. But I can't really remember what happened after that. I haven't got a clue what I did, where I went, how I got home. None of it. Apparently I was being a bit of a twat, shouting my mouth off and that. Which isn't like me. I'm usually quiet. Shy.

Next thing I know, it's the next morning and Mum's waking me up. I'm lying on the lounge floor. And all over the front doorstep, there's a pile of my sick. Mum and Dad go mental at me at first. And Kate, my sister, just sits there in her dressing gown and smirks. But they leave it at that. I still feel like an utter dick whenever I think about it.

Ash is waiting at the end of my road when I get there, slouching on his BMX. He's got a fag hanging out of his mouth. He really doesn't give a toss, Ash. If I smoked, there's no way I'd do it where people could see me, in case they told my mum and dad.

'All right, J?'

'Hi, Ash,' I say.

'You ready to get wasted or what?' Ash says. He's got a mad grin on his face.

'Yeah. Course,' I say. But in my head I'm thinking, *I'm not sure how wasted I want to get. I don't want to wake up on the lounge floor again.*

We start pedalling along the pavement, and then out on to the main road. It's the quickest way to the rec: along the main road, past the pub and the police station and the fire station and the memorial hall.

We pedal in silence for a bit, get some dirty looks from an old couple walking their dog cos we're riding on the pavement and they have to move out of the way.

'Hey, J,' Ash says. 'You know who texted me earlier?'

I shake my head.

Ash lets go of his handlebars. 'Lucy Crow!' he says. I can tell, even though I can't see his face, that he's got a massive cheesy grin. So would I if Lucy Crow was texting me.

'Jesus. Why?'

'Ah, you know,' Ash says. He takes hold of the handlebars again and pulls a wheelie. He manages to keep the wheelie going for ages before he lets the front wheel come back down to the pavement. 'She wants me.'

'Really?'

Ash nods. 'Yeah. She'll have to join the queue, though.'

I roll my eyes. Ash doesn't realise how lucky he is. He has girls literally throwing themselves at him and he acts like he couldn't care less.

'What about you?' Ash says. 'Anyone you like?'

I don't answer right away. I feel shy for some reason. I bet I'm even blushing. 'Don't know,' I say. Even though I do know. There is someone. But I don't want to tell anyone. Not even Ash. Especially not Ash.

'There must be someone.'

I shrug. 'I can't figure it out.'

'What?'

'Girls. Women,' I say. 'It's all foreign to me. Do you know what I mean? I don't know how to make girls like me . . .'

Ash smiles. He nods his head. He makes a face like some wise old man who knows all the answers. 'Well, you've come to the right place,' he says. And then he laughs.

He puts his brakes on and stops. I stop beside him. We're right outside the new flats that they've been building for months.

Ash looks right at me. 'The thing with girls, J, is that they're different from us. It's like they come from an alien planet or something.'

I nod. I thought I was gonna get a straightforward answer that solved all my girl problems. Looks like I was wrong.

'There's only one rule where girls are concerned,' Ash says. 'And it's a simple rule: never try and understand what a girl is thinking because you'll always get it wrong.'

11

I laugh. I wonder if he'd say that stuff to a girl. Actually, he probably would, knowing Ash. And then she'd probably get off with him. 'OK,' I say. 'But the thing is, I can't even go and speak to girls. My mouth just clams up.'

'Why?'

I shrug my shoulders. 'Dunno,' I say. Although to be honest, I do know. It's cos I don't want them to ignore me or turn me down.

Ash starts cycling again, slowly. After a few seconds he takes his hands off the handlebars and puts them in his pockets. 'Talking to girls is easy, J,' he says. 'All you have to do is use the Jedi mind trick on them.'

'Huh?'

'You know, like in *Star Wars*.'

I nod. I know what the Jedi mind trick is, but I have no idea why Ash is going on about it. 'What are you talking about?'

'Look, J, we may not be able to understand what goes on in girls' minds, but it's very possible that they can read our minds. So what you have to do is imagine that you're the Jedi, right? You are Obi-Wan Kenobi.'

'OK.'

'And the girl – whoever it is – is like a stormtrooper. She's the one that's standing in your way – you know, stopping you getting where you want to go . . .'

I make a really dubious face. Ash sometimes talks utter shit like this.

He stops his bike again. We're right close to the rec now.

'What you have to do is use the force. Like in *Star Wars* episode four . . . You know, the bit where Obi-Wan Kenobi and Luke are in the hover car and the stormtroopers have stopped them, looking for droids.'

I nod.

'And Obi-Wan starts talking to the stormtroopers and telling them what to think, like, "These are not the droids you are looking for." They start repeating it back to him like it was their idea in the first place, right?'

'Yeah. And?'

'Well, you're like Obi-Wan. All you have to do, young Jedi, is use the force. Jedi mind trick.' Ash taps his head and smiles.

'So I start telling girls that these are not the droids they're looking for and all my girl problems are solved?'

Ash laughs and shakes his head. 'No, Jedi, you make them believe what you want them to believe,' he says. 'Your problem is that you spend too much time worrying, and girls pick up on that stuff. If you go over and talk to a girl thinking she's gonna turn you down, she will. But if you go over to her all confident, she'll pick up on that. They'll do exactly what you want. Just don't show them any weakness or doubt.'

'I don't know about that.'

'It works,' Ash says. 'Just block any doubt out of your mind and you can make any girl believe anything you want her to. Try it.'

I shake my head. I can't imagine myself being all cocky and confident like Ash. It wouldn't suit me. Girls would just laugh at me. 'It wouldn't work.'

'Want a bet?' Ash says. He starts cycling again, alongside the railings of the rec. 'I'll prove it to you. You point a girl out to me today, and I'll use the Jedi mind trick on her.'

I smile. 'OK,' I say. 'Anyone?'

Ash nods. 'Yeah. Be kind, though.' He stops and opens the gate to the rec, wheels his bike through. 'No chavs or mingers.'

I smile. 'All right, deal.'

Ash laughs. 'Watch and learn, young Jedi. Watch and learn.'

We cycle across the rec to the bench, where three others are already gathered.

Ash

How do you describe the rec on a Friday night? Easy. One word: mayhem.

It's quite funny the way the rec is. We have our own bench, over on the left-hand side of the rec, kind of hidden away a bit. Our bench is like the alternative bench. It's got a load of band names written on it in marker pen. And some other stuff like *GT 4 AB* – you know, boyfriend and girlfriend stuff. My tag's on there too: *Layzee Eyez*. The chavvy kids hang out on the other side of the rec, near the road. They sit on the wall and smoke fags and wear tracksuits. We don't really mix much, the indie kids and the chavs. Just kind of respect each other's space instead. And then

15

there are the older kids, the ones who think they're something special, turning up in their souped-up Peugeots and Fiestas, parking up near the chav girls and then taking them for a ride. If you catch me doing that when I'm seventeen, please just shoot me. I want to be out of this hole by then.

Tonight there're ten or so of us hanging out by the indie bench. Usually someone's brought some booze from home. Sometimes I raid Dad's drinks cabinet. He's a whisky drinker – gets through a bottle or two a week. He doesn't miss the odd bit now and then. But tonight I haven't got any on me. So there are only two options open to me: 1. stay sober, or 2. go and get an older kid to buy some booze for me. And seeing as option 1 is not really what I have in mind for tonight, I walk over to the wall where the chavs in their hoods and trackie bottoms and the boy racers in their cars are hanging out. Joe and Rabbit don't have anything to drink either, so they come over with me, out of the far gate and on to the pavement.

The kids on the wall are all the same kind of age as me. Some of them are younger. I don't really like any of them much, but I nod and say, 'All right?' They nod back. It's best to stay on nodding terms with them. Sometimes they can be useful. But not when you need to get served.

I walk over to the parked cars. Glenn Moulting's in his Peugeot 306. He used to go to our school. Got kicked out before he did his exams, though, for starting a fire in the changing rooms. He's a bit of a psycho – shaved head, tattoos. But he's all right if you know him. If he knows you. He's eighteen now, works down on the industrial estate, driving a forklift truck. And he's used his wages to soup his car up – lowered suspension, new bodywork, put in some massive woofers. It looks fucking lame. And right now, he's playing some horrible house track and smoking a fag. There's a girl from my year sitting in the passenger seat and a couple of younger girls in the back drinking alcopops. I lean in through the window.

'All right, Glenn,' I say.

He looks at me and nods. He doesn't smile. He just blows a smoke ring. He truly is a cock.

'Can you go into the offie for us?'

He makes a face, like I'm kind of insulting him. But then he smiles. 'OK,' he says. 'Cost you a pack of fags, though.'

I shake my head. 'Joking, aren't ya? Can't afford that. You think I'm made of money or something?'

He sighs. 'All right, five fags . . .'

I shake my head. 'Three.'

He looks at me, then out of his windscreen, thinking. He sighs. Then he turns back to me and smiles. 'Four and you've got a deal,' he says. 'But I want some skins as well.'

'Deal,' I say. 'Get us some two-litre bottles of cider will you, Moulty? The cheapest they got. Lightning White.'

He nods. I pass him the money. 'Don't know why you drink that shit, though,' he says. 'It's as rough as a badger's arsehole.'

I laugh. 'It's the only thing I can afford. And it gets me wasted!'

Glenn laughs, gets out of his car and goes across the road to the offie.

I nod to Kelly, the girl from my year at school that's sitting in the front seat. She's got a can of cider in her hand. Just as I'm about to start talking to her, there's a noise. Engines. I look up at the road. A silver car goes racing past, well over the speed limit. Idiot – he'll get caught on the speed camera. A few seconds later there's another car, a BMW or something. It goes flying through the town centre as well, out towards the woods. By the time they're gone, I can't be bothered to talk to Kelly. So I just stand there and wait, light a fag.

A couple of minutes later, Glenn comes back out with a blue carrier bag stuffed full of rough cider. He hands it to me and I give him the fags. 'Pleasure doing business with you,' he says. He gets back into his car, starts the engine and then wheel-spins away.

'What a tosser,' Rabbit says. 'Just cos he can drive he thinks he's the dog's bollocks.'

I laugh. 'You can talk.'

Rabbit laughs. 'Yeah, the difference is that I don't play shitty house music and have a load of underage girls in the back of my car.'

'No,' I say. 'But that's cos all you've got in your car is a shitty radio. And you're only allowed to drive your car around the tracks in the forest with your dad in the passenger seat. No self-respecting girl in the world would be seen dead in the back of your shit-brown car.'

'Jealous,' Rabbit mutters under his breath as we walk back over to the bench.

When we get there we share the cider out. I open mine and take a swig. I wince. It tastes rough as hell. But for the price and the alcohol content, you can't go wrong. If there's a cheaper way to get drunk, I haven't found it yet.

Joe

It's late o'clock. I look at my watch. Nearly one in the morning. Me and Ash are on our way home, pedalling slowly through the woods. It's the only way to get back home at this time really, cos if you take your bike along the main road you're asking for trouble. If a police car goes past they'll stop you straight away. I heard that if you don't have lights on your bike, they take your bike off you and make you go to the police station with your mum and dad to pick it up the next day. Can you imagine how humiliating that would be?

And if the cops think you've been drinking it's worse. Much worse. If they smell booze on your breath and you have a bike on the road, they take you back to your house. I can just imagine what Mum and Dad'd do if I turned up at the door with the police. My life would be over. Grounded for ever. So, the woods it is. The police never bother going in the woods.

As it happens, tonight I'm not that drunk anyway. Just a bit merry. All I had was a little cider. Not like Ash, who's off his face, as usual. Right now, he's weaving around on his BMX, trying to pull wheelies, falling off, laughing like a maniac and babbling total shit.

We're sticking to the wide tracks, the ones that have been made for the logging lorries and JCBs and whatever else to drive along. Trying to take the winding paths through the trees in this light would be suicidal. It's difficult enough to find your way on the wide tracks, even when the moon's full and bright like tonight. All I can see is the moon reflecting light on to the gravelly path and beside the path, the big ghostly silhouettes of trees against the dark blue of the night sky. I'd say I know pretty much every inch of this part of the forest – I've travelled through here thousands of times before. But at night-time it's different. Still. Secretive. Not spooky exactly. Just like it could be hiding anything and you wouldn't know.

As he cycles along, Ash takes his hands off his handlebars, pats his pockets and pulls out a squashed packet of fags and a lighter. He stops for a second, takes out a mashed-up fag, puts it in his mouth and

21

lights up. He takes a long drag and then starts pedalling again. 'Told you about the Jedi mind trick, didn't I?'

I nod my head. Ash managed to pull Meg. She's amazing. Really tall and slim and . . . Let's just say that most lads would give anything to spend an hour with her. Well, actually, even a few minutes would do.

'All you have to do is believe in yourself,' Ash says. 'Simple as that. Show them no weakness.'

If only. If I'd gone up to Meg, I wouldn't have known what to say. She'd have laughed in my face.

'Hey,' Ash says, 'you can come over to mine if you want, when we get back.'

I shake my head. 'Nah,' I say.

'There's more booze,' Ash says. He tries to pull his bike into a jump over a ridge in the track that's been left by lorry tyres in the mud. 'My dad's got some whisky. He won't miss a little bit.'

I shake my head. 'Nah. I'm too tired.'

We continue in silence for a bit. I shiver as I pedal. It's cold out here. I want to get home quick. I look down at the track. By the side, I can make out tyre tracks in the mud and the grass. They're always there. Mostly from logging lorries, I guess. And some of them could be from Rabbit driving his car around. Although, to be honest, as he's not allowed to go out in his car without his dad, they're probably not his tyre tracks. He has to drive sensibly.

I'm looking down at the tracks when I hear Ash's wheels skid on the loose stones of the path as he comes to a halt a few metres up ahead. 'Fuck me,' he shouts.

I look at him. He's pointing up ahead, over towards the left-hand side of the track. My eyes focus in on what he's pointing at. 'Jesus.'

A car. A silver car smashed into the trees. The bonnet is crumpled up like a concertina. There are tyre marks coming off the track across the grass verge and mud right up to where the car came to a stop. The tree it hit is bent over, leaning against the trees around it.

Ash chucks his fag to the ground. We both pedal like mad over towards the car, jump off our bikes when we get close and run the rest of the way.

Up close, I can see it's got a dent and a long scratch along the passenger side, like someone crashed into it and scraped it. I look in through the passenger side window. No one's in the car, but the airbag on the driver's side is hanging out of the steering wheel. And the driver's door is open. I run round to the other side. There are more dents and scratches in the bodywork. I look inside. There's a stain on the airbag. Blood, maybe – it's difficult to tell in the dark. The front windscreen's shattered into millions of pieces, but it hasn't fallen out.

23

Ash comes round to the driver's side as well. 'Shit,' he says. He stands and stares, shocked. Like me.

I stand back from the car. I feel weird. My head's kind of rushing, like everything's in fast forward apart from me. I turn and stare at the inside of the car for a minute and then I turn away and look up at the trees. I need to think straight. I need to try and calm down. My heart's racing like mad. 'Do you think we should call the police or something?'

Ash stands and thinks for a second. Then he nods and checks his pockets. He takes his phone out. He presses a button and then stares at the screen. 'Bollocks,' he says. 'Battery's dead. You got yours?'

I've already got my phone out. I look at it. No signal. I hold it out for Ash to see and run my hand through my hair.

'Well, what shall we do, then?'

I shrug. I look around at the car, at the track, at the woods. 'I dunno,' I say. 'There's not much we can do. Maybe we should see if we can find whoever was driving the car, see if they're still here. They could be hurt.'

Ash nods. 'Yeah, OK,' he says. 'Good idea. We could check the woods.'

So we both walk into the darkness between the trees. Ash goes off to the right and I walk straight ahead into the woods. It's difficult to see anything at first. It's darker among the trees than on the path. But after a little while, my eyes get used to the gloom and I can see well enough to dodge the trees and undergrowth. There's no sign of anyone, though. I look around at the floor of the forest, at the undergrowth, searching for any sign that someone's been through: a footprint, trampled plants, bloodstains, anything. But it's almost impossible to make out any detail. So I give up looking at the ground. I just stand up tall and still instead, looking all around me. Nothing. No sign of anyone. Whoever was in the car must have gone. Walked away.

I look over at Ash. He's making his way back towards the car and the bikes. I decide I might as well do the same. We're not gonna find anyone out here.

'See anything?'

Ash shakes his head. 'Nothing,' he says. 'They can't have been hurt that bad. They must have gone already.'

I nod and we both get on our bikes. We start cycling along the path again. And I start thinking. How could someone just drive off the path and hit a tree? It's not like the trees are right next to the path cos there's a big grass verge in between. You'd have to be a shit driver not to be able to stop yourself coming off the path and hitting the trees. And come to think of it, what the fuck was a car doing in the woods in the first place?

Rabbit drives around the forest, but that's cos he lives there. There are gates to stop cars at most of the entrances – Rabbit's dad has to have a special key to open them.

We cycle on in silence. I guess we're both thinking about it.

'Shall I check if I've got a signal now?' I say after a while. 'Report the car . . .'

Ash shakes his head. 'Nah,' he says. 'It was probably just a joyrider or something. If we call the cops, we'll have to hang round till they get here and stuff, freezing our bollocks off. Anyway someone'll find it in the morning and call the cops. Let's just leave it for them.'

I guess he's right. We keep cycling, silently. And all the while I keep looking towards the trees, half expecting to see someone. Though I don't know why, cos it's not like I can see anything, just the black outlines of trees. Maybe Ash is right, maybe someone just abandoned the car and ran off. You see a lot of abandoned cars round here. Mostly up on the verge by the side of the roads.

'You gonna go to Rabbit's party next weekend?' Ash says.

'Yeah, course.'

'He told me to invite whoever I want,' Ash says.

'Right,' I say absent-mindedly, still looking into the

woods. There's no one there, just thousands of silhouetted trees.

'As soon as I get back, I'm gonna charge my phone up and I'm gonna start inviting the fittest girls I know.'

I don't say anything. Something in the grass at the edge of the trees has caught my attention. Something dark, on the ground over on the left-hand side of the path. I put my brakes on. Ash hears them and stops up ahead of me.

'What you stopping for?'

I point off to the left. 'Down there. There's something on the ground.'

We both jump off our bikes and walk over to the trees. As I get nearer I can make out that it's a bag. A holdall. Ash gets to it first, bends down and pulls it towards him. He looks at me and then undoes the zip on the top of the bag, opens the flap and looks inside.

'Clothes,' he says. He pulls the clothes out of the bag. There's a white T-shirt, some jeans and a navy blue sweatshirt. But then something else catches his eye. 'Holy shit,' he says.

'What?'

But before he has a chance to answer, I catch a glimpse of what it is in the moonlight. Money. Loads of it. Banknotes. Fives and tens and twenties and fifties.

27

'Unbelievable,' Ash says. 'Fucking hell. We're rich!'
He takes a fifty out of the bag and gives it a kiss.

I shake my head. 'This is mental,' I say. But I don't
say anything more cos I'm not sure what to say. There
are a million things I can think of, but right now I'm
not sure which is the right one.

'There must be thousands in here,' Ash says, staring
into the bag, picking up handfuls of cash, then letting
them drop back in.

I nod my head. 'Whose is it? Has it got a name?'

Ash looks at the bag. There's a name tag on it. He
turns it over and leans in close to read it. 'Nope,' he
says. 'Nothing written on it.' He lets go of the tag.

'What kind of idiot drops a bag full of money and
doesn't notice?' I say.

Ash shakes his head. 'I dunno. A rich one, I guess.'

'What shall we do with it?'

Ash stands and stares at the bag with a grin on his
face.

'We could take it to the police,' I say.

Ash looks at me. He screws his face up, like he's
thinking about it. 'You serious? Now?' he says. 'It's
the middle of the bloody night. The police station's
closed.'

'There'll be someone on duty, though, won't there?'
I say.

Ash shrugs. 'Even if there is, we've been drinking.

28

They'll smell it on us,' he says. 'They'll take the bag off us and then get our parents to come and pick us up.'

I sigh. I guess he's right. 'So what do we do, then?'

'Easy. Take it home.'

'We can't do that – it isn't ours. That's stealing.'

Ash shrugs. 'No, we'd just be looking after it. We wouldn't be taking it or anything.' He pauses and looks around at the forest, as though whoever the bag belongs to is gonna turn up and take the money any second. 'Anyway, we can't just leave it here, can we? Someone else would find it and keep it.'

I don't say anything for a bit. I'm thinking. I sigh. 'OK. We'll take it to yours. I don't want it in my house. And only till the morning, though, till we decide what to do with it.'

Ash puts the clothes back in the bag and zips it up. He gets to his feet. 'Come on then,' he says. 'Let's get it back to mine before someone else takes it.'

About ten minutes later we turn on to Ash's road. There was no sign of anyone on the way back through the woods. No one looking for a bag stuffed full of cash. No one staggering around dripping with blood, looking like they'd been in an accident, either.

Ash's house is on the road next to mine. The road's totally silent and still and dark as we pedal down it. All the houses have their curtains drawn. All the lights are off. We turn into Ash's drive and gently put our bikes down in the little patch of garden out front. We don't say a word as we walk up the steps to his house. Instead we look all around us, just in case someone's watching. I feel bad, like we're doing something really awful, like we're criminals. My heart's thumping against my ribcage. My hands are sweaty. I want to get inside Ash's house quick before someone sees us and the bag. It feels like we're stealing, even though we're not really.

Ash looks at me. Then he puts his hands in his jeans pockets and takes out his keys. He's silent. He slides the key really carefully into the lock and twists it. He steps inside the house, looks around, listens for any sound. He pokes his head round the lounge door to check no one's there. Then he turns and beckons. I look around me and step quietly into the house.

Ash pushes the front door shut ever so quietly and locks it behind us. The hallway's dark. He looks at me and points over to the stairs. I nod and let him go first, tiptoeing upstairs, holding the bag in front of him. He keeps stopping, straining his ears to hear his parents. But the whole house is silent. At the top of the stairs, he stops again. He looks around. All the bedroom doors are closed. He turns to me and then points to his bedroom door. I nod. We creep up the rest of the stairs and then, when he's at the top, Ash turns right and silently opens his door. He waits for me to get inside and then shuts the door behind us.

Ash chucks the bag down on his bed and switches on a lamp. The room fills with dim light. He looks around his room and his eyes settle on the swivel chair at his desk. He walks over to the chair, wheels it over to the door, jams it underneath the handle and then pushes down a lever on the side of the chair to lock the wheels.

He takes a deep breath and then blows it out slowly, running both hands through his hair. He looks completely sober now. I feel totally sober too. He turns to look at me. We both smile.

I can already think of a few things I'd do with the money. If we kept it.

Ash walks back over to his bed and pulls the bag towards him. He unzips it, pulls the flap on the top of the bag open and takes the clothes out. A smell of aftershave wafts up my nose. I look in the bag, half expecting it to be empty this time, or filled with blank pieces of paper or something. But it isn't. It's still full of money. I shake my head in disbelief and smile at the same time.

Ash picks the bag up and tips the money out on the bed. It doesn't all come out at first, so he has to shake it. But after a few seconds the bag's empty and the bed is covered in cash. And that's not all. There's a

31

clear plastic bag as well, filled with weed or something. Ash scoops the money up in his hands and lets it all shower down on us. 'I've always wanted to do that,' he says. He picks up the plastic bag and looks at it closely for a second, opens the top and gives it a sniff. Then he kisses it and smiles. 'This just gets better and better.'

I stare at the money all over the bed and the floor. There's just loads of it. God knows how much is there. Thousands probably. 'Let's count it,' I say quietly.

Ash looks up at me and smiles. He nods. 'You count the fifties, I'll do the twenties.'

So we crouch there, by the side of his bed, counting the stack of fifties and twenties. And when we're done with that, we do the fives and the tens as well. Ash goes over to his desk and grabs a piece of paper and a pen. He notes down the amounts. And then he adds them all up. 'Fuck me!' he says with a smile. 'That's more than twenty grand!'

I shake my head. This is too much to take in. Twenty grand! How can you lose twenty grand?

Ash smiles. He's worked something else out on his paper. 'If we were gonna split it, we'd get ten thousand and ninety-seven pounds and fifty pence each,' he says. He looks at me. He's smiling like crazy. Like he's just won the lottery.

I shake my head. 'Jesus,' I say. 'That's a lot of money.

How can someone not notice they lost that much money? That's just mad.'

Ash shrugs. 'I'll tell you one thing,' he says. 'If I had twenty grand, I wouldn't leave it lying round in the woods for someone to find. Would you?'

I shake my head. 'No way.'

From outside the room there's a noise. A door opens. Footsteps cross the landing. Another door opens and then shuts. Then there's a ping as the bathroom light goes on. And then the sound of Ash's mum or dad going to the toilet.

Ash looks at me and laughs. 'Quick, help me put it all back in the bag!'

We grab enormous handfuls of cash and stuff it back into the bag along with the clothes and the bag of weed, until there's nothing left on the bed.

Out on the landing, I hear the toilet flush, the door open and the light go off. More footsteps, then a closing door.

Ash grabs a handful of fifties out of the top of the bag. He shoves some in his pocket and offers the rest to me.

I put my hand out and he puts the money there. I look at him. 'What?'

Ash smiles. 'We deserve a reward, even if we end up giving it back,' he says. 'Don't you think?'

I look down at my hand, at the money. Two hundred

quid. I think of all the stuff that I could do with it. I smile and put the money in my pocket.

Ash smiles too. He gets up and grabs the bag, takes it over to his wardrobe. He shoves the bag up on a shelf right to the back. Then he grabs his clothes from the floor and shoves them in, hiding the bag. 'Let's not tell anyone,' he says. 'Not yet.'

I nod my head.

'You'd better get going,' he says. 'Get some sleep.'

'I'll come round tomorrow morning,' I say. 'Then we can decide what to do.'

Ash nods.

SATURDAY

Joe

I wake up and look at my clock. It's nearly ten. Light's streaming in through the window where I didn't pull the curtains properly last night. I stretch and rub my eyes. I feel rubbish. I didn't sleep properly last night. I couldn't switch my brain off. When I got in I was buzzing, thinking about the money: who it belongs to, why it was just lying there in the forest, what I'd spend it on if it was mine. And if I wasn't thinking about that, I was thinking about the crashed car. I fell asleep eventually, though. The last time I checked it was after three.

I sit up in bed and stare into the distance, thinking. I feel a bit weird, kind of nervous. About the bag and the money and the car, like I've done something I shouldn't have. I get out of bed and pull my dressing gown on, walk over to my computer and switch it on. I drum my fingers on the table as I wait for it to start up, look out of the back window at Mum in the garden, hanging out the washing, pegs in her mouth.

My computer eventually comes to life. Straight away I go to the search engine and think about what to type in to find out about the money. I try 'bag full of money'. Which is obviously a mistake cos right away it comes up with about 25 gazillion results. Far too many to search through. And all the top results are just about songs called 'bag full of money'. So I add 'Dorset' to the search term and press Enter. This time there are only 24,000 results. But they're still all about song lyrics.

So I sit back and think. What if the money in the bag was stolen? I mean, why else would there be twenty grand in notes in a bag? Normal people don't carry that kind of money with them, do they? Normal people have bank accounts and debit cards and internet banking and stuff. I type 'stolen money Dorset' into the computer, press Enter and watch as the results come on to the screen. I scan through them. The second one looks promising: 'Money stolen in armed robbery'. I click on it. The Dorset police website opens up. The story's from a few months ago. It doesn't say how much money was taken. But I don't think it has anything to do with the money we found. It's too long ago. If it was stolen a couple of months ago, they wouldn't still have it lying around, would they? I look back at the results, try the next one, about some money stolen from a funeral. But the link's broken. I look through a couple of pages of results, but they're all links to stories of highwaymen and people stealing chickens off farms. So I try a new search: 'Stolen bag money Dorset'. I press Enter. The results are useless – they're all about handbags being stolen and stuff.

I give up on the bag and try and find out about the car instead. I search 'car crash Fayrewood'. The results come up. There are 2,920 matches. They're all for things like car insurance and car repair shops and stuff. No good. Not what I'm looking for. I sigh. Nothing about the car in the forest last night. Nothing about the bag of money.

I sit and stare into space. I think about where I could find out about the crash last night or the money. Then I have an idea. I turn back to the computer and go to the website of the local paper, *The Bournemouth Press*. If the crash is gonna be anywhere, it'll be on here. The website comes up and I look through the list of top stories. There's nothing on there about the car or the money, just some stories about a body being washed up on a beach and something about a fire.

I close the website. I stare at my phone on the desk, then pick it up and check to see if I have any messages. But I have no signal. I get up and move around my room cos that's the only way to get a signal in here. I eventually manage to get a signal over by the window. No messages.

I put my phone on the windowsill and go downstairs to the kitchen. Mum's in there loading the washing machine.

'Morning, Joe,' she says. 'Sleep well?'

'Yeah,' I say. It comes out like a grunt. I don't look at her. I just go to the bread bin, get a couple of slices out and put them in the toaster.

'Do you want a cup of tea?' Mum says. 'I was just about to make one.'

I nod. 'Yeah.' I stand and wait for my toast to pop up.

Mum stands by the sink and fills the kettle, looking out of the window. 'Did you have a good time at the rec last night?'

I nod. 'Yeah, all right.'

Mum nods as well. There's silence for a bit. 'You feeling OK this morning?'

I nod my head. 'Yeah. I'm fine,' I mumble.

Mum turns the tap off and plugs the kettle in. She looks at me and smiles. 'Did you get woken by the sirens in the night?' she says.

I look at Mum. I shake my head. And I start to panic. 'What sirens?'

Mum shrugs. 'Early this morning,' she says. 'Just after four. They sounded like they were in a rush.'

I look away from Mum. What if they were something to do with the crashed car and the bag of money? What if the police are looking for the money? I feel like asking her questions about the sirens – how many cars it sounded like, where they were going – but I don't say a thing. We're both silent. She takes some plates out of the dishwasher, while I start panicking about sirens.

'We're going to Bournemouth in a bit,' Mum says as she stacks some plates in the cupboard, 'so be quick with your breakfast.'

'I said I'd go over to Ash's,' I say.

Mum shakes her head. 'You're coming to Bournemouth with us. We need to get you a new shirt for Claire's wedding.'

I sigh. 'What? Why?'

Mum laughs. 'Because you'll look a bit silly without one on.'

'I've got loads of shirts already,' I say.

Mum nods her head. 'But none that are suitable for a wedding.'

I sigh again. 'Can't you just buy me one? I don't have to be there, do I?'

Mum nods. 'Of course you do. It won't take long, promise. Then you'll have the rest of the day to yourself.'

My toast pops up. I open the cupboard and get a plate. Mum opens the fridge and passes me the margarine.

'Thanks,' I grunt.

Mum looks up at me and smiles. 'Honestly,' she says. 'Living with teenagers is like living with monsters sometimes.'

I spread the butter on my toast and look for the Marmite.

The kettle boils. Mum starts making the tea. 'Oh,' she says. 'And don't forget Sally and Edward are coming over this evening.'

I look at Mum. I roll my eyes.

'You will be here, won't you?'

I sigh. 'Do I have to?'

Mum shrugs. 'Well, it would be nice if you were,' she says. 'They haven't seen you for about six months. I think Darren and Samantha are coming too.'

I sigh. My annoying cousins. Just what I need. I nod my head and take my toast through to the lounge.

After breakfast and a shower, I go to my room. I still feel kind of odd. I need to know what the sirens were for. I need to know that they weren't anything to do with what we found last night. I grab my phone and send a text to Ash. **Sorry, got to go to Bournemouth. See you later.**

Then I hear footsteps stomping up the stairs and an impatient voice. 'Hurry up, Joe. We're leaving.' It's Kate, my sister. I can't remember the last time she said something to me in a normal voice without shouting or sighing or being annoying.

'Coming,' I shout back. I grab some socks and pants and the jeans I was wearing yesterday and pull them all on, then snatch up a T-shirt from the back of my chair and pull that on as well. I race down the stairs, stuff my feet into my trainers by the door and leave the house.

Mum, Dad and Kate are already in the car when I get outside. Dad starts the engine as soon as I close the car door and then backs out of the drive. It's silent apart from the radio, which Dad always has tuned to Radio 4. It sounds much too boring to even bother listening to. Beside me, Kate's already got her earphones in, listening to music. Straight away I wish I'd brought mine with me. Instead, I sit and stare out of the window, daydreaming as we drive through Fayrewood, watching the old ladies taking their dogs for walks, little kids being pushed in their buggies by their mums and the older kids messing around on their bikes.

But then, as we start driving along the main road towards the middle of town, the car slows and stops. I look out of the front windscreen. There's a traffic jam. This must be a first. I don't think I have ever seen a traffic jam in Fayrewood before. It's not that kind of place.

'What on earth's all this in aid of?' Dad says.

No one answers. Eventually the traffic starts moving more quickly.

'Bloody hell,' Dad says. He points over to the right, at the new flats.

'What's going on?' Mum says.

Up ahead there are police cars and fire engines and all sorts outside the flats.

'That must have been what the sirens were for last night,' Dad says. 'Looks like the flats have burned out.'

'Oh dear,' Mum says, half covering her face with her hands. 'How awful.'

It's awful and completely selfish, I know, but I can't help but feel relieved that the sirens were for this, not the car and the bag. At least no one will have been hurt – the flats aren't even finished yet.

We gradually creep forward. As we pass the flats, I wind down my window and stare. The air smells strange. A burnt smell. The front of one of the flats is completely blackened. All the flats around it are partly burned out too. Behind me, I can sense Kate leaning across to stare out of my window. And then we're past the flats and the traffic speeds up.

'You know who's done that, don't you?' Dad says, as we head out the other end of town.

No one answers him.

'The developers!' Dad says eventually. 'They must have run out of money. Insurance job. Bet you.' He laughs, looks across at Mum for a reaction. 'Looks like they made a pig's ear of doing it, though – they've only burned one flat!'

'Don't joke about it, Rob,' Mum says. 'Someone could have been hurt for all we know.'

'Doubt it,' Dad says. 'The flats aren't finished. There won't have been anyone in there. You wait until they've carried out an investigation. They'll find it's arson. It'll be on the news by the end of the week, mark my words.'

Mum doesn't reply. She looks out of the window instead.

Ash

When I get downstairs into the kitchen, I see a note and twenty pounds on the work surface. I pick them up. The note's in Mum's handwriting.

Dear Ashley,

Gone to work and then going straight to Swindon for June's 50th. There's a portion of Bolognese in the fridge – just heat it up and boil yourself some pasta. Should be back by teatime tomorrow. If you need to phone, me and Dad have our mobiles. Make sure you lock all the downstairs doors and windows before you go out, etc.
Love, Mum
PS get yourself a DVD with the money.

I look at the twenty-pound note and smile to myself. This is small change to me now. Still, I put it in my pocket. I go into the lounge, roll myself a joint, have a smoke and then play some video games. But I can't really be arsed with it this morning. I feel kind of itchy, if you know what I mean. I can't sit down, can't sit still. It must be the thought of the money just sitting there upstairs, waiting for me to spend it. I send a couple of texts out, see if anyone wants to meet. I don't bother sending one to Joe cos he's gone to Bournemouth. Dylan sends one saying he's visiting his grandad and Rabbit doesn't answer.

I sigh. Fuck them all, then. I'll go out on my own, have some fun. I climb the stairs, go to my room, pull the holdall down from my wardrobe shelf and take some money out. Two fifties. I stare at them. Before yesterday I'd never even held a fifty before in my life. And now I've got loads of them. I grab a few more and stuff them in my jeans pocket. I'm gonna go shopping, I think. Why not? What's the point of just having the money here doing nothing? I might as well spend it. I take out the bag of weed as well, hold it up and look at it, then open the bag and smell it. I should divide it up. If I got caught with this lot while I was out, I'd get done for dealing. Possession with intent or whatever you call it. I zip the top of the bag back up.

I leave my room with the bag of weed and go down

to the kitchen. I open the drawer next to the cooker and help myself to a load of sandwich bags. If I was being really anal about it, I'd get some electric scales out and use those too. But I don't have any, so I just share the weed out between the bags. There's got to be roughly an eighth in each.

When I'm done, I take most of the bags upstairs and hide them away in a drawer. I grab my rucksack, shove a jumper and some weed in there, then rush back downstairs and out the door. I pick up my bike and helmet and I'm on my way.

Joe

'I'm gonna go now,' I say to Mum as she puts the shirt over her arm and starts walking towards the tills. 'Where shall I meet you?'

'Back at the car,' Mum says. She looks at her watch. 'Ticket runs out at one, so make sure you're back by then.'

'OK.'

'Can I go round town on my own as well?' Kate says, all of a sudden not dragging her heels behind Mum. 'Please.'

Mum shakes her head. 'Not yet, Kate. We need to get you some shoes.'

Kate sighs heavily.

'I'm confused,' Dad says. 'I thought buying shoes was the reason women lived.'

Kate sighs again.

I smirk and head out of the shop. What a waste of time. I have no idea why Mum needed me to be there for that. All we did was go to one shop and find the first shirt that had a reduced sticker on the price label. A plain white shirt. As though I don't have a load of those at home already. It wasn't even as though she made me go into the changing rooms to try it on. All she did was hold it up against me. A waste of my time.

I don't mind coming shopping usually. I mean, I don't like walking round with Mum and Dad and Kate, but walking round the shops I want to look in is all right. Even if I never have any money to spend in them. Today, though, I'd rather not be here. I want to go and see Ash. I want to talk to him about what we saw last night. About what we found last night and what we're gonna do with it. I keep changing my mind. I know what I should be thinking: hand the bag over to the police. It's what we should do. But is it the right thing to do? I mean, if we took the bag to the police, what would happen to it? Would they actually find who it belongs to? I don't know what to think.

I head to the other end of town, where there are some shops I like looking in: music shops, skate shops, computer games shops. I have my hands in my pockets as I walk, feeling the fifties that Ash gave me yesterday between my fingers. And just the thought of having two hundred pounds in my pockets makes me smile to myself.

First I stop off at the skate shop. Not that I have a skateboard, but I like the music and the clothes that go with skating. There's some punky music playing really loudly in there. I think it's that band Ash keeps on about. Clustered around the counter are a load of skater kids, all dressed in uber cool clothes. They're the kind of kids that make me feel uncool just by looking at them. The kind of kids that look as if they were born looking like that. I start looking through the T-shirts. They're all really expensive. Thirty, forty, fifty quid. But they all look great. I'd love to turn up to the rec wearing one of them. Just for a change. I feel the fifties in my pocket and think about buying one of the T-shirts. But I resist.

Instead, I walk over to the trainers and take some high-tops down from the rack. I sneak a look at the price. £84.99. I put them straight back. They look great. But I can just imagine what Mum and Dad would say if I spent that much on some trainers. They made enough of a fuss about paying forty quid for the ones I'm wearing now. I keep browsing through the sale trainers. As I turn away from them, I catch a glimpse of myself in the mirror: scruffy T-shirt, faded jeans and scuffed-up, out-of-shape trainers. It's kind of depressing. I look tragic.

'Can I help you, mate?'

I jump. It's the guy that runs the shop. 'It's OK,' I say. 'Just looking.' It's what I always say when someone in a shop talks to me, like an automated response. The shopkeeper's just about to walk away when I change my mind. 'Actually,' I say, 'can I try some of those on?' I point over at a pair of trainers in the sale.

The shopkeeper smiles. 'Course,' he says. 'Size?'

'Eight.'

He goes off to get the trainers and I sit down on a bench. And I start feeling panicky and paranoid. Can I do this? Can I really spend the money we found? Won't Mum and Dad work out that something's going on?

But before I can make a decision, the shopkeeper comes back in, holding a shoebox. 'Size eight. Last pair,' he says. He hands one of the trainers to me.

I take off my skanky old trainers and immediately wish I had a better pair of socks on. Mine have holes in them.

'These are a good little pair of trainers,' he says. 'Look, you've got loads of support around the ankle and the foot. Ideal for skating. Do you skate?'

I shake my head as I pull the trainers on. 'Not really.'

'They look good as well,' the shopkeeper says with a smile. 'What do you think?'

I stand up in them and look in the mirror. They look great. I nod. 'I'll take them,' I say, before I have time to think twice about what I'm doing.

The shop assistant smiles. 'Good choice. I've got a pair of them myself.'

A minute later I'm standing by the counter next to the impossibly cool kids as the shop assistant rings up the sale. And I'm feeling kind of nervous. Stupidly nervous. Like he's gonna see the fifty that I'm gonna use to pay and he's gonna know where I got it from. It's stupid, I know.

'That's thirty-nine ninety-nine,' the shop assistant says.

I nod and smile and put my hand in my pocket. I breathe deeply. I need to stay calm. It's just like Ash says about talking to girls: act confident, like this is nothing out of the ordinary, and the assistant will think this is normal.

I pull the fifty out of my pocket and hand it over.

Beside me I can sense the cool kids look at me. One of them whistles. 'Jeez, man,' he says, 'you must be loaded.'

I look at him and smile. I can feel myself blush. I try and think of something cool to say back, but my mind's blank.

'Can you lend me some?' one of the others says, then laughs. 'I'm skint.'

I smile again. I feel hot and flustered. I can feel my heart racing. I want to get out of here. I grab the bag with my new trainers off the counter, mumble 'Thanks' and walk as fast as I can to the door.

Out in the street, I take a deep breath. I can't believe how uncool I was back in there. I nearly gave myself away. All I had to do was hand the money over and I went to pieces. I start walking, not even thinking about where I'm going next, but a few seconds later I hear someone behind me.

'Oi, mate!'

At first I just ignore it, but then, with a sinking feeling, I start thinking maybe it's someone after me. I turn round to see it's the shopkeeper. Shit. I knew it. He's sussed me.

He runs over to me. He holds out his hand. 'You must be seriously loaded,' he says. 'You didn't take your change.'

I look down at his hand. There's a receipt, a ten-pound note and a penny lying there.

I hold out my hand and take the money off him. 'Thanks,' I say. 'Sorry. My mind's somewhere else.'

The shop assistant smiles. 'Know that feeling. Enjoy the shoes.' And he heads back towards the shop.

Ash

There is literally nothing to do in Fayrewood on a Saturday morning, unless you're old and you spend half your time popping sedatives and the other half popping down the supermarket. Which is the reason, right now, that I'm in Rangbourne instead. Rangbourne's a little town about five miles away, but it's way better than Fayrewood. There's a skatepark and some proper shops there – like a bike shop and a skate shop.

I head to the skatepark first. It's totally empty. I ride around for a couple of minutes, taking in all the ramps and the jumps. But I can't really be arsed with it this morning. So I bring my bike to a halt and just sit there for a bit, staring into space. Leaves and empty crisp packets swirl around the park on the gusts of wind.

My mind drifts for a bit. But wherever it drifts to – school, girls, BMX tricks – it always ends up back in the same place. Last night. The car and the bag and the money and the drugs. It's crazy. I don't know what to make of it all. I mean, it didn't come from anyone's savings, that's for sure. Whoever it belongs to is a criminal, that much is obvious. Why would anyone else carry that much cash and that much weed? And it makes me feel weird to think that now it's sitting on the shelf in the wardrobe in my room.

But why should I feel weird about it? I haven't done anything wrong. I didn't steal the money. I didn't buy the weed. It isn't wrong to find stuff, is it? And it would be criminal not to use the money.

I start pedalling through the skatepark and towards the centre of town. I ride along the pavements, through the roads with all the posh old Victorian houses on them, towards the shops. I cross over the one-way system and take a short cut through the alleyway that stinks of piss next to the supermarket. I come out of the other end on to the market square. I cycle straight across it. It's busy with old ladies and families dragging their little kids round the shops. I dodge in and out of them all. Some old lady tuts at me and shakes her head as I go past. I just ignore her.

I come to a stop outside the bike shop – Slack Rob's Bikes. I open the door and wheel my bike inside, right up to the counter. Slack Rob's standing behind the counter, as always, reading a magazine. He's playing some crap punk band over the sound system. He looks up at me and smiles.

'Ash,' he says.

I smile. 'All right, Slack.'

'What can I do you for?'

'I want a new frame,' I say.

Slack Rob nods and comes out from behind the counter. He leads me over to the back of the shop, where all the bikes are. 'You got anything in mind?' he says.

I shrug. 'Not really.'

Slack strokes his little goatee beard. He looks at me. 'How much you got to spend?' he says.

I pause for a second, think about how much I want to spend on it. I have four hundred quid on me. I'm not sure whether I should spend it all. Four hundred is a lot of money. But, you know, fuck it. I should be enjoying this. There's plenty more where it came from. 'Four hundred,' I say.

Slack does a double take. His eyes open wide in surprise. 'Wow,' he says. He nods and strokes his beard again. 'OK, OK . . . Let's have a little look, then, shall we?'

Slack takes me through pretty much the whole range of bikes and frames and stuff, going through all the talk about what materials they're made from, which riders use them and all that blah. He treats me like I'm royalty or something. Even when other people come into the shop, he keeps them waiting while he serves me. It's amazing how much respect you get when you've got a bit of money. Eventually I go with a frame that costs 350 quid and get a new helmet as well.

I follow Slack up to the counter. He rings the frame and the helmet through with a smile on his face. 'Three hundred and ninety-four pounds ninety-eight, please, Ash,' he says.

I smile at the sound of that. I mean, I actually have enough money in my wallet to pay for all this. Me. Ash. I take my wallet out of my pockets, open it up. I take the fifties out and count them, all eight of them. I pass them over to Slack.

He looks at them like he can't quite believe his eyes. 'Shit, Ash,' he says. 'Where'd you get this sort of money from?'

I give him a look back, like I don't think it's a big issue. 'What?' I say. 'My nan died and left it to me.'

Slack's face changes straight away. 'Sorry, man,' he says.

I nod. 'That's OK,' I say. 'It wasn't your fault she died.'

Slack takes the money and puts it in the till. He counts out my change and gives it to me. Then he helps me out of the shop, carrying the new frame for me and holding the door open.

After that, I go along the road to the burger bar. It's well old-fashioned but it's kinda cool for Rangbourne. I walk up to the counter and order myself a quarter-pounder with cheese and chips and a lemonade and then go and sit down at a table by the window, where I can keep an eye on my bike outside.

As I'm waiting for my food to be brought to me, I sit and look at my new frame. It's a street one, which basically means that it's really sturdy and hard-wearing. At the moment it looks shiny and clean and the paintwork is smooth, but give it a couple of weeks of hard riding and it'll look different.

There's a knock on the window. It startles me. I look up. It's Jack from school. He smiles and then comes in and sits down at the table opposite me. He looks at my frame.

'Nice,' he says. 'Jeez, man, how much was that?'

I shrug. 'About three fifty.'

The waitress comes over with my food and puts it down on the table. Right away, Jack helps himself to some of my chips.

'Where did you get the money for that?' he says through a mouthful of chips.

I take a bite of my burger and chew it before answering. I look Jack in the eyes. 'Found a bag full of money in the woods, didn't I?' I say with a smile.

Jack laughs. 'Yeah, very funny,' he says. 'Seriously, though, where'd you get it?'

I chew and then swallow some chips. 'Inheritance,' I say. 'My nan left it to me.'

Jack nods and grabs a couple more chips from my plate. 'I didn't know your nan died.'

I shrug. 'Why would you?'

He shrugs and grabs another chip from my plate. I take a swig of my drink, which is too cold and bubbly and makes my eyes water for a second. We sit without talking for a while, as I stuff my face with burger and chips and Jack helps himself to my chips.

When all my food's gone, we leave the burger bar and wander in the direction of the skatepark. It's still empty when we get there. We find a bench and sit down. And as I'm sitting there, I remember the weed in my bag and I suddenly fancy a smoke. So I take it out and start rolling up. It takes Jack a little while to notice.

'Is that what I think it is?' he says.

I look up at him, smile and nod.

I finish rolling it and spark it up. I take a couple of drags, holding the smoke down in my lungs each time. And then I pass it to Jack. As he smokes, I look out over the park. And I feel pretty good. I can't believe my luck. How many other sixteen-year-olds can say that they have twenty grand and a big bag of weed?

Jack passes the spliff back to me. I take another couple of drags and then pass it back to him. And we sit in silence, smoking, staring into space for a couple of minutes.

After I've stubbed it out, Jack looks at me. 'You got any more?'

I nod my head. 'I've got loads.' For a second I think about telling him exactly how much I've got. But I decide not to. 'Why?'

'I'll buy some.'

I take a deep breath and look out over the skatepark. I hadn't thought about selling any, but I guess I can't smoke the whole lot on my own. And it can't do any harm to sell a little bit to a friend. I look at him and nod. 'Yeah, all right,' I say. 'Why not?'

Jack smiles a hazy smile.

I pull the plastic bag back out of my rucksack and pass it to him. He takes it and puts it straight in his pocket.

'How much?' he says.

'Fifteen.'

He smiles even wider and gets his wallet out.

Joe

When I get back to the car Kate's already there, leaning against the door, reading a book that she's bought this morning. She looks up at me as I walk towards her and almost instinctively, I hold the bag with my trainers in it behind my back.

'All right, loser?' I say to her.

She sticks her fingers up at me and then goes back to her book. And I think, good, she didn't notice the bag.

Until she opens her mouth and says, 'What did you buy?'

'What?' I say. I feel panicked. 'Nothing.' Which is just about the stupidest thing I have ever said, as I obviously bought something.

'Yes you did,' Kate says, still without looking up. 'You've got a bag.'

I look down as though I'm noticing the bag for the first time. 'Oh,' I say. 'Just bought some trainers.'

Kate looks up immediately. 'Trainers? Where'd you get the money for them? Did Mum and Dad give you the money?'

I shrug. I prepared my story as I was walking through town because I knew Kate would ask this kind of question. But right now the lie I've made up doesn't seem all that believable. 'Kind of,' I say. 'I saved up my pocket money for a while.'

Kate raises an eyebrow, like she doesn't believe me.

'Where else do you think I'd get the money?'

She shrugs and goes back to her book.

And we don't speak again. A couple of minutes later, Mum and Dad turn up. Dad's carrying all the shopping bags.

'I hope the credit card company's got enough money to pay for this little lot!' he says.

The car unlocks with an electrical *clunk* and Dad starts putting the bags into the boot.

'What have you bought?' Mum says to me.

I don't say anything right away. I was hoping she wasn't going to notice.

'He's bought some trainers,' Kate says.

I sigh. Trust Kate. She can be a right pain in the arse sometimes.

'Did you?' Mum says, getting in the passenger seat.

I get in the back. 'Yeah,' I say. 'I saved up. I needed some. Mine are falling apart.'

Mum nods her head. 'Fair enough,' she says.

I smile. How easy was that? I've got away with it. Maybe keeping the money will be all right. Maybe I can keep it a secret from everyone. Just as long as I'm careful.

Ash

I'm sitting on my own on the bench at the rec, staring at my bike, looking at my new frame. Which, by the way, looks wicked. It feels good to ride as well.

I see Joe come in through the gate at the far end of the rec and then close it behind him. He cycles across the grass towards the bench.

'Hi, Ash,' he says as he puts his bike carefully on the ground and then comes and sits next to me.

'All right, J?'

Joe looks at my bike. I can sense what he's thinking. I know what he's gonna say even before he opens his mouth. 'Is that a new bike?'

I shake my head. 'Nah. New frame.'

'Looks good,' Joe says. 'Did you buy it with . . . you know?'

I nod and smile. 'Yeah.'

'How much?'

I don't answer right away. I'm not sure how Joe'd react if I told him how much it really cost. Time for a white lie, I think. 'Two hundred,' I say.

Joe raises his eyebrows. 'Two hundred?' He whistles, like that's a lot of money. Which I guess it is. Although not if you've just found a bag with twenty grand in it.

I nod. And I can tell that he's a little bit pissed off with me, just from the tone of his voice. He doesn't say it in so many words, though. He just looks down at his trainers. And so do I.

I smile. 'Are they new?'

He nods and goes slightly red. And I know, even without asking him, that he spent some of the money from the bag today as well.

'Nice,' I say. 'They're cool.'

Joe mumbles something that I think is 'Thanks'.

We're both quiet for a while. I watch some kids who are having a kickabout, using their bikes as goalposts. One of the kids gets hacked to the ground and starts rolling around as though he's been shot or something. He gets up as soon as he's awarded a penalty.

68

'I guess this means we should keep the money,' Joe says after a while. 'Now that we've spent some of it. We can't exactly take the bag to the police with some of the money missing.'

I look at him and nod. I smile. 'Yeah, I guess you're right,' I say.

He looks across the rec and nods. 'Yeah,' he says. He pauses. 'Did anyone ask you any questions about where you got the money from?'

I shake my head. It's easiest to lie. 'Not at all. You?'

He sighs. 'Kind of,' he says. 'My sister did. She asked where I got the money for the trainers. I told her I saved my pocket money.'

I nod. 'Good thinking. Did she buy the excuse?'

Joe looks at me. He smiles. 'Yeah.'

I smile back at him. 'Nice one,' I say. 'We just have to be careful, that's all. Just make sure we don't let anyone suspect us of anything. And then we're loaded!'

'It made me think, though,' he says, 'that we should probably try and ration the money.'

I look at him.

'So we don't draw attention to ourselves,' he goes on. 'My sister got suspicious enough just cos I spent forty quid.'

I nod. Maybe he has a point. 'OK. How much do you reckon, then? Hundred quid a week?'

He shakes his head. 'Too much.'

'A hundred's not too much,' I say. 'No one in a shop's gonna get suspicious about that.'

Joe shakes his head, though. 'No,' he says. 'It should be less than that. Kate and my parents would get suspicious if I started spending that much every week.'

'My mum and dad wouldn't,' I say. 'They couldn't give a toss. They hardly even notice I'm there anyway. How about fifty quid, then? No one'll notice that.'

Joe shakes his head again. 'Thirty.'

'Forty.'

Joe thinks about it for a second. 'Thirty-five,' he says after a bit.

'Deal,' I say. Thirty-five quid is nothing, but I know I can get away with spending more than that a week. This way, I let Joe think he's in charge.

We shake on it.

We fall silent and look out across the rec at the little kids playing football. And as we do, I wonder whether I should tell him that I sold some of the weed to Jack. But something stops me from saying anything. So I sit quietly and I stare at the football without really following the game.

'Do you believe in fate?' Joe says eventually.

I look at him, wondering what the hell he's talking about. He stares straight back at me. I shrug. 'I s'pose. Why?'

Joe looks away from me, across the rec. 'I was just thinking, maybe we were meant to find the money,' he says. 'Maybe it was fate. Maybe someone up there wanted us to find it.'

'What do you mean? God?'

Joe shakes his head. 'Not like that. I just mean, like, what if we found it so that we can do some good with it?'

'We've done that already, haven't we?' I say. 'My bike looks wicked with the new frame. And your trainers aren't too bad, either.'

Joe turns back to me again. 'You know what I mean,' he says. 'Look, we both know that this money isn't just someone's life savings that they lost by accident. No normal person carries that much cash and a big bag of weed on them, do they? It must have belonged to someone dodgy.'

'Right. So?'

Joe sighs. 'I can't explain . . .' he says. 'We got lucky when we found it, but maybe we should use it to do some good instead, not just spend it all on ourselves. Do you see what I mean?'

I nod slowly. I think I see what he's getting at. Although, to be honest, I'd rather spend the money on myself.

'You know what karma is, don't you?' Joe says.

I nod. 'Yeah, I think so.'

'If something good happens to you, you should go and do something good in return. And if you do that, more good things will happen. But if you do something bad, then bad things will happen to you.'

I nod. But I don't believe in it. 'We're already doing more good with it than whoever had it in the first place,' I say. 'It's not like we're gonna use it to fund a criminal empire or anything. We're not gonna do bad things with the money.'

Joe looks at me, his right eyebrow raised. 'Don't you see what I'm saying?'

I sigh. 'You want us to give the money to charity or something,' I say.

Joe shrugs. 'Not necessarily,' he says. 'But I think we should think carefully about what we use it for. We shouldn't just use it to buy loads of stuff we don't need.'

I nod. 'OK,' I say. Even though I fully intend to spend the money on things I don't need.

The football from the kids' game rolls over towards us. Joe jumps down from the bench, runs over to the ball and kicks it back over to the kids. Except instead of going straight to them, it curls over to the right, so they end up having to chase after it. He comes and sits back down.

'What you doing tonight, J?' I say.

Joe's shoulders kind of droop. 'Family meal,' he says.

'Why don't you come over to mine, then?' I say. 'My parents are gonna be away all night. I'm gonna invite Rabbit and Dylan too.'

Joe sighs. 'Can't,' he says. 'Mum says I have to look after my dumb cousins.'

'Bring them round.'

He shakes his head. 'Nah,' he says. 'You'd understand if you'd ever met my cousins.'

We go home the back way. Mainly cos I wanna check out the place where the car was last night. Joe took a little bit of persuading, but now we're on our way through the woods. Because it's Saturday afternoon, there are loads of people out for a stroll or walking their dogs. And it makes me think: if we hadn't picked the bag up yesterday, there's no doubt that someone else would have found it by now. And the chances are that they'd have kept the money for themselves, just like me and Joe.

We see the car up ahead, the silver Vauxhall Astra. Only we also see something we weren't banking on. There's a policeman there as well. We keep on cycling, trying not to stare too hard. We don't look at each other, don't say a thing to each other, just keep riding innocently as though we just happened to be cycling through that way.

It's not until the crashed car and the policeman are out of sight behind us that we finally speak.

'What were the police doing there?' Joe says.

'Dunno,' I say. 'Probably just checking out the car crash, I guess.'

'I s'pose,' Joe says. He doesn't sound too convinced, though.

'Probably just putting one of those Police Aware stickers on it.'

Joe nods. We cycle on for a bit, neither of us saying anything. We come out of the woods and out on to the main road.

'You don't think it had anything to do with the bag, do you?' Joe says after a while. He sounds kind of anxious.

I shake my head. 'Nah. Relax, Joe. Probably some old codger was taking his dog for a walk and found the car, called the cops and then they had to come and take a look at it. End of story.'

Joe kind of nods. 'Yeah.'

'Besides,' I say, 'the bag and the car probably didn't have anything to do with each other. Just coincidence.'

Joe

I go into the kitchen, partly to see if there's any food that I can scavenge but mainly to try and get away from Darren and Samantha, my annoying cousins. Mum's in there, cooking and looking stressed.

'Can I have some food?' I say.

Mum doesn't look at me. 'No,' she snaps.

I stand in the doorway, wondering whether I dare ask again. And as I think, I watch Mum go over to the fridge, look inside for a few seconds, take a pot of cream out and stare at it. Then she puts it back in the fridge and makes an angry kind of grunting sound.

'Are you OK?' I say.

Mum sighs and pushes the fridge door closed. 'I am slowly losing the will to live,' she says through gritted teeth.

Mum always gets stressed when Edward and Sally come round and she has to cook. Mainly because my Aunt Sally, Mum's sister-in-law, is always so sneery and competitive. Everything in their house is just so. Not like in our house, where everything is more 'whatever'.

Mum comes over to the counter, grabs her purse and opens it. 'I bought single cream instead of double, Joe. Take this and go to the shop for me.'

She holds out a five-pound note.

I stare at her and sigh. I'm about to protest when it dawns on me that if I go to the shop for Mum I'll get away from Edward, Sally, Darren and Samantha for a bit. I grab the money. 'Double cream, right?'

Mum nods. 'Five hundred mills.'

I take the money and turn just as Sally walks into the kitchen and blocks my way. 'Anything I can help with, Beverley?' she says.

Mum shakes her head. 'No thanks, Sally,' she says. 'Everything's under control. But I forgot the double cream. Joe's just going to pop to the shops and get me some. Not much I can do till then.'

'Oh,' Sally says in her sneery way. 'I see. Right. Well, I'm sure Darren and Samantha would like to go for a walk as well, Joseph,' she says, before adding, 'if you don't mind, that is . . .'

My heart sinks. I try not to make it too obvious that I'd rather chew on my own eyeballs than go to the shops with Darren and Samantha. 'OK,' I say with a fake smile. 'I'm going now. Are they ready?'

I stand in the kitchen as Sally goes and gets my cousins. I open my wallet to put Mum's fiver in there. And when I do, I see one of the fifties that Ash gave me. I get a momentary pang of guilt. I try to stop it by closing my wallet and putting it in my pocket. And then I listen as Sally forces Darren and Samantha against their will to come with me.

A minute later and we're walking towards the centre of town, silently. Kate's with us as well. She got rounded up by Sally too, so now she's walking along, her head bowed in a sulk. And as I walk, I kick a stone along in front of me to avoid having to look at or talk to my relatives. Because if there's one thing that me and Kate actually agree on, it's that we both hate Darren and Samantha.

The stone that I've been kicking falls off the edge of the pavement and disappears into a drain.

'How can you live in a shithole like this?' Darren says.

I look at him. The way Darren asks the question makes me feel defensive, even though I kind of agree that Fayrewood is a shithole. 'What?' I say. 'Fayrewood's all right.'

Darren makes a face at Samantha, like I've just said something stupid. 'Yeah, right,' he says sarcastically. 'It's full of old people. It's like a waiting room for heaven.'

I shrug. He's right. I'm not gonna tell him that, though, am I? And I can't be bothered to get into an argument with him.

'At least where we live is in London,' Darren goes on. 'There's much more to do there.'

Samantha rolls her eyes. 'Stop boasting, Darren,' she says.

'I'm not,' Darren says. 'It's a fact. It's way better than this shitty little place.'

All of a sudden, Kate looks up. 'You don't live in London,' she says. 'You live in Surrey, along with all the other spoilt little boys and girls that go to public school.'

Darren doesn't say anything right away. He stares at Kate and narrows his eyes. 'Who asked for your opinion, lanky?' he says.

Normally, when someone points out that Kate's freakily tall, I would laugh and join in. But when it's Darren, I feel more like defending Kate. But I don't have to. She sticks her tongue out at him and then carries on walking sulkily. And we all walk another fifty or so steps without another word.

In fact, no one says anything until Darren spots the crowd that's gathered on the pavement outside the flats and says, 'What's going on there?'

'There was a fire last night,' I say. 'At the new flats.'

Darren smiles. 'Cool,' he says. 'Let's go and have a look.' And he starts marching off along the pavement at about three times the speed he was travelling before.

Samantha turns to me and shrugs her shoulders. And Kate just mopes along the pavement beside us.

We catch up with Darren by the scrum of people. There's a policeman and a policewoman in front of the tape. And in front of that, there's someone from the local TV news being lit by a bright light, with a camera pointed at her face.

Darren turns to me. 'Turns out Fayrewood's not as boring as everyone thought.'

I nod my head without really thinking. But instead of looking at Darren, I'm looking beyond the cameras and the crowd and the police tape at the flats. There are loads of vehicles, including a fire investigation van and a couple of police cars. There are loads of people walking around too. They must all be police. Some of them are in white overalls.

I stare for a while, wondering how it burned down and whether Dad's theory is right or not. But then I remember the cream. I look round to find the others. Kate's right next to me. Darren and Samantha are both standing behind the TV presenter, Samantha looking bored and Darren waving over the reporter's shoulder at the camera. Me and Kate walk over to them.

'Come on, Darren,' I say, grabbing him by the arm. 'We've gotta go and get the cream.'

He laughs. 'I want to get on TV,' he says. But he starts walking with me around the crowd. 'Did you see that reporter? She's gorgeous.'

I ignore him. Even though he's right – she is.

We go into the small supermarket opposite the rec. I go straight to the back, to the fridges where they keep the milk and the cream and all that stuff. The others don't follow me, they just hang around near the magazines instead. I look along the shelves, grab two small tubs of double cream and take them to the counter. There's one person ahead of me in the queue. I look over at the magazines. Kate and Samantha are looking at the celeb magazines. Darren's pacing around near the doorway, like he can't wait to get out of here.

I step up to the counter, open my wallet, pay with Mum's fiver, put the cream in a carrier bag and take my change. And we leave the shop.

A little way up the road, Darren turns to me. 'Where'd you get all that money?' he says.

'Mum gave it to me,' I say.

'Your mum gave you a fifty to get some cream?'

I look at him. I feel like I'm about to blush. I look away from him, like it's no big thing. 'She gave me a fiver,' I say. 'I paid with a fiver.'

He smirks. 'But you had a fifty in your wallet.'

I panic. I don't know what to say. I can't think straight. I'm gonna drop myself in it.

'What's your problem, Darren?' Kate says. 'Haven't you ever seen a fifty-pound note before?'

I look at Kate. She's smirking at Darren. And Darren's staring back at her, his eyebrow raised. 'Jesus,' he says. 'Who rattled your cage again?'

Kate doesn't answer. She sighs and then turns away from Darren. Next to Darren, Samantha laughs.

Darren pretends to ignore her. 'Still doesn't explain where Joe got the fifty from, though, does it?'

I've had time to think of an excuse now. My heart's beating fast, but all I have to do is look him straight in the eyes and say it. 'I got it out of the bank today,' I say. 'I was gonna buy some clothes.' And even when it's out there, my heart is still beating like crazy.

Darren looks at me like he doesn't believe me. I try and hold his gaze. He stares at me for what feels like hours. Then he laughs and looks away. 'I think you should have spent it on clothes,' he says. 'It looks like you need some new ones.'

I don't say a word. I just keep on walking, feeling

flustered and pissed off and stupid. If Darren wasn't my cousin, I'd be really tempted to just smack him one.

Ash

I've eaten the Bolognese that Mum left. I couldn't be bothered to boil any pasta, so I had it cold on toast instead. And right now I'm lying on my bed, eyes closed. Not sleeping, just vegging out before Rabbit gets here.

I hear a noise. A ringing phone. I keep my eyes closed, try and ignore it for a while cos it's not my phone and it's not the landline. But it keeps ringing. And I realise that it's coming from somewhere in my room. I open my eyes and sit up. The ringing is coming from the corner of the room, near the wardrobe. My heart starts racing. I get up from the bed and walk to the wardrobe and all the while the phone keeps on ringing. It's one of the basic ringtones that you get on every mobile, a *bring-bring* sound. And as it rings again, I realise it's definitely coming from inside my wardrobe. I open my wardrobe and stare inside, trying to work out where on earth the ringing is coming from. And then I realise. The bag. There must be a phone in the bag.

I pull all the clothes off the shelf in my wardrobe and let them fall to the floor and then grab the bag and pull that down as well. I carry it over to my bed and drop it on top. Then I listen again. There are zipped pockets at either end that I didn't even notice last night. And the ringing is coming from one of them. I unzip the pocket just as the phone stops ringing. I take the phone out. It's a cheap one. A really old and clunky blue one.

On the screen it says, *You have 1 missed call*. I press the green button to see who it's from and see that it was another mobile number that called. I think about calling the number straight back to see who it was. I might be able to find out who the bag belongs to. But I don't do it. Instead, I open up the contacts. There are no names in there. Not even one. So I go to the text messages. Nothing there, either. I sigh, switch the phone off and put it back in the end pocket of the bag.

I look through the rest of the pocket. There's half a packet of mints in there. I put them back and rummage around again to see what else there is. But it's empty. So I turn the bag round and open the pocket at the other end. I shove my hand inside. And right away I feel something. Hard and cold. I wrap my fingers around it and take it out. And even before I see it, I realise what it is with a sinking feeling. A gun. A black handgun. I stare dumbly at it for a couple of seconds, like my brain's working in slow motion or something, before I realise what I've done. I've just got my finger-prints all over it. Shit. I start to panic. I don't know what to do. I don't even know what to think.

I hold the gun up to the light and look at it. There's a company logo on the handle. *Pietro. Beretta.* On the barrel there are some words engraved: *Made in Italy* and *9mm*. There's an Italian word as well, *Gardone*. I don't know what it means. Maybe the name of a place. I put my finger on the trigger and then look down the barrel, aiming at my wardrobe. I've never held a gun before in my life. I never thought I would. It feels strange. One pull of the trigger and someone could die.

The gun feels heavy and powerful. I get an urge to pull the trigger right now, just to see what happens, what it feels like. But I don't. Instead I lower my arm and look at it. I've seen people use guns like this a million times in films and on TV and stuff. I could probably name every part of it. But it feels weird to have a gun right here in front of me. I wonder whether it's loaded. I fiddle around and the magazine slides out. I count the bullets. Six. It chills me, seeing the bullets, thinking that any one of them could end someone's life. I slide the magazine back in. I look at the gun again, at the safety catch. I flick it off and then back on. I sit and stare at the gun for ages, trying to make sense of it all. My heart's beating like mad. I don't know what to do.

I close my eyes and try and stop my heart from pounding so hard. And then I try and rationalise this. Because the simple fact is, nobody knows that I have this gun. Not even Joe. And as long as I hide it, no one will ever know it exists. This doesn't change anything. I can deal with it. I just have to stay calm and not do anything stupid. All I have to do is keep it hidden. And then dispose of it somehow.

Downstairs, the doorbell rings. I sit up with a start. I stuff the gun back into the end pocket and zip it back up. The doorbell rings again, impatiently. I grab the bag off my bed and take it over to the wardrobe, reach up and put it on the shelf, just as the knocker on the front door goes. I shove my clothes back in front of the bag and then shut the door.

I leave my room and run down the stairs. I take a second to compose myself and then open the front door.

'Ash!' Rabbit says, barging past me.

I close the door and follow him through to the lounge, where he's already sitting on the sofa, taking a bottle out of a blue carrier bag and inspecting the label. It's white rum.

'You got any glasses?'

I ignore his question. I take a second, just to stay calm. And I realise I have to act completely normal, so Rabbit doesn't think anything's up. 'What you drinking that shit for?' I say, smiling.

Rabbit opens the bottle and takes a swig, makes a face and then grins. 'Because, my friend, it was in my dad's spirit cabinet. And it gets you wasted. Fast.'

'It's what girls drink,' I say.

Rabbit laughs. 'Nothing wrong with being in touch with your feminine side,' he says. 'As long as you're getting wasted!'

I smile. 'All right. I'll get some glasses.' Because I need a drink right now, even if it's this rubbish.

We sit and shoot the shit about music and girls and all kinds of stuff. And we down the rum quickly. And pretty soon I'm starting to feel pissed. I start to feel better about the gun. Cos I can deal with it. I will deal with it.

After a while the conversation turns to next weekend.

'You coming to mine Friday?' Rabbit says. 'My dad's in London all weekend.'

I smile. 'Course,' I say. 'I've invited everyone I know.'

Rabbit laughs. 'What, your mum and dad?'

'Yeah. Very funny,' I say. I take a gulp of neat rum. It tastes disgusting. 'No, seriously. I invited a few people. You don't mind, do you?'

Rabbit shakes his head. He drains his glass. 'Nah.' He picks up the bottle and peers at it. It's already nearly finished. He takes the cap off and pours the rest out, some into my glass and the rest into his.

'Down it?' I say.

Rabbit nods and smiles. 'Down it!' he says, holding his glass up.

So we do, at the same time. Down in one. It makes me shudder. But when it's down, I get a warm feeling in my stomach. And the world starts to feel fuzzier.

'Right,' I say. 'More booze!'

Rabbit smiles. He's starting to look a bit drunk.

'My dad's got loads of whisky. Want some?'

Rabbit nods his head. I go over to Mum and Dad's drinks cabinet and take out a half-full bottle of whisky. I'll buy them some more tomorrow. It's not like I can't afford to. Not that Dad would notice anyway. He gets through loads of the stuff.

Me and Rabbit start to get through the whisky damn

88

quick ourselves. Shot after shot of the stuff. And pretty soon we're completely wasted. Wankered. Rolling around the floor. Slurring. Talking rubbish.

I get up and kind of stumble over. I laugh.

'You're pissed!' Rabbit says.

Which is a bit rich, seeing as he's also lying on the floor.

'Come with me,' I say.

Rabbit grins. 'Where you going?'

'Upstairs. My bedroom.'

Rabbit starts to laugh like a madman. Eventually he manages to say, 'No way, bender boy! I'm not into all that!'

I shake my head. 'Don't be an idiot,' I say. 'I've got something I want to show you.'

He starts laughing again. 'Listen, Ash, if it's your dick, I don't want to see it!'

I shake my head. I start walking towards the door. 'Stay here if you want,' I say. 'Just means there'll be more for me.'

I start walking up the stairs. And sure enough, after a couple of seconds, Rabbit starts following me, falling all over the place. 'So what is it?' he says. 'What you got up here?'

I push my bedroom door open. Rabbit follows me inside. He sits down on my bed.

'What is it?'

I don't answer. I just go over to my drawers and pull

out a bag of weed. I take it over to Rabbit, chuck it down in his lap.

His mouth falls open. 'No way!' he says. 'Jesus. Is that what I think it is?'

I nod my head. 'Oh yes,' I say. 'And it's good stuff as well.'

There's a massive grin on Rabbit's face. 'Well, don't be shy,' he says. 'Let's have a smoke!'

SUNDAY

Ash

I get woken up by the bloody message tone on my phone. I can hear it somewhere near my head. I reach out my hand and feel around, but I can't find it. So I open my eyes. And I realise right away that I'm not in bed. I'm not even in my room. I'm in the bloody lounge, lying on the floor. I raise my head up a bit and look around. My phone's on the floor, near the sofa. I sit up and groan. I feel like shit. I pick it up. There's a message from Mum. **Hope you are OK. We'll be back at teatime. Mum x**

I sigh. Was it really worth waking me for that? I put my phone in my pocket and look around the room. Rabbit's sleeping on the sofa, snoring. There's an empty bottle of rum and a bottle of whisky lying on the floor. And some others as well, ones that I don't remember drinking, like a half bottle of vodka. At least it explains why my head's spinning and I feel like I'm gonna vom. There's loads of fag butts and ash in the vase on the table as well. Mum and Dad'll kill me if they come back when the house is like this.

But right now I can't even think about stuff like that. What I need is sleep. And water or something. I stand up, not too steady on my feet. I walk through to the kitchen. And as soon as I get in there, a smell of vomit fills my nostrils. I put my hand up to my face and cover my mouth and nose. I go over to the sink and there it is: a big pile of sick. It makes me gag. I don't remember doing that. Must have been Rabbit. I look away from it and try not to breathe the smell in. I grab a mug from the draining board, fill it with water and then gulp it down. I fill it straight back up again and gulp it all down.

I turn and go out of the kitchen, clutch at the wall to steady myself. I head up the stairs to my bedroom. When I get in there it's a total mess. My clothes are all over the floor, the bed and my drum kit. And the money from the bag's spread all over the place. As I stand there, I kind of get a flashback: me and Rabbit standing in my room, throwing the money around as though we're millionaires. Oh shit. I hope he doesn't remember. Joe'd kill me if he knew I'd told someone else.

But I'm too fucked to think about it right now. My bed's calling me. I pull everything off my bed, get in and pull the covers over me.

I wake up a couple of hours later. Just after eleven. And I still feel like shit. My head's swimming. I think I might still be pissed.

I lie in bed for a while, looking around my room at the mess, at the money. And I get a pang of something as I look at the money. Guilt, I guess. Not guilt that I have the money. More that I might have let Joe down, that Rabbit knows our secret – if he can remember what happened last night. I mean, there are worse people to know your secrets than Rabbit. He wouldn't tell anyone. But . . .

I jump out of bed. I've gotta tidy this stuff up. If anyone saw all this money and the weed, that would be it. So I start picking it up, handfuls of notes at a time, stuff it back into the bag. As I'm doing it, my head pounds and my stomach feels like it's filled with acid. But I have to do this right now.

When I'm done, I pick the bag up and shove it back into the wardrobe and I let out a sigh. I think about getting back into bed. But then I remember Rabbit asleep downstairs. Maybe I can find out if he remembers seeing the money. Subtly, of course. So I leave my room, go down the stairs to the lounge.

Only Rabbit's not there any more. He must have woken up and let himself out. The room's a total mess. I turn and go into the kitchen with my hand over my mouth so I don't have to smell the sick. I put the tap on, aim it at the sick and leave it running so it'll wash the puke away. I look under the sink, grab a black bin bag and go back through to the lounge.

Joe

Sunday lunch in my house is like a sitcom where everyone says and does the same things every week, like they're characters rather than real people. It's comforting in a way, I guess. Sometimes it's even funny and me and Kate take the mickey out of it all. But sometimes it's just plain annoying, simple as that.

And here we are again, Sunday lunch. Dad's picked Granny up from her bungalow and Mum's cooked the dinner.

Dad brings some of the plates into the dining room, where me and Granny are waiting. He puts a small one in front of Granny. She looks down at her plate with a shocked expression, like she's never seen anything so delicious-looking in her whole life. She does it every weekend.

Dad puts my plate down in front of me. 'Thanks,' I say. I look down at it. It's pork, roast potatoes, carrots, cabbage, broccoli. And I feel hungry as hell.

'The broccoli, spuds and cabbage are home-grown,' Dad says.

'Ooh, nothing but the best service in this restaurant,' Granny says to me as Dad goes back through to the kitchen.

I smile back, like I've never heard her say that before.

Kate comes and sits down at the table. Her plate's already on the table waiting for her.

'Hello, Katherine, dear,' Granny says.

Kate doesn't look up. 'Hi, Granny,' she says. She's staring at her plate. At the pork. She does this every week too.

Mum and Dad both come into the dining room. Mum's carrying her and Dad's plates and Dad has the gravy boat in one hand and a bottle of wine in the other.

'What's this?' Kate says.

Mum puts the plates on the table and sits down. Dad goes round the table, filling glasses with wine.

'You know what it is,' Mum says. She doesn't look at Kate. She gets the pepper from the middle of the table and grinds some on her food.

'It's meat!' Kate says. She makes it sound like someone shat on her plate. Every week the same thing.

'I should hope so too,' says Dad, sitting down. 'I paid good money for that at the butcher!' He winks across the table at me and Granny.

Granny chuckles to herself and loads her fork with food. I keep my head down. I'm not taking anyone's side in this now. I'll wind Kate up about it later instead.

'You know I'm a vegetarian!' Kate says. 'I don't eat meat. It's murder.'

Mum puts down her knife and fork and sighs. 'Look,' she says. 'When you're sixteen you can make your own decisions. Then you can be a vegetarian or a vegan or a fruitarian or a Rastafarian or whatever you like.'

Kate sighs. She pushes the meat towards the edge of her plate, so that it looks like it might fall off on to the table. 'I'm not eating it,' she says. 'You can't make me.'

Mum shakes her head and picks up her knife and fork again. 'Fine,' she says.

There's silence for a while. Everyone sits and eats. Everyone except Kate, who just kind of pokes her food around her plate.

After a while Granny stops eating and looks over

101

at Kate. 'Come on, love,' she says. 'Eat up, won't you?'

Kate doesn't answer. She doesn't even look up.

'You need meat. Your body needs the protein,' Granny says.

Kate still doesn't look up.

Dad stops eating. He looks at Kate. 'Your grand-mother is speaking to you, Kate,' he says. 'Stop being rude, please.'

Kate sighs. She slowly lifts her head and looks at Granny. 'I'm a vegetarian, Granny,' she says. 'Or at least I would be if they let me.' Kate nods her head towards Mum and Dad.

Granny looks her in the eyes. 'Look, Katie,' she says. 'I understand why you'd want to be a vegetarian. I've seen all the TV programmes with the chickens and the pigs and what have you. It's appalling when they keep them in cramped conditions. But not all animals are kept like that. And your dad bought this from the butcher. It's free-range.'

Kate tuts. She says something under her breath, something like, 'You don't understand.'

Granny pretends not to notice. 'Besides, love,' she says, 'you're a growing girl. You need a balanced diet. You need protein and iron and –'

'I'm not stupid,' Kate snaps at Granny. 'Meat isn't the only kind of food that has protein and iron, you know.'

'Right,' Dad says in a raised voice, like he's gonna shout at Kate. But he doesn't shout. He doesn't say anything for a few seconds. And when he finally does open his mouth, he just says, 'Let's change the subject, shall we?'

And we don't talk about it any more.

In fact, we don't talk about anything. The only noise in the dining room is the clunk of knives and forks on plates and the disgusting crunching noise as Granny eats a bit of crackling. The sound makes me cringe. I hate other people's food noises.

A minute or so later, Granny puts her knife and fork down, has a gulp of wine. She puts her wine glass down carefully. 'There was a big fuss by those new flats when we drove into Fayrewood,' she says.

Mum picks up her wine glass and takes a sip and nods. 'We drove past yesterday. Awful, isn't it?'

Granny nods. 'Oh, yes,' she says. 'Police cars and all sorts, weren't there, Robert?'

Dad nods. He doesn't say anything till he finishes his mouthful. 'Yes,' he says eventually. He turns to Mum before he carries on talking. 'There are more camera crews down there now, Bev. A real scrum of them.'

'Really?' Mum says. 'I wonder why that is.'

Granny and Dad both shake their heads.

103

'It'll be what I said,' Dad says. 'They'll have found out it's an insurance job. You wait.'

I spend the afternoon in my room, trying to start some revision by drawing up a revision timetable. Downstairs, Granny's watching a documentary about elephants or something while she does the ironing. She does it every week, to lend a hand, she says. Dad's in the garage, trying to tidy it up. And Mum's in the living room with Granny, yakking. Kate's in her room doing her homework.

At about half four, there's a knock on my door.

'Come in,' I say. I'm lying on the floor highlighting the different subjects in fluorescent pens.

Granny pokes her head round the door. 'I'm off now, Joe, love,' she says.

I look round and smile at her. 'OK,' I say.

She walks into my room. 'Why don't you work at your desk?' she says. 'You can't do your homework on the floor.'

I smile again. 'It's all right,' I say. 'I'm only doing my revision timetable.'

She smiles. 'You've always been a clever lad,' she says. She pats my head like I'm a five-year-old. 'You'll make something special of your life, I know it.'

I don't know what to say to that. So I just smile again.

Granny comes right over to me and kisses me on the top of my head. 'You're a good lad,' she says. 'See you on Thursday.'

'Bye,' I say. And I get back on with my work.

Around teatime, when I'm in my room and I've finished the timetable, I'm lying on the bed strumming my guitar when I hear Dad's car pull up outside the house. I go downstairs.

'All right, Dad,' I say as he comes into the hallway.

He puts his keys into the bowl near the door, takes off his jacket and hangs it up. 'Hey, Joe,' he says. He's got a strange look on his face. Like something's wrong. 'I don't know what's going on out there, but there are more TV trucks down near the flats.'

'You were right probably, Dad,' I say. 'Maybe they found out it was an insurance job.'

Dad shrugs. He goes through to the lounge and I follow him. 'Let's put the goggle-box on and have a look.'

We sit down on the sofa. Dad grabs the remote control and flicks it to the news. They're showing a story about an England batsman who broke his finger in training.

'Nothing,' Dad says.

But along the bottom of the screen, there's a rolling

news thing. It says, *BREAKING NEWS: A BODY HAS BEEN FOUND IN BURNT-OUT FLATS IN A DORSET TOWN.*

'God,' I say. 'They found a body. It's down at the bottom, Dad.'

Dad reads it as well. 'Bloody hell,' he says. He shakes his head.

We both sit in silence staring at the screen. And I'm thinking, *I wonder who was inside the flats? I wonder if I know them.*

The story about the cricketer comes to an end. The newsreader in the studio looks straight into the camera. 'Breaking news now,' she says. 'And a body has been found in the remains of a fire in an unused block of flats in the East Dorset town of Fayrewood. Fire crews were called to a fire at the flats in the early hours of Saturday morning. Police have today revealed that a body was found in the aftermath of the blaze by fire officers. They are treating the fire and the death as suspicious. Our correspondent Judith Lawson is at the scene . . .'

Dad turns to look at me. His eyebrows are raised. 'I don't believe this,' he says. 'Not in Fayrewood.'

I don't say anything. I just look back at the TV. There's a reporter standing on the pavement less than half a mile down the road. In the background you can see the police tape sealing off the unfinished road that runs down towards the flats. And in front of the tape are a few policemen and policewomen standing around.

'Details are scarce so far,' the reporter says. 'But a police spokesman has said that they are treating the fire, and therefore the death, as suspicious. No formal identification of the body has taken place yet. But we understand that the body is that of a man.'

'Bev,' Dad calls to Mum from the sofa, 'come and watch this.'

I sit there and stare at the screen. There's an aerial view of the town. For a second I try to find our road and our house on it, but before I can, the camera zooms in on the flats. People are scurrying around outside them. They look like ants from the camera angle.

Mum comes into the room. 'What is it?' she says. She stands behind the sofa and stares at the TV.

'They found a body,' Dad says, 'in the flats.'

Mum gasps. 'No,' she says. 'How awful! Who is it?'

Dad looks up at her. He shakes his head. 'Don't know. They've said it's suspicious. It's a man is all they've said so far.'

'That's horrible,' Mum says. She turns away from the screen. 'Oh, that's made me feel unwell.'

The news story ends and they go on to a story about a suicide bomber in Israel. Dad flicks over to another news channel. But it's just the adverts. He switches the TV off.

'Well,' he says, 'let's just hope that it's no one we know.'

Ash

Mum and Dad pull up outside the house. I get off the sofa and run upstairs. I don't want to be downstairs when they get in and realise that I've been smoking and drinking and chucking up while they've been away. I look out of my bedroom window. From up here, I can see Mum and Dad having a go at each other in the car. I watch as Mum shakes her head, shouts something and then gets out. She slams the door shut behind her and marches up to the front door.

I keep watching the car as I hear Mum open the door and come into the house. Dad doesn't go after Mum. He sits in the driver's seat and looks at his mobile. He puts the phone to his ear and then has a conversation. I watch as he gesticulates, but I have no idea what he's saying or who he's talking to.

After a bit Dad puts his phone away, gets out of the car and opens the boot. He pulls his and Mum's suitcases up to the door.

Almost as soon as he comes into the house, I hear him and Mum having a go at each other again. Their voices come up through the floor. I can just about make out what they're saying.

'I'm working all the bloody hours under the sun to stop my bloody business going tits up. And all you can bloody do is moan!' Dad shouts.

I sigh. I hate it when they argue, which at the moment is pretty much all the time.

'When you are here you're always bloody drunk,' Mum says.

'Ha! The words pot, kettle and black spring to mind,' Dad says. 'You can bloody talk!'

I can't be doing with this. I go and put some music on, bang it right up, drown Mum and Dad out. And then I go and sit behind my drum kit. To think that I was worried they were gonna come in and have a go at me because the place was a mess. They couldn't care less about anything but themselves. I start playing along to the track, good and loud, so I can't hear anything else.

About a minute later, my door swings open and Dad stands in the doorway. He says something, but I carry on playing. I look away from him. But out of the corner of my eye, I see him move into my room. He comes and stands in front of me. I stop playing, look at him and roll my eyes. 'What?'

'Can you keep the noise down?' he says. But it doesn't sound much like a question to me, more of a threat.

'Why? Can't you hear yourselves shouting?'

Just for a second, Dad looks like he's gonna explode and shout at me. But he doesn't. He just breathes deeply. 'You making a noise isn't going to help the situation,' he says.

I kind of snort with laughter, though it isn't funny.

'Please,' Dad says. He's trying to stay calm with me.

I roll my eyes and get off the drum stool, go and sit on my bed. 'Fine,' I say. 'I'll be quiet so that you and Mum can enjoy your argument.'

Dad's eyes narrow for a second. 'Thank you,' he says. But instead of leaving my room, he keeps on standing there. 'How was your weekend?' he asks.

I shrug. 'OK.'

Dad rocks on his heels. 'Good,' he says. 'Good.'

And then there's a silence. I don't even look at Dad. I can sense him standing there with his hands in his pockets. 'Have you done your homework?' he says eventually.

I shake my head. 'We didn't get any,' I say. Which is a lie. 'I've only got one week left.'

'Well, you should be revising, then,' Dad says. 'The next month or so is gonna be one of the most important times of your life.'

I lie back on my bed. 'I know,' I say. I'm not really in the mood for the lecture right now. 'I'll start revising next week.'

Even without looking I know Dad's hanging around in my room, not saying anything. He stays there for a while. And then, still without saying a word, I hear him walk out of my room and back downstairs to go and carry on his argument with Mum.

MONDAY

Joe

When I go downstairs for breakfast, Mum and Dad are both in the living room watching TV. I stand by the door, looking in at what they're watching. It's the news. It's about the fire at the flats. My curiosity gets the better of me and I walk in.

Mum turns round. 'Oh, morning, love,' she says.

Dad's still watching the TV. He points at the screen. 'Hey, Joe, have you seen this?'

I read the rolling news bar at the bottom of the screen: *DORSET POLICE CONFIRM THAT THEY HAVE LAUNCHED A MURDER INQUIRY FOLLOWING THE DISCOVERY OF A BODY IN A BURNED-OUT BLOCK OF FLATS.*

I'm not sure what to say. This is weird. Stuff like this doesn't happen in Fayrewood. It's not that kind of place.

'They're doing a post-mortem as we speak,' Dad says, still watching the screen.

'It's horrible,' Mum says.

I nod.

Dad puts the TV on standby with the remote and then goes and switches it off at the wall. He turns to me and Mum. 'There's a press conference this afternoon,' he says. He shakes his head and sighs in disbelief. 'Come on, then, let's get some breakfast.'

Ash

I've been thinking. About what Joe was saying at the rec. About karma. About how we can do some good with the money. It took me ages to think of it, but it's obvious really. Right under my nose.

Which is why, instead of getting ready for school right now, I'm sitting on my bed counting the money. Mum and Dad have already had a row and both left for work.

I count out twenties. A hundred of them. Two thousand pounds. Then I put them in a big brown envelope, lick the sticky bit and seal it. I pick up a pen, hold it in my left hand and write the name and address. Back in middle school I broke my arm playing football and I had to learn to write with my left hand for a while. I haven't written with my left hand for years. My writing looks uneven and spidery. Which is just how I want it to look. No one will be able to trace it to me.

When I'm done writing the address, I stick a stamp on the front and stare at it for ages, wondering if this is the right thing to do. And then I get ready for school.

Joe

It's all anyone's talking about at the bus stop. The fire. The body. The murder inquiry. Everyone has their own theory about what happened and who was in the fire. There's even a rumour that it was our head teacher, Mr Watts.

About quarter past eight, which is when the bus is due, Ash walks up the road towards the bus stop, carrying a brown envelope. As he goes past the postbox, he puts it in and then comes over and stands next to me.

'Last week of school!' he says. He lets his bag slide off his shoulder and fall on the ground.

I smile. 'I know. I can't believe it. We're nearly free men.'

'About bloody time,' Ash says. 'I can't wait for this week to end. Actually, to tell you the truth, I can't wait for the next two years to be over. I'm gonna get my A levels and then get out of this dump for ever.'

I nod. 'Yeah.'

'Hey, you hear about the flats?' Ash says.

'Course,' I say. 'It's mad, isn't it? Murder in Fayrewood.'

Ash laughs. 'It's like the hood in Fayrewood nowadays.'

'Like New York or something. The Bronx.'

Ash smiles. 'Too right. I can just imagine it,' he says. 'Old Mrs Reilly from down my street, cruising down Marshland Road on her mobility scooter.' He starts miming driving a mobility scooter. 'She sees someone from a rival gang – Mrs Webster from the WI. She reaches into the basket of her scooter and pulls her piece. AK47!' Ash mimes an old lady pulling out a gun in slow motion.

I can't help but laugh.

'Bang, bang, bang!' he says. He blows the smoke away from the top of the imaginary weapon. Then he laughs.

As we're messing around, the bus pulls into the stop. The brakes hiss and the door swings open. The Year Eights get on first. Me and Ash wait and get on last. Ash goes right up the bus to where a couple of Year Eight kids have sat on the back seat.

'Shift,' Ash says. He indicates with his thumb. 'Down the front of the bus where you belong, little boys.'

One of the young kids makes a face at Ash and sticks up his middle finger. Ash lifts his hand as though he's gonna slap the kid round the face. The kid laughs and gets up from the seat and so do his mates. Ash uses his hand to ruffle the kid's head and then breaks out into a grin.

'Gotta admire that in a kid,' he says. 'Takes balls to stand up to your elders and betters.' He looks at his hand. He sniffs it. 'He could do with washing his hair, though!'

He holds his hand out for me to smell. I turn away.

The bus moves down Marshland Road, turns right at the end and then on to the main road. It trundles along the road, through the middle of the town, stopping at the lights. The bus slows as we get near the flats. Everyone moves over to the right-hand side of the bus and looks out of the window. The block of flats is still cordoned off and it's surrounded by police and reporters and TV cameras. There are still police standing around; some in uniform and some in suits and ties. There are others in white boiler suits as well. They must be forensics or something.

The bus moves past and everyone sits back down.

As we drive along the road out of town, Ash's phone beeps to say he has a message. He reads it right away and sighs.

'What's the matter?'

He looks out of the window. 'Nothing,' he says.

And neither of us says another word all the way to school.

Ash

Rabbit is the first person I see when I get into the playground. And I feel uneasy as soon as I see him. He gives me a really angry look. And I start to dread what's gonna happen. See, he sent me a text on the bus, saying, **You better be able to explain this**. And it can only mean one thing. It has to be about Saturday night and the money. Though why he's angry about it, I don't know.

'Follow me,' he says quietly, so no one else can hear.

So we sneak away from everyone else, Rabbit leading and me following. And all the time I'm kind of hoping that this is about something else – about something I said the other night when he was round, or some girl he fancies. But I don't ask what he wants. I just follow.

We walk right past all the mobile classrooms and then go round the back of the last one – Mr Robert's French room, where some of us go at break time to have a smoke. Rabbit doesn't usually smoke though, only when he's drunk. There's no one else here right now.

Rabbit turns and looks at me. He puts his hand into his pocket and pulls out his mobile. He looks at it, presses a few buttons and then holds it up for me to see. And as soon as he does, my stomach ties itself in knots. There's a picture of me on there, holding a gun. The gun. Trying to look like a gangster or something.

'Explain this!' he says. He sounds angrier than I think I've ever heard him before.

'Shit!'

'That's your fucking bedroom,' he says. 'I must have taken that photo on Saturday night.'

I take a deep breath and look away. Shit. I don't remember that photo being taken.

'That sure as hell isn't my gun,' Rabbit says, 'so it must be yours. Now explain. Where the fuck did you get a gun from?'

I open my mouth to speak, but don't say a word. I'm not sure what to say. 'It's not what it seems.'

Rabbit stares impatiently at me. He looks like he's gonna hit me any second.

So I tell him the lot. About me and Joe and how we found the car and the bag and the money. Except I don't tell him the complete truth. There are parts of this he doesn't need to know. Like the fact that there was twenty grand in the bag. I tell him five hundred instead. Don't know why, it just comes out. And I tell him how I found the gun the next day, just before he came round.

'I don't believe this,' he says when I've finished. He runs his hands through his hair, looks at the picture on his phone again and then back at me. 'Fuck!' he says, kicking at the floor. 'Did I touch it as well? Are my prints on it?'

I shrug. 'I don't remember much from Saturday night. I don't know.'

'You haven't got any pictures on your phone?'

'I don't know,' I say. 'I haven't looked.'

'Fucking well look now, then,' he says.

I get my phone out of my pocket. Rabbit comes and stands at my shoulder. And sure enough, when I open up my pictures, there's one of him wearing my shades and holding the gun, pointing it at the lens.

He kind of wheels away as soon as he sees it. He kicks at the fence. 'Shit. Shit. Shit.'

Neither of us says anything for a second. I keep flicking through the photos on my phone. There's another one of Rabbit smoking a spliff, with a handful of money.

Rabbit takes a long, deep breath and then blows it out slowly. It's ages before he finally speaks. 'This is serious.'

'I know.'

He shakes his head like he can't take all this in. 'My prints'll be all over the gun.'

I nod. 'Both our prints are on it.'

'Did you say that you didn't find it till Saturday afternoon?'

'Yeah. When I heard the phone ringing I checked through the bag and found it.'

'So does Joe know?'

I shake my head. 'No. And I don't intend to tell him. He'd freak out.'

'No shit, Sherlock,' Rabbit says. 'Course he'd freak out.'

'He'd go straight to the police,' I say.

'Yeah?' Rabbit says. 'Maybe that's not such a bad plan.'

I shake my head. 'No way.'

'Why not?'

'Because me and Joe have already spent some of the money. Because me and you have already smoked some of the weed. Because it's gonna look a bit weird that we found the bag on Friday and waited until now to hand it in . . .'

Rabbit doesn't say anything. He looks at the ground, where the grass has been worn away by the feet of all us smokers, at the fag ends. It feels like hours before he looks back up at me. 'In that case, we need to get rid of it,' he says.

'What? Sell it?'

He shakes his head, looks at me like I'm mad. 'No. Get rid of it. Hide it somewhere where it's never gonna get found.'

'Like where?'

'I don't know. Throw it in the sea or something.'

'Throw it in the sea? How we gonna do that? The sea's ten miles away.'

In the distance, I hear the school bell going for the start of registration.

'Well, what about the woods, then?' he says. 'We could bury it.'

'That's better. That could work. You won't tell anyone, will you?' I say. 'No one else can know this.'

Rabbit nods. He doesn't look at me. He seems stressed and angry.

'I'll cut you in on the money if you want. A hundred quid?'

Rabbit looks at me now. There's something in his eyes, as though he's deciding whether he's gonna hit me or not. 'I don't want anything to do with the money,' he says. 'I just want that gun to go away and never be found.'

'Course.'

'I'll come over to yours after school,' Rabbit says.

As soon as I get home, I go straight to my wardrobe and take everything out. I hold the gun in my hands, turning it round and round, staring at it for ages, wondering who it used to belong to. Whether it's killed anyone. And I feel creeped out by the thought that the object I'm holding might have ended someone's life. So I check the safety catch is on and put it back in the bag. I lie on my bed.

From downstairs, I hear the door knocker. I run down the stairs two at a time. I pause before I open the front door and I realise how nervous I feel, how serious this situation is. Rabbit is standing on the step. He doesn't smile as I answer the door; he doesn't even say hello. He walks into the house without saying a word, a weird mix of fear and determination on his face. I close the door behind him. And then we stand in the hallway, looking at each other, awkward.

'So how do we do this?' I say.

'We should try and wash our prints off the gun first,' Rabbit says.

'Can you get rid of fingerprints?'

Rabbit shrugs. 'I don't know. I've never had to clean

my prints off a gun before,' he says. He starts off sounding sarcastic, but halfway through his voice changes and he sounds serious, scared. 'I saw it on some detective show once. It worked when they did it.'

'What do we need?'

'Bleach,' Rabbit says. 'Cloths and rubber gloves or something so we don't have to touch the gun with our skin.'

I nod. 'Right.' I head straight to the kitchen, to the cupboard under the sink, where Mum keeps all the cleaning things. I grab a bottle of bleach, a brand new cloth and two pairs of rubber gloves, and we head straight back out of the kitchen, up the stairs to my room.

I drop the cleaning stuff on my bed, chuck a pair of rubber gloves to Rabbit, put a pair on myself and then take the gun from the bag.

'We should do this in the bathroom,' Rabbit says. He picks up the bleach and cloth and we go into the bathroom.

I pull the door closed behind us and lock it, then put the gun down on the edge of the basin with a metallic *clunk*.

Rabbit shrugs. 'I dunno how to do this exactly,' he says. 'We need to make sure that we get rid of any trace of us on the gun, though. No prints, no clothes fibres.'

131

I nod.

'We'll have to get rid of all the cleaning stuff after-wards too,' Rabbit says. 'All we need to do is dump it in a bin somewhere. No one'll find it.'

'OK.' I take a deep breath. My heart's racing faster than ever. This is making me feel like we've done something bad, like we used the gun to kill someone, even though all we did was find it. I have to remind myself that what we're doing is the right thing to do now. It's the only thing we can do without having to go to the police. So we don't get in shit up to our necks. We have to do this. There's no other choice. And I need to focus.

I squeeze some bleach on to the cloth. I take the gun off the basin and start cleaning it, scrubbing at the handle first, then the barrel. I turn it over and do the other side. We're both silent, staring intently at it. I'm even holding my bloody breath. We exchange a serious glance, but that's it. After a bit, I stop scrubbing. I turn the gun round and round in my gloved hands, inspect-ing every inch of it. But I can't tell whether our prints are off it or not. So I squirt some more bleach on to the cloth and start scrubbing again.

'We can't afford any mistakes,' Rabbit says. 'We have to do this right.'

I nod. I feel panicked. How can we ever be sure that the gun is clean?

Downstairs I hear a key in the front door. The door opens and then closes.

We both freeze.

'What's that?' Rabbit whispers.

'Mum,' I say. 'She must be back from work.'

Rabbit doesn't say anything for a second. I can see him taking deep breaths, trying to compose himself. 'Shit.'

'It's all right,' I say. 'The bathroom door's locked.'

I go back to cleaning again. And then when I'm done, I look at Rabbit and say, 'Do you want to have a go, make sure it's clean?'

Rabbit shakes his head. 'No. Let's just get rid of it.'

'Yeah. Right.'

'We need a plastic bag or something,' Rabbit says, 'to put all this stuff in.'

'Wait here,' I say. 'I'll go and get one.'

Rabbit takes the gun from me. He holds it awkwardly, like it's gonna go off or something. I take off the rubber gloves and leave them on the floor with the bleach and unlock the bathroom door. As soon as I'm outside I look up and see Mum's just about to go into her bedroom. She turns and looks at me. Behind me, the lock clicks shut on the bathroom door. Mum's brow kind of furrows, like she's confused.

I roll my eyes. 'Rabbit,' I say. I'm about to come up

with some excuse, about why we were in the bathroom together, but something stops me.

Mum nods. 'Is he all right?'

I nod. 'Yeah, course.'

Mum rolls her eyes, opens her bedroom door and
goes inside.

I rush along the landing, down the stairs and into
the kitchen. Mum keeps plastic bags in one of those
bag for life things, on a peg. I grab the first one that
comes to hand. I screw it up into a little ball. And then
I turn and run back up the stairs and knock on the
bathroom door. 'It's me,' I hiss.

The lock clicks and the door opens a crack. Rabbit
cranes his head out and looks around the landing.
'Come in,' he says.

I go into the bathroom and pass the bag to Rabbit,
who puts the gun, the cloth, the bleach and the rubber
gloves straight into it.

Then we leave the bathroom together. I look across
at Mum's door, kind of expecting it to open. But it
doesn't and me and Rabbit rush down the stairs, not
daring to breathe the whole time.

We go through the kitchen out into the back garden
and I search around for something to dig with. There's
nothing on the patio, so I go across the lawn into the
shed, grab a trowel and put it in my pocket.

We go back through the house and out of the front

door to get our bikes. Then we ride silently down my road, along the main road and into the woods.

Once we're in the woods we pedal for all we're worth, going deeper and deeper into the forest. And all the time I'm completely on edge: sweaty palms, racing heart, eyes and ears on stalks.

Eventually, when we've been cycling for about ten minutes, I put my feet down to stop myself. Rabbit does the same. We look around at the forest. We're quite near this abandoned building in the woods that we used to call the Old House, where we used to play when we were younger. This would be a good place. You hardly ever see anyone round here; no dog walkers or runners. No one will find the gun here.

I look over at Rabbit. 'What about here?'

He takes another look around us and then nods. 'Yeah,' he says.

'Let's walk into the trees a bit, though,' I say, 'away from the path.'

We wheel our bikes over to the right, off the path and into the trees and the undergrowth. I let my bike fall among the ferns, so it's hidden from view. Rabbit does the same. We start walking, dodging in and out of the trees, walking deeper and deeper into the wood, having to pick our way through brambles, bushes, long grass, ferns and fallen branches.

After a bit, it feels like we're far enough in, further

than anyone else would ever think to walk. So I stop. And I notice something on a tree. My tag. *Layzee Eyez*. I did it years ago, when we used to spend all our time in the Old House. I scratched it into the tree with a penknife. It looks pretty crap. Carving things into tree trunks isn't easy.

I turn to Rabbit. 'How about here?'

He nods.

I bend down and start getting rid of the weeds and ferns and stuff, so that there's a patch of earth to dig in. When there's a clear patch of earth, I plunge the trowel into the soil. It sinks in fairly easily. It's easy to dig and soon the hole's twenty or thirty centimetres deep and there's a growing pile of soil beside it. I stop and look up at Rabbit. He's holding the bag in his hand, staring down at me and the hole.

'How deep do you think we should make it?'

Rabbit looks at the hole and then at the bag, his face twisted into a look of concentration. 'Deeper,' he says. 'We need to make sure no one ever digs it up.'

So I carry on digging. And as I dig deeper, the soil gets harder to dig, especially since I'm using a stupid little hand trowel. I mean, you don't ever see this in the movies, do you? When someone in a film buries something, they always have a big spade, and even though it's always at night, they have the headlights of a truck or a car lighting everything up. The deeper I dig, the heavier the soil is; pale coloured and sticky, like clay. It's a bugger to move with the hand trowel. By the time the hole's about half a metre deep, I stop.

'Deep enough now?'

Rabbit nods, staring into the hole, a serious look on his face. 'Yeah,' he says. 'Move out the way.'

I stand up and take a step back as Rabbit steps forward. He stands over the hole, takes a glove out of the bag and pulls it on, takes the gun out of the bag and lays it in the bottom of the hole.

He takes the glove off and puts it in the plastic bag. 'Pass me the trowel,' he says.

I pass him the trowel and he starts filling the hole back in with the soil.

Joe

As soon as I get back to the house, I switch the TV on and then go through to the kitchen and grab some biscuits. I take them back to the lounge. The TV is already on the news channel, showing the press conference about the fire in the flats and the dead body. I sit on the sofa and turn the volume up.

There's a couple of policemen in uniform sitting behind a desk and a man in a suit next to them. Across the bottom of the screen, there's a little ticker thing, saying, *DORSET POLICE REVEAL THAT BODY FOUND IN FLAT IS THAT OF A 35-YEAR-OLD MALE WHO WAS WANTED FOR MURDER. POST-MORTEM*

CONFIRMS THAT VICTIM DIED OF A SINGLE GUNSHOT WOUND.

I shiver. It's horrible to think that happened half a mile down the road.

The news cuts from the press conference back to the studio. I put a biscuit in my mouth and start looking through the channels for something else to watch.

Ash

Me and Rabbit cycle back out of the forest and on to the main road. I feel very weird. I felt on edge when we cycled into the forest and when we were burying the gun, but now I just feel empty, vacant, as though the rest of the world is happening around me and I can't quite get a grip on it. As though I'm standing in the middle of the road as the traffic zooms past me on both sides. And I don't like it one bit.

I let Rabbit lead the way, along the pavement towards town. We're gonna get rid of the bleach and the cloth and the rubber gloves, put them in a bin somewhere, so they get taken away by the bin men. And then that's it. Nothing left to incriminate us. Well, except the

140

money and the drugs and the holdall. But they're easier to get rid of than a gun.

We go right past the turning to my house and then on into town, past the police station and the fire station. We slow as we pass by the new flats on the other side of the road. They're still taped off, still a couple of police on guard there. They stare at me and Rabbit as we cycle along the path. I look away from them, at the pavement in front of me. I feel as though they can tell what we've been up to, like they can read our minds. There aren't many reporters out there, though. Just a couple standing around looking bored, waiting for something to happen. Someone should tell them that you can wait a long time in Fayrewood for anything to happen. Well, normally, anyway.

We keep cycling, till the police and the flats and the reporters are well behind us and out of sight, and I feel a little better. I'll feel better still when we've got rid of the stuff.

We cycle past the rec, left at the mini roundabout, down to the supermarket. Rabbit turns to me as he's cycling, points off to the side of the supermarket, where there's a little covered walkway and a precinct of shops. We head straight towards it.

We lean our bikes against the newsagent's window and look around, check no one's watching. There are loads of people about, but they're all too busy pushing trolleys and loading up their cars to look at us. I check there are no CCTV cameras, either. There aren't. So we walk along the precinct, right to the end and off to the right, behind the shops. There are five big industrial bins there.

'Open it up for me,' Rabbit says, standing at the nearest bin.

I reach across and pull open the enormous lid of the bin. And immediately a rancid kind of smell hits me. I hold the bin open with one hand and use the other to cover my nose. Rabbit checks again that no one's watching. Then he peeks into the bin, moves a few things around and drops the bag with the cloth, the bleach and the gloves in. He covers it over with a couple of bin bags and a box and then steps back. I let the lid fall. It closes with a thunk. And then we get out of there as quick as we can, round the corner and back to our bikes.

We stop again when we get as far as the rec, where we go over to a bench. Rabbit sits down on the bench without saying a word and stares into space.

'You all right?'

He nods. 'Yeah.'

But I don't think he is. He probably feels like I do: dirty, guilty.

'Neither of us ever tells anyone what happened today. Understand?' he says. 'Not even Joe.'

I nod. 'Definitely.'

We sit in silence for a while. I take out a cigarette and light it, smoke it to the filter and then throw it to the ground.

'What are you gonna do with the rest of the stuff?' Rabbit says eventually.

'I don't know,' I say. 'Just keep it, I guess.'

'Maybe you should hide it somewhere,' he says. 'Get it out of your house in case anyone finds it.'

I don't answer right away. Cos he's probably right. I can't just go on hiding the money in my room. Imagine if Mum found it. But at the same time, I don't want to let go of it. Twenty grand. Well, seventeen and a bit grand now. Where do you hide something like that?

'I'll talk to Joe,' I say.

TUESDAY

TUESDAY

Ash

I get up before my alarm goes off. Which is not like me at all. And the first thing I think about is the bag. I guess that shouldn't be such a surprise, seeing as it's on my mind most of the time. I go over to my wardrobe and pull it down. I open the main part of the bag and take the clothes out. A navy blue sweatshirt, some jeans and a white T-shirt. They all smell of some horrible aftershave. I look at the labels in them. The T-shirt and the sweatshirt are both large and the jeans are a 36 inch waist. Whoever they belong to is much bigger than me.

I put the clothes to one side and look at the money. I shake my head, like I still can't quite believe that we found it. I think about the envelope full of money that I posted yesterday and I wonder where it is right now. And then, with a jolt, I think about the gun and I feel sick and nervous.

I shove the clothes back into the bag and zip it back up. And I turn the bag round, open the end pocket. I take the phone out. And without even thinking about what I'm doing, I switch it on. It takes a while to come on, but as soon as it does, it makes a noise. There's a message. I freeze. For a second I think about switching the phone off and putting it straight back in the bag. But I know I'm not gonna do that. I'd just spend all my time wondering what was in the message.

So I open it.

What have you done with my money? I will find you.

I stare at it for ages, read it over and over again, look at when it was sent, look at the number that sent it. And I start to panic. What if whoever sent this message knows who I am? They could be waiting for me when I step out of the door.

I try to compose myself, remind myself that nobody knows this bag is here. Just me, Joe and Rabbit. And neither of them would tell anyone else about it. There's no way that anyone can know we have the money. No way. Cos if they'd been in the woods on Friday night, they'd have taken the money for themselves. And that's the only time the bag's been outside. Whoever sent the message doesn't know who has the bag, otherwise they'd have it back by now. They're just trying to scare me.

I switch the phone off, put it in the bag and then put the bag on the wardrobe shelf. I go back to my bed and lie down, stare at the ceiling. I definitely have to talk to Joe today. I want to get the bag out of my house.

Joe

Me and Ash have been friends for ever. We met at playgroup (though obviously I can't really remember much about that) and then we were at the same first school and middle school. Now we're at the same high school. Except, I guess, soon we won't be at high school any more. I know where I'll be next year: back here in the sixth form, doing my A levels. I don't know what Ash is gonna do. He says he doesn't want to be at school any more. He hates teachers and being told what to do. To be honest, so do I. Doesn't everyone? But it's something you have to do if you want to get a degree, get a decent job and all that stuff. And I want to do that.

But I'm getting away from the point. The point is that me and Ash have always been close. When we were little, we were inseparable. We hung around together in school, swapped stickers and football cards and all that. And then as soon as school was over, we'd go round to each other's houses to play. It helped that we live so close to each other, but I'm sure we'd have been good friends anyway. We just got on well, without having to try.

When we were in Year Eight, a new kid started at our school. Kurt. His parents had moved to Fayrewood from London. God knows why you'd want to move to Fayrewood from London, but there you go. Anyway, when he started school, everyone thought he was just about the coolest person they'd ever met. He had everything that people wanted. He always had the best trainers, new football shirts, loads of sweets and he had a cool haircut. And he just happened to be the best footballer in our year at school as well. All that stuff sounds so crap now, but back then it meant everything.

It didn't take long for him to figure everyone out, to work out who else was cool and who wasn't. And straight away it was obvious that he wanted Ash to be his best friend. So the three of us hung out together for a little bit, maybe a week. But like everyone knows, two's company and three's a crowd. And as far as Kurt was concerned, I was the one who was making things crowded. So he started treating me like a joke. And me being me, I didn't stand up to him, I just let him go right on ahead and make me feel like shit.

It was just little things, like Ash and Kurt would sit next to each other in class so I was on my own. And they'd have all these in-jokes that I was never in on. Which hurt, because it used to be Ash and me that had those in-jokes.

It sounds weird – it sounds kind of gay (which it isn't) – but I was lost without Ash. I had no one to back me up. I hated it.

But as much as I tried to keep my head down and ignore it, I couldn't. And one day, it came to a head. It was during a PE lesson. A football lesson. Our teacher, Mr Watson, picked two teams, gave us a ball and left us to it. I was on one side, Ash and Kurt were on the other.

Their side scored first. Kurt tackled someone – I can't remember who – on the edge of his own area, and then set off on a run. He went past loads of players. He was really showing off, like he always did. On the edge of our box he passed it to Ash, who looked up and passed it first touch back into Kurt's path. Kurt walloped it and scored. 1–0.

After that, their side scored another one. I think it was Mark W, who played for the school team. And we thought we were in for a real hiding. As the game went on, they went close a couple of times, but they didn't score again. And my team started to get back into it.

I was playing on the wing. And the ball came out to me. I went tearing up the wing, went past a few players and then cut inside, into the box. And Kurt was in front of me, watching the ball, waiting for the right time to tackle me. I tried a couple of tricks, trying to make him commit himself. But he just watched the ball. Finally, I decided to play the ball past him and run. As I ran, after the ball had gone, Kurt stuck out his leg and brought me down. A clear-cut penalty.

'Bollocks!' Kurt said. 'He dived.'

I didn't say anything. I didn't want to get into an argument with him. I knew I wouldn't win that. But the rest of my team did argue the point. And even though Kurt kept insisting that I'd dived or fallen over, we claimed a penalty.

Robbie stepped up and smashed it into the back of the net. And we were back to 2–1. As we celebrated, I caught a glimpse of Kurt looking at me, giving me evils.

For the rest of the game, any time I got the ball, Kurt would be there, trying to hack at my legs. It kind of got to the point where I didn't even want the ball to come to me.

But just as the lesson was about to finish, I couldn't avoid it. The ball dropped at my feet in the opposition team's penalty area and I suddenly found myself one on one with the goalie. I can remember how fast my heart started to beat. I had the chance to level the game. I tried a stepover and sent the keeper the wrong way. Suddenly I had an open goal. All I had to do was roll the ball over the line. I swung my leg and kicked the ball. The ball hit the post and bounced back out. The keeper dived on the ball. And that was that. I'd missed an open goal.

I buried my face in my hands, totally humiliated. I could feel my cheeks burning with shame, with embarrassment. And I could hear Kurt laughing and shouting. I tried really hard not to look at anyone.

The whistle went for the end of the game. We'd lost. A couple of people came over and slapped me on the back. I didn't know who they were cos I still couldn't bring myself to look at anyone. And I could still hear Kurt taking the piss out of me. There were other people joining in too.

I trudged off the pitch on my own. And as I heard people taking the piss, chanting my name, I thought to myself that I just had to ignore them, pretend that I wasn't bothered, and then they'd stop. All I had to do was try and act cool.

Only, when I got back to the changing rooms, I was

met with a barrage of noise and people chanting my name and laughing. And I couldn't handle it. I felt like I wanted to run away and cry. I sat down on the bench and got changed as quickly as I could, not speaking to anyone, not looking at anyone. The noise and the laughing and the chanting didn't stop.

When I'd finished changing, I swung my bag on to my shoulder and walked through the changing room, head down. Before I reached the door, Kurt stepped into my path. The whole changing room seemed to hush, as though everyone was looking in our direction. He stepped right up into my face.

I tried not to look back at him, but he was so close I could smell his breath. I couldn't ignore him. So I stared back into his angry eyes.

'If you ever dive again when I tackle you,' he said, with a real snarl in his voice, 'I'll kick your head in.'

'I can't help it if you tackle like a girl,' I said. I still don't know why I said it. I don't know what possessed me, but the words just seemed to blurt out of my mouth.

A couple of people laughed. Everyone else just kind of gasped, like, how dare I say that?

Kurt looked angry for a second. And then he smiled. 'Yeah? You can talk. You missed an open goal, you donkey. You couldn't hit a barn door with a banjo!'

It sounded like everyone in the changing room laughed. And suddenly something inside me kind of snapped. I leapt forward and grabbed Kurt. Somehow I managed to pick him up, like a karate move. I threw him over my shoulder on to the floor. I looked down at him for a second. He looked shocked, lying there. I turned away, picked up my bag, which had fallen on the floor, and walked towards the door.

Just before I reached the door, I felt an arm on my shoulder. I turned. It was Kurt. He swung his arm, punched me in the stomach and I doubled over.

'Don't mess with me, dickhead,' he said, almost spitting it out.

I didn't say anything. Even if I'd wanted to, I was too winded.

As Kurt turned to go back to where he'd been changing, Ash came striding over with his bag on his back. He looked angry and as he reached Kurt, he pushed him hard in the chest. Kurt was taken completely by surprise and went flying back on to the floor.

Ash didn't say a word to Kurt. And Kurt didn't retaliate. A second later, me and Ash were out of the changing room.

And that was it. Kurt and Ash didn't speak after that. A couple of months later, Kurt had moved again.

Ash

I wait till lunchtime to talk to Joe. We're out on the field, sitting in the sunshine.

'I've been thinking,' I say casually.

'First time for everything,' Joe says. He doesn't turn round to look at me, but stares at some Year Eights who are throwing piles of cut grass at each other.

'About the money,' I say.

Joe's head turns right away. He looks nervously around to make sure no one's listening in. 'What do you mean?'

'I think we should hide it somewhere,' I say.

He stares straight back at me, a kind of confused expression on his face.

'I mean, if I keep it at mine, what happens if someone finds it? What if my mum tidies my room or something?'

He nods his head. 'Good point.'

'If we hide it somewhere else, even if someone finds it, there's nothing to link it to us, right?'

'Yeah,' Joe says. 'OK. Where?'

I shrug. 'Somewhere no one's gonna find it. Like the Old House in the woods.'

Joe watches the Year Eight kids as he thinks about it. After a while he nods. 'All right.'

I smile. 'OK,' I say. 'We should do it tonight.'

'Straight after school?' Joe says.

I shake my head. 'No. We should move it after dark, when there's no one around to see. Meet me at mine at one in the morning.'

Joe sighs and shakes his head. 'One in the morning? You're joking.'

But I know he'll be there.

When I get in through the door, I can see Mum in the kitchen.

'Hi, Ashley,' she says. 'Tea?'

'Yeah, please,' I say.

She fills the kettle and puts it on. And while she's doing it, I stare at her. Thinking. Wanting to say something, but not wanting to be too obvious.

'Did you have a good day?' I ask her as she gets the mugs out.

She plonks the mugs down on the surface and then looks at me, like she doesn't quite understand. 'What are you after?'

I shake my head. 'Nothing,' I say. 'Just being nice. There's no law against that, is there?'

Mum opens the fridge and gets some milk out. 'No,' she says, pouring some into each mug. 'Sorry.'

'So did you?'

'Yeah. Not bad,' she says. 'A bit weird.'

It's quiet for a while. Mum finishes making the tea and then passes me a cup.

'Thanks,' I say. 'What was so weird about your day?'

Mum sighs and looks into the distance. Then all of a sudden she looks at me and says, 'Come on, let's go and sit down in the lounge.'

So we go through and sit down. Mum takes a sip of her tea and then she looks at me seriously. 'I got some post today,' she says.

'That *is* weird,' I say sarcastically.

Mum rolls her eyes. 'No, Ashley, I got some very strange post today.'

'What?'

I get an urge to look away from her, so that she can't read the look in my eyes, so that I can't give anything

159

away. But I fight the urge and look her straight back in the eyes.

'An envelope filled with money,' Mum says. 'Two thousand pounds.'

I try and look surprised, confused. 'What?' I say. 'Why?'

Mum shakes her head and takes another sip. 'I don't know,' she says. 'There was no letter with it and I didn't recognise the handwriting on the envelope. It's a complete mystery.'

I smile. 'That's great,' I say.

Mum raises an eyebrow. 'Is it?'

I nod. 'Yeah,' I say. 'You and Dad are always arguing about money.'

Mum sort of laughs, though I don't think she thinks it funny. 'If it wasn't money, we'd row about something else,' she says. 'Anyway, two thousand pounds wouldn't even pay off the interest!'

'But it'll help, won't it?' I say.

Mum takes another sip of tea. 'It would,' she says, nodding her head. 'Except I can't keep it, can I?'

I have a sinking feeling. 'Why?'

Mum raises both her eyebrows. 'Because it isn't mine, Ashley.'

'Did it have your name on the envelope?'

'Well, yes, but . . .'

'Then it's yours, isn't it?'

Mum sighs. She takes another sip of tea. 'If I knew

160

where it came from, then perhaps,' she says. 'But I've been thinking about it and I have no idea who might have sent it.'

It's silent for a while. Mum sits and drinks her tea. And I start wishing that I hadn't tried to do something nice. She wasn't meant to get suspicious. This never happened to Robin Hood.

'Perhaps I should take it to the police,' Mum says.

I sit up right away. 'What? Why?' And I realise as soon as I've done it that I'm not acting very cool.

But Mum doesn't seem to notice. She's in her own little world. 'Because,' she says, 'it's a bit strange, isn't it? Money turning up in the post like that, addressed to me.'

I nod. This has gone wrong. She was supposed to take the money and use it to help pay some debts or something. It was meant to make her and Dad happier. She was s'posed to be so happy that the money was there that she wouldn't even think about where it came from. Bollocks.

'Maybe you should just keep it somewhere safe,' I say. 'Use it if you need to. Don't take it to the police.'

Mum sips her cup of tea then puts it down on a coaster. She sighs. 'We'll see,' she says.

I'm up in my room after tea. Mum's downstairs watching TV. Dad's still at work, as usual. I push my swivel

161

chair across the room and wedge it underneath the door handle, so no one can get in. I walk over to my wardrobe and pull the bag out. I unzip it. I pick up a wodge of notes and look at them. I smile. It feels kind of mad to be getting rid of it all. Well, I guess we're not getting rid of it exactly . . .

But there's still a part of me that wants the money here, where I can get to it. I look at the notes in my hand. I count them. Three fifties, eight twenties and five tens. Three hundred and sixty quid. I put my hand in the bag and pull out two more twenties. Four hundred pounds. Joe will never know it's here and not in the bag. I fold the money up and hide it in the drawer of my bedside cabinet underneath a couple of old magazines.

Joe

It's five to one in the morning. The house is still. Mum and Dad came upstairs just before eleven and Kate's been in her room all night. I can hear her snoring right now. I've been thinking about what's going to happen tonight, making a plan for how to get out and then back into the house without anyone noticing. And I have to admit that I'm feeling nervous.

But now it's time for action. No going back. I'm wearing black from head to toe. It'll make me harder to spot if there's anyone out there. I get up off my bed, open my door and go out on to the landing, closing my door carefully behind me. The landing's dark. I stand still for a couple of seconds, making sure that no one's stirred. But everything's quiet, apart from the snores.

I creep down the stairs, treading as lightly as I can, sticking to the outsides of the steps where they don't creak. And then, as soon as I'm downstairs, I head for the door, unlatch it and pull it open. I feel the blast of cooler air before I even step outside. I leave the house and quietly pull the door closed behind me.

My bike is leaning up against the side of the house. I get on and start pedalling down the drive and towards Ash's house. I feel nervous. My stomach's churning. I don't want to be doing this. This feels like the most stupid sensible thing I've ever done. Being out in the woods in the early hours of the morning carrying a holdall full of cash. It's risky.

Ash is waiting on his bike at the end of his road. He's got a black hoodie on just like me, only his hood is pulled up over his head. On his lap there's a black bin bag, which I guess has the holdall inside. He's smoking a cigarette as I pull up beside him. He takes it out of his mouth.

'All right, Joe?' he says quietly. From the pocket of his hoodie, he pulls out a torch. He shines it up underneath his chin, making his face look ghostly.

But I'm not in the mood for jokes and messing around. I don't smile, I don't say anything, I just nod. I don't feel all right, no. I feel weird. And nervous.

And scared. I'll feel all right when this is all done and I'm back in bed.

Ash throws his cigarette to the ground and then looks at me. 'Let's do this,' he says. And he starts pedalling.

I sit and stare at him disappearing into the night for a second. He looks like he's in a film, as cool as you like. Maybe it is just like a film in his head – no consequences. Maybe that's how I should be. Maybe then my heart wouldn't be beating like a drum against my ribs. Before Ash is out of sight, I pedal after him.

Neither of us have any lights on our bikes. I have brackets fitted to my bike for them, but I didn't put my lights on tonight. I figured that we're not supposed to be drawing attention to ourselves. And shining a light would do that. But now that I'm on the road, I'm beginning to think that maybe I should have put lights on.

Just before we get to the main road, I hear something. It's a car. 'Ash,' I hiss. 'Car.'

I jump off my bike and flatten myself against the hedge. Ash does the same. We stand there, branches sticking into us, and wait silently. Slowly a silver car appears on the main road. It's a police car. It cruises past the end of the road and then accelerates off into the distance, out of town.

'Jesus, that was close,' I say, feeling sick and shivery with nerves.

Ash nods. 'Come on, let's go.'

We get back on our bikes and start pedalling again. On to the main road and then into the woods. Neither of us says a word. I catch a glimpse of Ash's face. He's looking straight ahead with a kind of steely, determined expression.

We follow the track for a while. There's no noise, apart from the sound of our bikes on the path. We head in the direction of the Old House. The trees tower over us on either side, silhouetted against the dark sky. It gives me the creeps. I can't help thinking about who might be lurking in the woods, what the darkness and the trees could be hiding. I want to get this over and done with as quickly as possible and then get back out.

Before long, we're not surrounded by pine trees any more, but by gnarled older trees, and I know that we're close to the Old House. We slow down and get off our bikes without exchanging a word. We wheel our bikes off the track and in among the trees. We leave them in the undergrowth and then walk the rest of the way. Ash takes a torch from his pocket and lights the way in front of him. I try to concentrate on the ground in front of my feet.

Eventually we pick our way through to the Old

House. Ash shines his torch on the front of the building. It looks even more rundown than it did last time I was here. There's so much ivy and stuff growing on the outside, it almost looks like part of the forest rather than a building. The windows and door are still boarded up, but the chipboard looks like it's rotting and about to fall off. Ash shines the beam of the torch on the grey chipboard rectangle that covers the front door. He goes on ahead, pulls the board off the front of the doorway and in we go.

Inside it's pitch black except for the beam of Ash's torch. He shines it around, lighting up one corner at a time. He leads us off to the left, into the room where we used to hang out back when we were in Year Seven or something. I shuffle along behind, disorientated by the dark, feeling like I'm gonna crash into something any second.

'Where shall we hide it?' Ash says, shining the torch slowly from side to side.

I follow the torch with my eyes, looking for a hiding place. But there isn't anywhere obvious. There's hardly any furniture – no cupboards or anything like that, just a couple of wooden chairs, a table and some old crates. But then the beam of light hits the side of the room, and I have it.

'What about the chimney?' I say.

We both rush over to it. Ash bends down, shines

the torch upwards and looks. 'There's a ledge up there,' he says. He steps out of the way so that I can look as well.

I take a look too. The ledge is just big enough. 'Do it,' I say.

Ash shoves the bag up the chimney until it rests on the ledge. He turns and shines the torch right in my face so I can't see. I put my hands in front of my eyes.

'There. It's done,' he says. 'No one's gonna find it there.'

I smile at him. I feel relieved.

'Let's get out of here,' he says.

Ash leads the way out of the house. We rush along through the undergrowth, among the trees, the beam from his torch bouncing around as he moves. We get back to our bikes and pick them up. Ash switches the torch off, sticks it back in his pocket and then we wheel our bikes back to the path. We jump on to them and start pedalling back through the forest as quick as we can manage, despite the fact that it's too dark to see the ground in front of us. And pretty soon, we're well away from the Old House.

But then, as we bomb along the path with pine trees towering either side of us, Ash skids to a halt and says, 'Did you hear that?'

I didn't hear anything, just the sound of my tyres. But I stop as well. And as soon as I do I can hear what he means. An engine. Tyres crushing small stones. There's a car somewhere near. I keep still and listen. It sounds like it's coming from the track up ahead of us. We both stare ahead, looking for any sign of a car. Nothing. Then I see the flash of headlights between the trees way up ahead of us, round a bend in the track.

'This way,' I say, running off to the right of the track with my bike. 'Quickly!'

We both run, carrying our bikes, in among the trees, until we're twenty metres or so in. We drop to the ground and hide down behind some ferns.

Up on the track the car moves slowly forward, its headlights on full beam. And I realise how exposed we are, that even hidden behind the ferns they might be able to see us.

As the car gets closer, I recognise it as a BMW. It's difficult to tell the colour, but it's definitely dark. Maybe black. Maybe dark blue or green. But what the hell is it doing in the forest at this time of night?

The wheels crunch along the path painfully slowly. Then they stop. And it feels for a second like my heart has stopped beating. The car is literally right in front of us, just twenty metres away up on the track. And I feel vulnerable, like whoever is in the car can see me, like they're looking right at me. Cos for all I know, they could be. Why else would they choose that exact place in the whole of the woods to stop? A shiver runs down my spine. I try and get as low as I can in the undergrowth, hide myself away. If I could tunnel downwards into the earth, I would. My eyes stay locked on the car, wondering who is in there and why they've stopped right in front of us, whether they've spotted us.

And then there's an electrical buzzing noise. The passenger side window opens slightly. I try to look inside, but it's too dark and too far away to make anything out. I close my eyes for a second, hoping that when I open them again this won't be happening any more. But when I do open them, the car's still there. As I stare at it, a glowing cigarette butt flies out of the window and on to the track. The window buzzes back up again. The engine roars, the wheels spin for a second and the car speeds off along the track. I let out a long breath. I can feel my pulse pounding through my temples.

Me and Ash stay silent and still after the car has gone. It must be a minute or more before it finally feels safe and we get to our feet, brush the leaves and soil off our clothes.

'Who was that?' Ash says.

I shake my head. 'I don't know. Didn't see their faces.'

Ash stares over at the track where the car was. 'Do you think they saw us?'

'I don't know,' I say. 'Maybe. Why else would they have stopped right in front of us?'

Ash doesn't say a word. He just stares after the car, down the track. And then suddenly he grabs his bike and starts wheeling it back towards the path. 'Let's get the fuck out of here,' he says.

I grab my bike and follow. 'Let's stick to the smaller paths,' I say. 'Just in case they come back.'

Ash nods and then bombs off along the track.

WEDNESDAY

Joe

I couldn't sleep last night. I got back home at about three in the morning. My heart was still beating at a million miles an hour and my head was rushing. I changed and got into bed, but there was no way I could sleep. So I just lay there and thought things through.

I was panicking about the BMW in the forest. I thought about who it could have been in the car. And there were three options that I managed to get it down to:

1. It was undercover police, patrolling the forest because of the abandoned car or something.
2. It was whoever the bag belongs to, looking for their money.

3. It was just some random person who happened
   to be driving through the forest.

I'd feel most comfortable if it was number 3, the random stranger, obviously. But let's be honest, that one is the least likely cos for a start why would they be driving around the forest? And secondly, why would they be there at two in the morning?

So realistically, I guess it had to be either the police or the owner of the bag. Which is bad news either way.

And then I started thinking about whether they saw us or not. When I first got back, I had convinced myself that they must have done. I was paranoid. But when I thought about it more, I realised that they couldn't have seen us. If they had, they would have done something, wouldn't they? If it was the police and they saw two teenagers hiding in the woods, they would have come and asked us what we were doing. And if it was the owner of the bag and they'd seen us, they wouldn't just drive on, would they?

I got some sleep in the end, when I'd tired myself out with thinking and worry, but I don't know what time it was.

All I know is that right now it's the morning, it's a school day and I feel tired. And I also feel weird about what happened last night, like I'm keeping a guilty secret. Which I guess I am.

I go downstairs and eat breakfast, though I don't manage to eat much. And when I'm done, I go into the lounge to watch TV for a bit and take my mind off everything before I get ready for school. I want to check the sports news cos the cricket starts tomorrow. First Test. Except Kate's already beaten me to it and she's watching some crappy R & B video on a music channel.

'Do you have to watch this?' I ask her.

She turns and fixes me with a stare, right eyebrow raised. 'Yeah,' she says. 'I do. First one into the lounge gets control of the remote. That's the rule.'

I think about getting hold of the remote control and changing channels anyway. Kate's not strong enough to get it back off me. But it's too early for that. So I go upstairs. I'll check on the internet instead.

In my room, I switch my computer on as I get dressed for school. Trousers, shirt, tie, jumper. And by the time I'm finished, the computer has played its little warm-up jingle. I go straight to the sports page to check the cricket news, but before I can read it, I notice the news box at the top of the page. My stomach turns as soon as I see it. *MAN KILLED IN DORSET FIRE LINKED TO ABANDONED CAR*, with a picture of a policeman standing in front of the taped-off flats. I click straight on the link.

Detectives investigating the death of a man in a fire at an unfinished block of flats in Fayrewood have released CCTV footage of the man and made a link to a car abandoned in nearby woodland. The body has been identified as that of Martin Garrard, who Hampshire police believe was involved in a shooting in Southampton on Friday night. CCTV footage released by Hampshire Police appears to show Mr Garrard emerging from the address where a Southampton drug dealer was shot dead. He is seen in the footage carrying a holdall and getting into a silver Vauxhall Astra. Dorset police have now confirmed that the silver Vauxhall, a stolen vehicle, was found crashed in woodland on Saturday morning and recovered by police. Forensic detectives are now examining the vehicle.

Earlier this week, detectives confirmed that Mr Garrard had been shot before the fire at the flats in the early hours of Saturday morning. Det Insp Michael McDermott said: 'We are treating this death as murder, and encourage anyone who may have seen anything suspicious on Friday night in Southampton or Fayrewood to contact us.'

Police are urging anyone with information to call Crimestoppers.

As soon as I've finished, I get up from my computer. I don't know what to do. I'm in shock. I run it through my brain, over and over, trying to work out what this means. Oh God. This can't be happening.

I go back to the computer and reread the story. At the bottom of the page there's a picture, a freeze-frame from CCTV. In the centre of the picture there's a Play button. I click on it and the CCTV clip starts. It's black and white and really grainy. It starts off with a view of a street, with front doors and parked cars on the road. It moves along jerkily for a couple of seconds, before a door opens and a man comes running out. And sure enough, he's carrying a holdall. It's so small, so blurry and jerky that I can't really make out whether it's the same bag that we found, that we hid last night. The man crosses the road and gets into a silver car. The same kind of silver car that we found in the woods. An Astra. The car zooms off and then the clip finishes.

I take a deep breath and blow it out slowly. I can't take this. This is too much.

I scroll back up the page, scan through it again. And I focus on the number. I pick my mobile up and stare at it, thinking. My thumb hovers over the numbers. But something stops me from pressing the buttons. My head is a blur of thoughts and feelings that don't make sense. I don't know what to do. Without thinking too much about what I'm doing, I punch the number into my phone. I take another deep breath, close my eyes and press the Call button. I put the phone to my ear. It rings. Once. Twice. Then there's a click on the other end of the line.

'Hello, you are through to Crimestoppers. Please hold and your call will be answered shortly.'

The line goes quiet for a few seconds and my heart starts to thump in my chest. Then there's another click on the line and another voice. 'Hello. Crimestoppers. How can I help?'

I gulp. I try and work out what I'm going to say. I open my mouth. I want to say something. But the words don't get as far as my mouth; they catch in my throat. And all the time I can feel my heart beating like mad in my chest, in my neck, in my temples.

'Is there anybody there? Are you in immediate danger?'

I breathe deeply, try and compose myself.

'Your call is in the strictest confidence. We won't ask you for a name. Your call will not be recorded or traced.'

I take the phone away from my ear. I can't do it. I press the button on my phone to end the call. I close my eyes and put my head in my hands.

You know what I'd really like to do right now? I'd like to go straight downstairs and tell Mum and Dad what's happened, just so they know. So they can help me. So that this is out of my hands. So someone else can make the decision for me. Except I know that I can't do that. Mum and Dad can never know what's happened. They would go spare. Whose parents wouldn't? Imagine it. *'Um, Mum, Dad, you know the dead body that was found in Fayrewood? Well, I found twenty grand and a big bag of drugs in the woods, and I didn't tell the police about it. Oh, and by the way, I think it probably belonged to the man who died in the flats.'* It wouldn't go down well.

I open my eyes and look around my room. There is only one thing I can do right now. I have to go and see Ash. We have to sort this out together. I get up and grab my school bag and coat off the floor. I go straight downstairs and out of the house.

Thirty seconds later, I'm banging on Ash's front door. I take a step back and wait for an answer. After a bit, the door opens.

'Hello, Joe,' says Ash's mum. 'You're early.'

'I know,' I say. 'Is Ash up?'

Ash's mum shakes her head and opens the door wider. 'No,' she says. 'Go on up, though. Maybe you can shift him.'

I climb the stairs and knock on Ash's door.

'What?' he shouts.

'It's me. Joe. Let me in.'

There's no answer, but a few seconds later the door opens and Ash peers round it. He's wearing his dressing gown. His hair's all over the place, like he's just got out of bed.

'What do you want?' he says. 'It's half bloody seven.'

181

I squeeze past him into his room and go and sit on his drum stool. 'Can I use your computer for a second?'

Ash looks at me, confused as hell. 'Yeah. Why?'

I don't answer. I just grab his laptop, switch it on and find the news story about the body and the car. I turn it round so Ash can see it properly. He walks over and leans in as he reads. The colour drains from his face.

'Shit,' he says.

I nod my head. I thought I'd feel better when I'd shown it to Ash. A problem shared is a problem halved, or whatever they say. But I don't feel better. I feel sick and nervous and guilty as hell. I feel like I'm drowning.

Ash doesn't say anything. He just stares into space, thinking, trying to take it all in.

'What do you think we should do?'

Ash shrugs and shakes his head. 'Shit!'

'We need to do something. We . . .' I say. But I stop cos I don't know what we need to do. It's not the kind of thing they teach you in school, is it?

'Christ,' Ash says. 'We've got the bag. We saw the car. I don't believe this.'

I nod. The guilty knot in my stomach tightens.

'I wonder if Rabbit's seen this,' Ash says.

I'm confused. 'What? Why?'

Ash stares at me for a minute with his mouth open, looking guilty. He glances away from me and runs his

182

hand through his hair. 'I fucked up, Joe,' he says. 'Rabbit knows what happened on Friday night.'

'What? How?'

Ash takes a deep breath. He looks down at the carpet. 'It was Saturday night,' he says. 'Rabbit came round. We got drunk. And I let it slip by accident.'

I don't say anything. I don't even move. I can feel the veins in my temple, throbbing, painful, like they're about to explode. I turn away from Ash, start pacing round his room. I can't believe he's telling me this. What the fuck? If he's told Rabbit, who's to say that he hasn't told other people as well? And what about Rabbit? He might have told someone else. Jesus. Loads of people could know by now. The whole story could be going around Fayrewood.

'You dickhead,' I say. I want to shake him. I want to punch his bloody lights out. I want to shout at him and let him know what a stupid, irresponsible little twat he's been. 'You stupid bloody dickhead!'

Ash doesn't say anything. He doesn't even look at me. He just looks down at his dressing gown and shakes his head.

'Rabbit could have told anyone,' I say. 'Someone could have told the police . . .'

'Sorry,' Ash says. 'What more can I say? I can't do anything about it now, can I? We've just got to deal with it. And Rabbit's not gonna tell anyone, is he? He's not stupid.'

I snort. '*You* bloody told someone!'

'Yeah,' Ash says. 'I know. Sorry.'

I sigh, sit down on the drum stool again. 'What does Rabbit know?'

Ash takes a deep breath. 'I don't know exactly. We were drunk,' he says quietly.

'You've talked to him since then, though, haven't you?'

Ash nods. 'Yeah,' he says. He looks right at me. 'I told him about what happened, how we found the car and the bag, how it was full of money.'

I put my head in my hands. And I think.

'I told him there was only five hundred quid in the bag, though. I offered to cut him in on it, to make sure that he didn't tell anyone else. But he wasn't interested in the money.'

I sit and stare into space, trying to work out what all this means. Does it mean that whoever had the bag got killed because of the bag? Did the man who died in the fire steal the bag from someone? Cos if he did, does that mean that someone's looking for the bag right now? That they might kill me and Ash for it?

And if we took it to the police, what would happen then? Would they even know that we spent some of the money? Would they know that we found it on Friday night and we've had it all that time cos we were gonna keep it? Would they care? I have no idea.

All of a sudden, Ash gets up. He marches over to his wardrobe and gets some clothes out, starts pulling them on in a hurry. Some jeans, a T-shirt, a hoodie.

'What are you doing?' I say. 'It's a school day.'

Ash stops, his foot still in mid-air as he pulls on a sock. 'Fuck school,' he says. 'We're not going today.'

I just stare at him. I've never skived off school in my life. But right now, that's the least of my worries.

Ash pulls his other sock on, then grabs some trainers off the floor and pulls them on as well. 'We're gonna do something about this,' he says. 'We're gonna sort this out once and for all. I'll phone Rabbit.'

I nod my head, even though my stomach feels like something's got a tight hold on it, squeezing it.

Ten minutes later we're riding through the woods. Ash is on his new bike and I'm on one of his old ones. It's started raining lightly. The sky above the treetops is slate grey.

We cycle without a word, heading right through the woods, back to the Old House, to the bag. It's only a few hours since we were here.

There's a problem with this, of course. My sister, Kate. She's going to notice that I'm not at the bus stop. She's hardly likely to keep quiet either. She won't tell the teachers – she's not that stupid. But she'll drop it into conversation in front of Mum and

Dad, you can bet. There's nothing I can do about that right now, though.

We stay well away from where we found the car last Friday, just in case the police are there, in case they're investigating where the car crashed.

By the time we get close to the Old House, it's really starting to piss down with rain. We jump off the bikes and wheel them into the undergrowth, throw them to the ground and run towards the Old House. Ash leads the way, his hood pulled up over his head.

He pulls the piece of boarding covering the door out of the way so we can get inside and then puts it back in its place behind us. He takes his hood down and sighs. He goes straight through to the room on the left, walks up to the chimney and pulls the bag down and out. A load of soot and dust comes with it and lands in the fireplace and on the floor. Ash carries the bag over to the table and puts it down. He opens it and checks the money is still there. Which it is. He looks up at me and nods.

'We should get rid of it,' I say. 'Once and for all.'

Ash looks back at me. He doesn't say anything right away, like he's thinking about something. Eventually he nods his head and says, 'Yeah. Maybe you're right.'

He opens the end pocket of the bag and takes a mobile out.

'Whose mobile is that?' I say.

He shrugs. 'It was in the bag when we found it,' he says.

I stare at the mobile. I think back to last Friday night. There definitely wasn't a phone in the bag. Not that I saw.

'It wasn't,' I say. 'I'd remember.'

Ash stares at the phone. 'I found it in the end pocket of the bag the other day,' he says.

'And you didn't tell me?'

He shakes his head and shrugs. 'Didn't think it was important.'

I snort with laughter. Not important! How dare he not tell me? We're in this together.

'Sorry,' he says quietly. 'I fucked up. Again.'

'Too right,' I say. 'We could have traced who the bag belonged to using the phone. We could have taken it to the police. You dick.'

He shakes his head. 'It's pay as you go. Can't trace that.'

I shake my head in disbelief.

Ash doesn't say anything or even look at me. He switches the phone on and stares at it. But as he's doing it, there's a noise from outside – branches breaking. Someone's near. Ash chucks the phone back into the bag and stashes the bag under the table.

'Get down, Joe,' he says.

So I do. He picks up a wooden chair and goes and stands near the doorway with it raised above his head. I keep down and watch him.

And then there's the sound of the panel covering the entrance to the Old House being shifted, and the whole place momentarily gets lighter.

'Jesus!' says a voice. Rabbit. 'I'm soaked.'

Ash breathes a big sigh of relief and lets the chair fall to the floor. I get up and dust myself off just in time to see Rabbit come through into the room. He's looking serious.

'What's this about?' Rabbit says. He pulls up a chair and sits down.

Ash goes over to the table and picks the bag up from underneath it, places it back on the table. Then he sits down. 'Did you see the news this morning?' he asks.

Rabbit shakes his head. Suddenly he looks worried, anxious. 'No, why?'

Ash explains the whole thing. And as he does, Rabbit looks more and more anxious.

'Oh fuck,' he says, when Ash has finished.

We both nod at him.

As we all sit in silence, I start feeling angry. Not with Rabbit. It's not his fault he got caught up in this. But with Ash. Because I trusted him. We were supposed to keep this a secret. We were supposed to be honest with each other. And in the space of a week he's gone and blabbed to Rabbit, and kept the fact that there was a phone in the bag to himself. I have an urge to go over and smack him in the face and then walk out of here. I should leave him to deal with this shitty situation. I feel angry enough to do it. But I don't. I close my eyes for a couple of seconds and let the anger pass.

When I reopen my eyes, I look over at Rabbit, sitting, chewing his lip, nervous. 'This is some real messed-up business,' he says to no one in particular.

Ash takes the mobile phone back out of the bag. He turns it round and round in his hands, staring into space.

We all sit, thinking, staring at the floor, at the walls. There are empty, faded cans and wrappers on the floor. I look up from the floor, at Rabbit. There's something that needs to be said before we can get any further. Before I can trust Rabbit. Only I don't want to have to ask it. I look over at Ash. He's just sitting there, turning the phone over and over in his hand. He's not gonna ask it. So I compose myself and then I open my mouth.

'Rabbit,' I start.

They both look over at me.

'There's something I need to know.'

Rabbit nods, like he knows what I'm gonna say.

'Have you told anyone else about this?'

'Course I fucking haven't,' he says. 'I'm not stupid.'

There's a pause for a second. Outside, a bird calls.

'You haven't let anything slip?'

Rabbit shakes his head.

'Cos it's easy to let things slip.' I look over at Ash.

Ash flashes back a look that's says, *'Fuck off.'*

Rabbit stands up. 'Look,' he says. 'Do you think I wanna be in this situation? Do you think I wanted to incriminate myself, to leave my fingerprints on –'

'Shut up,' Ash says, cutting Rabbit off. He's standing up too now, looking angry.

Rabbit stares over at Ash. There's a weird look between the two of them, one which I don't understand. Something's going on here. Something I want to know about.

They keep staring at each other. Neither of them looks away. There's a tension in the air, like before a fight. Eventually, Rabbit shakes his head, sighs and sits back down. Ash sits back down too.

'What was all that about?' I say. And I look from Rabbit to Ash.

They both keep their heads down, not wanting to look at me.

'Nothing,' Ash says. 'Just leave it, Joe. Rabbit's just being a dick.'

Still neither of them looks at me. 'It's obviously something,' I say. 'Tell me.'

Ash shakes his head. 'Leave it.'

190

And it's silent again.

Then, slowly, Rabbit looks up. He looks over at Ash. 'We should tell him.'

Ash stares at Rabbit like he's totally lost it. Like he's deciding whether or not to go and lamp him one.

'What?' I say. 'Tell me what?'

Ash doesn't even look at me. He stares at Rabbit like he wants to kick his head in. 'I said, "Leave it",' he says.

'Why?' Rabbit says.

'Cos . . .' Ash begins. 'Cos . . . he won't be able to handle it.'

That makes my blood boil. I can't believe he's talking about me like that when I'm here in the room. 'I won't be able to handle what?' I say.

Ash doesn't answer me. He's still staring at Rabbit in the gloom.

'He should know,' Rabbit says.

Ash shakes his head. 'No! I'm gonna smack you in the mouth in a minute, Rabbit. Change the subject!'

Rabbit rolls his eyes. 'Look, if we're gonna sort this out, we've gotta be honest, tell each other the truth.'

'Just tell me,' I say.

Rabbit turns to me. 'There was a gun,' he says. 'In the bag.'

I sit and stare at him. A gun? No. This is way too much. 'You're joking, right?'

Rabbit shakes his head. He looks down at his shoes. 'Fuck!'

It's silent again. And I struggle to take this in. A million things go flashing through my mind. Thoughts, questions. And the guilty knot in my stomach tightens so much that it actually feels like I'm gonna vomit.

'Happy now?' Ash eventually says to Rabbit.

Rabbit doesn't answer him.

'Where is it now?' I say. 'Is it here? In the bag?'

Rabbit shakes his head. 'We got rid of it,' he says. 'Cleaned all the prints off it and buried it in the woods.'

'Does anyone else know about it?'

They both shake their heads. 'No one,' Ash says.

No one says anything for ages. Not a word. We're all probably thinking the same thing. We're out of our depth. We're fucked. I stare at the cracks in the ceiling, where the light's coming in. I listen to the sound of the rain outside. And all I can think is that I want to be out of here. To leave all this behind and just run into the woods. To keep running till all this is miles away, just a bad memory. I'd give anything not to be me right now, to be an animal or a bird or something, without any worries. I'd give anything to be able to just fly away. Anything.

But that's not happening, is it? I'm stuck with this. I think for a second that maybe I can pick the bag up, take the money and make a run for it. I even get as far as wondering how long the money would last me and whether they'd track me down.

I look over at Ash. He's still staring at the bloody mobile phone. I start thinking about the news story earlier on. A shiver runs down my spine. The phone must have belonged to the body they found in the flats, Martin Garrard or whatever his name was. And the reason the guy in the flats died is probably sitting right here on the table. The bag. And then I realise something else. About the gun. The news said the guy was wanted in connection with a shooting in Southampton. That means that the gun in the bag could have been the murder weapon. It must have been. Shit.

Rabbit sits up and looks over at Ash as well. 'Whose phone is that?' he says.

'It was in the bag,' Ash says.

'Chuck it here,' Rabbit says.

Ash throws the phone to Rabbit. And then he puts his hands in his pockets and takes out his fags and lighter. He lights a cigarette and stares over at Rabbit as he starts to look through all the stuff on the phone.

I sit and watch them, hoping that someone else is going to make a decision – one that makes everything right, so this is all over with. But no one does. Ash smokes his fag right down to the filter. And Rabbit plays around with the phone. The dead man's phone.

'Fucking hell! Have you seen this message?' Rabbit says all of a sudden.

I shake my head. 'I didn't even know the phone existed until a minute ago,' I say to Ash. 'Ash doesn't tell me anything.'

Ash sighs. 'The message came the other day,' he says.

'Let me guess,' I say. 'You didn't think it was important?'

Ash shakes his head. 'I didn't want to worry you.'

I ignore Ash and hold my hand out to Rabbit. 'Let me have a look,' I say.

He pauses for a second, looks up at Ash and then passes the phone over kind of reluctantly.

I grab the phone and read the message. **What have you done with my money? I will find you.**

I read it through again, just to make sure I've read it correctly. 'They're on to us,' I say. 'Why the fuck did you keep this to yourself?'

'They're not,' Ash says. 'They don't know where the bag is. They don't know who has it. They're just trying to scare whoever found it. If they knew who we were, they would have found us by now.'

I don't say anything. I put the phone down on the table. I don't even know what to think. I feel scared. But what Ash said makes sense.

194

'Have you ever tried texting them back?' Rabbit says after a while. 'Or phoning them?'

'Don't be stupid,' Ash says. 'What would I wanna do that for?'

Rabbit shrugs. 'Dunno,' he says. 'Just an idea.'

The Old House falls silent again. Rabbit picks the phone off the table and looks at it. Ash lights another fag. I stare around the room and wish I'd never seen the bag in the woods, that someone else had found it and got into this mess.

'Maybe Rabbit's right,' Ash says. He starts pacing around the room, taking drags from his fag.

'What?' I say.

Ash stops and looks at me. 'What Rabbit said about the numbers on the mobile. Why don't we phone them or text them or something?'

I stare back at him. That sounds like a really stupid thing to do. 'I don't understand,' I say. 'How is that a good idea? That sounds like suicide. If we do that they'll know who we are.'

Ash stamps out his fag. 'The easiest way out of this is to get rid of the bag, right? If we give it back to whoever it belongs to, we're out of this. The police would have no reason to come after us. And neither would the people who wanted the bag so much that they killed the man in the flat.'

I nod. He has a point.

'Pass the phone here,' he says to Rabbit. 'If we phone the number that sent this message, we could arrange to give the bag back to them.'

I shake my head. 'No way.'

'But we'd get rid of the bag,' Ash says. 'Think about it. No more money, no more stress, no more –'

'They'd kill us, for fuck's sake!' I say. 'They'd think we took the money in the first place.'

Ash doesn't reply. He stares at me instead.

'They're gonna be pissed off that someone took their money, aren't they?' I say. 'And seeing as whoever took the bag last time ended up dead, I don't think they're the most understanding people on the planet, do you know what I mean? I can't imagine them waiting to hear the end of our explanation.'

Ash doesn't say anything. He glares at me, sighs, then turns away. He must realise it's a crap plan.

Rabbit just stares into the distance. Until all of a sudden he sits up straight and looks at me, then Ash. 'It's not such a bad idea, actually,' he says.

Ash turns round. 'Thank you,' he says.

'Except we have to make sure that there's no way they can track us down. If we do it on our own terms there's no reason why they should ever know who we are.'

'So how exactly do we do that then, genius?' I say.

'Easy,' Rabbit says. 'We take the bag somewhere

196

right now and hide it. Then we get well out of the way before we give them the call. We tell them where the bag is. Then that's that.'

I nod. It sounds like a plan. It sounds like it can't go wrong.

Ash has a wide smile on his face. 'You are a fucking genius,' he says. 'Let's do it. We could just leave it here and then call them.'

Rabbit shakes his head. 'No,' he says, 'it's too close to home. We need to find somewhere else.'

Ash

I grab the bag from the table and zip it up.

'Let's go,' I say.

I start off towards the door, Joe and Rabbit following behind.

It's still raining outside. We pick our way through the undergrowth and collect our bikes. In no time at all, we're riding back along the tracks. I have the bag resting on my lap. It feels kind of exposed there cos someone could see it if they go past us, but I have nowhere to hide it at the moment.

'Where are we going with it?' Joe asks as we pedal along.

No one says anything. I think about it. It needs to be somewhere out of the way, where no one's gonna come across it by mistake, where no one's gonna sec us drop it or see the pickup. And also somewhere we can get away from quickly.

'What about the golf course?' Rabbit says.

It's not such a bad idea. The golf course is right on the edge of town, and being rainy today no one's gonna be there.

'Where would we hide it, though?' Joe says. 'If we put it out on the course, one of the golfers could find it.'

'Where do you suggest then?' Rabbit says.

Joe doesn't answer right away. He just pedals along through the puddles that are starting to form on the track and thinks. 'What about the common?' he says eventually. 'There are loads of little clay pits. It'd be easy to hide the bag there. No one would find it. Only if they knew where to look.'

I nod. It's a better idea. There'll be fewer people there. And it'll be easy to hide it.

'OK,' Rabbit says. 'Let's do it.'

We cycle through the forest and then out on to the main road and turn right going out of town. There's not much traffic on the roads, which is just as well given that I have a bag full of money on my lap and Rabbit and Joe are both in their school uniforms. We're hardly inconspicuous.

We take a left off the main road and then follow the smaller road down to the common. We leave our bikes leaning up against the fence and go inside, through the gates.

The common is basically a fancy word for a bit of grass with some gorse bushes and some kind of pits on it. It's nothing special really. Except that there are some lizards and snakes that live there, so the place is protected. If there weren't, they would have built some houses or a supermarket on the land by now. There are lots of pieces of corrugated iron on the common which they put there for the snakes. Fuck knows why snakes like corrugated iron, but apparently they do. Joe always used to try and get me to come down here with him when we were like ten or eleven, to look under the metal sheets. But to be honest, me and snakes don't get on. I'm not exactly scared of them, but they don't make me feel too good.

We walk across the common dodging cowpats, checking around us to make sure no one's watching what we're doing. We head off the main path, through some low, scrubby gorse bushes.

'There,' Joe says, pointing at a metre-square sheet of corrugated iron. 'We can use that.'

We all stop and stare at it. Joe and Rabbit both look back at me.

'What?' I say. Cos I know what their looks mean – that I should be the one to pick up the sheet. I shake my head. 'I'm not picking it up. I'm taking enough of a risk just carrying this bag. You two do it.'

They stare at each other.

Rabbit shakes his head and puts his hand up, like he's surrendering. 'Don't look at me,' he says. 'I'm scared of snakes. There's no way you'll get me touching it.'

Joe sighs. He mutters something under his breath. And then he gets down on his knees, an arm's length away from the metal sheet. He stretches out and gets hold of the corner.

I take a step back.

He starts to lift the sheet slowly, peeking underneath. I can't see anything at first, but then he throws it right back. I just about have a heart attack.

'Ha!' he says. 'Nothing there!'

I shake my head. 'Bastard,' I say under my breath.

Joe and Rabbit grab hold of the sheet and start walking with it over towards a pit in the ground. They drop it on the ground.

'This'll do,' Joe says. 'Throw it in there and we'll cover it.'

I open the bag and take the phone out, close the bag up again and then throw it into the little pit. Joe and Rabbit pick up the sheet and lift it over the bag and the pit and then drop it. They stand back. There's no way that you would guess a bag is hidden under there.

'Right,' I say. 'Let's get the fuck out of here and make a phone call.'

We're back in the Old House. Me and Rabbit are sitting on the chairs, Joe's on an upturned crate. I can feel them staring at me but I don't look back at them. I stare at the phone instead. The dead man's phone. And all of a sudden it doesn't seem like such a good plan. I feel sick just thinking about it.

I press the buttons, go to the inbox. And then I dial the number that sent the message. I put the phone up to my ear. The phone rings. My heart thumps. I don't know what I'm going to say to them. Which is not like me. I normally know what to say in any situation. But not this one. It keeps on ringing, over and over and over. And I start thinking, what happens if nobody picks up? What do we do then? Leave a message on voicemail? Go and get the money back?

Just as I'm getting ready to hang up, there's a click at the other end of the line. Then background noise. But no voice.

'Hello?' I say. 'Is there anyone there?'

I hear some noise at the other end. It sounds like cars going past. And then a voice. 'Who's this?' It's a deep voice. A London accent.

And I realise I still don't know what to say. I can't

tell him my real name. 'Layzee Eyez,' I say. The first thing that pops into my head.

'Lazy what?' demands the voice at the other end.

'Layzee Eyez,' I repeat.

The man laughs – a deep, intimidating laugh. 'Jesus, your mum and dad must have had a sense of humour,' he says, and he laughs again.

I don't say anything. I look at Joe and Rabbit. They're leaning forward on their seats, staring at me, wanting to know what's going on.

'Enough with the introductions, Lazy Eyes,' the man says. 'Down to business. Where the fuck did you get this phone?'

My heart is pounding. I can't think straight. 'Found it,' I say. I sound really weak. Like a little kid.

'You found it?' he says. 'Some people might call it finding, others might call it stealing.'

'I found it,' I say again. 'I know where your money is as well.'

At the other end of the line the sound becomes muffled, like someone's put their hand over the mouthpiece or something. There's talking going on, but I can't work out what they're saying. I look at Joe and Rabbit again. Their eyes are begging me to tell them what's happening.

'Right,' the deep voice says. 'Let's talk. You can start by telling me where my money is.'

'Fayrewood,' I say. 'Fayrewood Common.'

I hear the man breathe in deeply and then out again. 'Where?'

'The common. You need to go to Redlands Way in Fayrewood,' I say. 'Go into the common through the first entrance.'

'Yeah.'

'Turn off the path to the right as soon as you're inside, go through the gorse bushes for about ten metres. You'll find a sheet of corrugated iron over a pit. The bag's hidden underneath.'

There's nothing but background noise at the other end of the phone for a while. 'You better be telling me the truth,' the voice says. It sounds more threatening now.

'I am,' I say. And again I sound feeble.

'Because if this is a trick, if this is a set-up, I will hunt you down and kill you,' he says. 'Do you understand me?'

'It's not a trick,' I say. 'I found your money but I don't want it.'

There's more background noise at the other end – cars whooshing past. And then the phone goes dead. I slowly lower it and switch it off. I look at Joe and Rabbit.

'There,' I say. 'It's done.'

Neither of them smiles. Neither of them says a word. They both look like they're in shock. Like I feel.

I drop the phone on the floor.

'What you doing?' Joe says.

I don't answer him. I just slam my foot down on the phone. It doesn't smash like I imagined it would, just kind of slides underneath my foot. I lift my foot and slam it down again and again till it comes apart.

'What did you do that for?' Joe says.

I bend down to pick the pieces up. 'Why d'you think?' I say. 'Now they can't phone us back. That's it. We don't have to worry about it ever again.'

Joe nods. He comes over and helps me pick up the pieces.

After I've dumped the phone pieces in a dog shit bin, I go home. I don't really feel like hanging out with Joe and Rabbit right now. There's an atmosphere between us all. Everyone seems pissed off with each other. I'd rather be on my own. Mum and Dad are both at work, like always, so the house is silent and empty when I get in. I go upstairs and put some music on shuffle, try to relax a bit. I take out the weed, roll myself a spliff and have a smoke. And I start to feel a bit better about what we've just done.

God knows how long I sit there doing nothing, staring into space and listening to music. I must have gone into a kind of daze. But that's interrupted when I hear something from outside. A car. It sounds like Dad. I jump up off my bed and go to the window. And sure enough, I see Dad's car pull into the drive.

Shit! What's he doing home? He should be at work. Maybe he forgot something. What if he realises that I'm here instead of at school? I duck down from the window, crawl over and switch my music off. And then I lie on the floor beside my bed, so that even if Dad opens my bedroom door he won't be able to see me.

As I'm lying on the floor, I hear Dad's voice outside. Who's he talking to? Maybe he's just on his phone. But I hear someone else. A woman. She laughs. It doesn't sound like Mum.

From downstairs, I hear Dad's key sliding into the lock and the front door opening. I hear his voice again, laughing and joking, but I can't make out what he's saying. And then the woman's voice again. She giggles. The front door closes behind them. What are they doing?

They carry on talking, but I still can't work out what they're saying. I hear them go into the kitchen and get some glasses out. I lie still, my cheek pressed against the carpet, holding my breath, listening, trying to work out what on earth is going on. And then I hear footsteps coming up the stairs, running up the stairs. And I hear Dad's voice again, but clearly this time.

'Come on, you dirty cow,' he says.

The woman giggles again.

And I know exactly what's going on. I hear the spare bedroom door open and then slam shut. I lie still for a couple of seconds. My blood starts to boil. I can't bloody believe that Dad would do this. Bastard. I feel so angry. I just want to go in there and punch his lights out. Pull them away from each other and chuck them both out on to the pavement.

There are noises coming from the spare bedroom. I try not to listen. I can't hear this. No way. I get up from the floor and go over to my drawers. I grab some weed and get out of my room. I creep down the stairs, ignoring the noises and voices from upstairs. I open the front door. But before I go outside, I look back up the stairs. My blood begins to boil again.

'BASTARD!' I shout up the stairs.

And then I close the front door, get my bike and go.

Joe

It's nearly five o'clock when I hear a car pull up outside the house. Someone dropping Kate off from netball practice. The car door opens. I hear Kate say something and then close it. The car accelerates away down the road. I hear Kate open the front door, slam it closed behind her and then come running up the stairs. She knocks on my door. She comes barging in before I can even shout, 'Go away.'

'How come you weren't in school today?'

I look up at her. I knew this would happen. I've been trying to think of an excuse all afternoon. But the truth is, I can't think of one.

'I was.'

She raises an eyebrow. 'You were not. You weren't on the bus this morning.'

I look away from her, pretending I'm not interested or worried by her accusation. 'I got a lift,' I say.

'Liar,' she replies. 'Who with?'

'What's it to you?' I say. 'I don't have to answer to you.'

She shakes her head. She's acting like she's my mum. 'No,' she says. 'But you'll have to answer to Mum and Dad, though, if I tell them.'

I sigh. 'I got a lift with Ash,' I say. 'I went round there this morning and he was running late, so his Dad ran us into school.' Which is a pretty good lie considering I made it up on the spot.

She doesn't say anything back right away. I look at her and smile.

'I didn't see you in school,' she says eventually.

'So?' I reply. 'You never see me in school. You're in Year Nine and I'm in Year Eleven.'

'I'm gonna ask someone if you were on the bus home after school,' she says. 'I bet you weren't.'

I pretend to act cool. 'Go ahead,' I say. 'Ask whoever you like.'

She narrows her eyes at me. 'I know you're up to something,' she says. She stays standing there for a couple of seconds, like she's going to say something else, but she doesn't and eventually she turns and goes to her room.

Ash

I've been at the rec most of the afternoon, smoking and thinking. About my dad. What a total bastard. How could he do that to Mum? How could he do it to me? Although, to be honest, I don't think I want to know the answers to those questions. I don't want anything to do with Dad full stop.

Maybe I should have realised. He's always getting home late. Him and Mum are always arguing. They always have done. Maybe Dad's been having an affair for years. I wonder if Mum knows. I don't think she does. Surely she wouldn't still be with him if she knew. Would she? Making excuses for him, saying he's working late and all that?

I get up off the bench and grab my bike, start pushing it across the grass. School must be finished by now, cos there are a load of primary school kids on the field playing football. I walk my bike round the edge of the pitch they're playing on. I keep my eyes fixed on the ground. And a question pops into my head – one that I don't want to have to think about. Shall I tell Mum what I heard? Or shall I just keep quiet, let Dad drop himself in it? Cos if I tell Mum what happened this afternoon, I could ruin her life. And I'd be grassing myself up cos I'd have to explain what I was doing at home in the afternoon instead of being at school. Fuck it. Maybe I'll just drop some hints, let her work it out for herself.

I look up. There are a load of kids on the wall near the main road. I decide to head away from them. I don't feel like talking to anyone at the moment. All I feel like doing is hitting my dad right in the middle of his face. I wheel my bike round the outside of the playpark, towards the gate at the end of the rec. But as I get near the gate, I hear footsteps behind me.

'Ash!' a voice calls.

I turn round. It's Mark. Manky Mark, as we call him behind his back.

I stop walking as Mark rushes up to me and then stops.

'Hey, listen, man,' he says in his stupid homeboy voice. It's stupid cos it's so obviously fake – his dad has the broadest Dorset accent you can imagine. But Mark tries to sound like he was born in Jamaica or somewhere. 'I heard you was selling some gear.'

I look back at him. 'Who told you that?'

'Jack,' he says.

I nod my head, don't say anything.

'You still got any?'

I don't answer right away. I look beyond Mark, over at the playpark. I don't have the money any more, so I might as well make something out of having found the bag. I look back at Mark. 'Yeah,' I say. 'A bit.'

Mark smiles. 'How much is it, man?'

'Twenty quid,' I say.

He smiles and puts his hand in his pocket. 'You got it on you?'

I feel in my pocket. I have some. I grabbed it as I left the house. When I left the house, I was thinking about smoking the whole fucking lot. I only had one spliff, though. I nod. I close my fingers round the bag, shake Mark's hand and he takes the weed. He pushes it up his sleeve and then puts his hand in his trouser pocket. He takes his hand out and passes the money to me. Then he winks at me.

'Nice one, Ash.' He walks off, back to the wall.

I put the money in my pocket and push my bike along. I stop when I get to the burned-out flats. I look across the road at them, at the scrum of reporters who are still there. And I think about the bag and the man found dead in the flats. It makes me feel a little sick that we had the bag, that I held the gun, that we found the car. The car could have been the fucking murder scene. The gun could have been the murder weapon.

I start pedalling again. I wonder whether the guy I spoke to has found the bag, whether we should go back and check. Cos what if they haven't? What if they couldn't find it? Someone else might have done. They could have taken it to the police.

I stop my bike and send a message to Joe. **Meet me at end of yr road in 2 mins. Gonna check if bag has gone.**

I think about sending it to Rabbit as well, but his house is too far away. I don't want to have to wait for him to get here. I'll let him know when we've checked.

Joe

My first reaction is to say, '*Fuck you. I'm staying here.*'
Cos I'm still pissed off about earlier, about the gun and
about Rabbit knowing what happened on Friday night,
about the mobile phone and the text message Ash
didn't show me. I don't feel like seeing him or talking
to him right now. I want him to know that I'm pissed
off with him.

But I also want to know what's happened to the
bag. I have to know that it's been taken, that it's out
of our hands. It'll set my mind at rest. So I grab a
jumper, go downstairs, out of the front door and get
on my bike.

When I get to the end of the road, Ash is already

there. He's sitting on his bike, leaning back, his hood up over his head.

'Hi, Joe,' Ash says as I brake and stop just in front of him.

I make a point of not making eye contact, not answering. I just nod my head once.

We cycle in silence, turn left on to the main road and cycle out of town, take the turning down towards the common. The road is clear, which makes me feel better. At least whoever it was that Ash spoke to on the phone earlier isn't sitting there waiting for us. We cycle along the road till we come to the entrance to the common. We get off our bikes and lean them up against the fence, look around us. Ash adjusts his hood and then we go in. We head straight off, round the gorse bushes, almost running.

I can see before we get to the pit that the bag isn't there any more. The sheet of corrugated iron has gone and the pit's empty. Ash walks up to it and peers down inside. I hang back, look around the common. There's no one here. And now that we know the bag's gone, I'd rather not be here.

Ash turns on his heels. 'Well, that's the end of that then,' he says. He doesn't sound happy about it. He sounds kind of angry.

I nod. 'Yeah. Come on, let's get out of here.'

'Hang on a minute,' he says. 'Come and help me.'

He starts walking off round the pit, where the sheet of corrugated iron has been thrown. I follow him. We pick it up and take it to where it was before, to the patch of light-coloured, flattened grass. We put it down and then we get away from the common as quickly as we can.

When we're back on the main road, cycling home, Ash takes his hood off and looks at me. For a second I think he's gonna say something, like maybe, *'Sorry about lying to you.'* But he doesn't. He looks ahead again and keeps on going.

We get to the top of Ash's road without exchanging a single word. We both stop. We sit on our bikes. A few moments pass without us looking at each other or even speaking. It feels sort of awkward. I look up at Ash. He's kind of slumped over the handlebars of his bike, looking down at the tarmac. He looks totally pissed off. I feel like I should at least say something to fill the silence, if nothing else.

'Do you think they'll notice there's stuff missing from the bag?'

Ash looks up all of a sudden. 'What?'

I stare back at him. There's a weird look on his face and I don't know what it means. 'The money,' I say. 'We spent some of it. Do you think they'll notice?'

He keeps looking at me with that weird expression on his face. It's like he's accusing me of something. Then he looks away again, at someone's front garden.

He shakes his head. 'Who cares?' he says. 'They don't know who we are, so they can hardly come and ask for it back, can they? It's over.'

I suppose he's right. I hope so. I put my foot on the pedal and my hands on the handlebars and I go home.

Ash

Dad's car isn't in the drive any more. Probably just as well. Cos if I saw him right now I'd probably do something stupid – something I'd regret for the rest of my life. I leave my bike out the front and go inside, run straight upstairs to the back bedroom.

The room looks like nothing's been touched. All the sheets are pristine, like no one's been here, like Dad didn't come back with someone. Like I imagined it all. I begin to doubt myself. Maybe I did imagine it.

I turn and leave the room, go back down the stairs, into the kitchen. I heard Dad in here earlier. The draining board's empty. I open up the dishwasher and pull out the drawers with a dull clunk. Nothing in there except the plates from last night, a couple of mugs and the breakfast stuff from this morning. No sign that anyone's been home during the day. I shove the drawers back, close the dishwasher. And then I just stand, staring, not really even thinking. Lost. Empty.

After a while I go over to the cupboard, grab a pint glass and fill it with water. Then I head back up the stairs to my room and shut the door behind me. I go over to my iPod and switch it on, turn it up loud.

A bit later I hear the front door shut and Mum putting her keys down on the worktop in the kitchen.

'Ashley, I've got your tea here,' she shouts up the stairs.

My mind is made up. I wait a second, try and prepare myself. Not that anything could prepare me for this. And then I go downstairs, taking each step slowly. As I get to the bottom the smell of Chinese takeaway hits my nose. Mum's in the kitchen, getting plates and bowls and cutlery out, opening takeaway cartons. She looks up and smiles as I walk towards her. I think about coming straight out with it. Telling her now. I open my mouth and try and think what to say. But I can't do it. Maybe it's the smile on her face. Maybe I'm just too much of a coward. I don't know.

'You OK, Ashley?' Mum says without looking at me. 'I got some takeaway in.'

I look at the food so I don't have to look at Mum. 'Chinese?' I say, cos I don't know what else to say.

'Yeah. Barbecued ribs, sweet and sour pork, special fried rice, beef in oyster sauce,' she says, pointing at each of the cartons. 'Thought we could have a treat. Your dad won't be back till late as usual, I expect.'

I look up at her for a second, expecting to see a look in her eye, like maybe she knows what I know about Dad. But she's not even looking at me, she's just scraping the food into bowls. I walk past her. 'Do you want a drink?'

'Yeah,' Mum says. 'I've been dying for a coffee all afternoon.'

So I grab the kettle and fill it, take it over to the side and plug it in. I fetch two mugs and the jar of coffee and spoon some into each cup. And then I stare out of the back window into the garden. My mind starts to wander, about what happened today. About the bag. About Dad. It's been some shitty day. And it can only get worse.

'Penny for them,' Mum says.

I turn round. 'Uh?'

'Your thoughts,' Mum says. 'Penny for your thoughts. You were miles away.'

I nod and smile, but it isn't a real smile. I try and think of something to say. Do I tell her now? I look away from her. 'Just thinking about exams and stuff,' I say.

Mum smiles. 'Listen,' she says, 'don't you worry about that. Whatever grades you get, we'll both be proud of you.'

Which is a lie. I know. Cos Dad has been on my back for weeks about revising and making something of my life. But I smile back at Mum anyway, or at least I try. 'I know. Thanks.'

Mum goes through to the lounge carrying a tray of Chinese food. I stare out the back door at the garden, wait for the kettle to boil, cursing myself for not saying anything to her. When the kettle boils, I make the coffee and carry the mugs through to the lounge.

'Thanks, love,' Mum says.

I put my mug down and help myself to some food. Normally if Mum had brought Chinese home for tea I'd pile my plate high cos I love Chinese food. But right now I don't feel hungry. I don't feel like eating at all.

Mum's put the TV on. There's some talent show blaring out. I sit and watch as I try to eat. There's a man on there juggling chairs. It looks impossible. He drops one and then they all come tumbling down to the ground. He gets buzzed out by the judges.

Mum laughs. 'That wasn't very good,' she says. 'You at least should have rehearsed if you're gonna go on national telly.'

I nod my head. Although, to be honest, I couldn't give a shit about talent shows. They're lame.

221

I scoop a forkful of special fried rice into my mouth as the next act comes on. It's a father-and-son act. They say they're gonna tap-dance. Jesus.

'Oh, I like these,' Mum says, watching the screen, her fork hovering above her plate.

'Mum,' I say.

'Yes?' she says. She keeps staring at the screen as the dad and his kid tap-dance.

'What time's Dad gonna be home?'

Mum doesn't answer. I don't know if she's even heard me – she's just staring at the screen and smiling. 'What?' she says. 'Oh, your father? I don't know. Late, I should think.'

I don't say anything. I just think. She can't have a clue what's going on, what Dad's really up to, otherwise she wouldn't say it like that, would she? She'd be angry, bitter. She'd feel like I do.

'Why's he always working late?'

Mum sighs. She turns and looks at me. The adverts come on the TV. 'To keep his business afloat,' she says. 'It's not easy running your own company.'

I sigh. I want to go over to Mum and shake her. I want to shout the truth at her. I don't want to keep this secret on my own. I want her to know.

'Sometimes he comes home at eleven at night, though, Mum,' I say. 'He can't be working right through till then, can he?'

Mum takes a sip of her coffee and puts the mug back down on the side table. 'What do you mean?'

'Well, who else is gonna be around at that time?' I say. 'What business can he be doing?'

Mum raises an eyebrow. 'There's lots he can be doing,' she says. 'Accounts. Phoning clients in America. All sorts.'

I sigh. I can't believe she's defending him. I have to tell her. She turns back to the TV as the next act on the dumb talent show starts. 'Mum,' I say. My voice comes out uneven.

'Yes,' she says. She doesn't look at me.

'There's something I need to tell you.'

She still doesn't turn round.

'Something important.'

Mum turns to look at me. She smiles.

I open my mouth. 'I . . .' I stop. I don't know how to say this. 'I . . . Dad . . .'

Mum sighs. 'Come on,' she says. 'Spit it out. I'm missing my programme.'

I look down at the floor. I can't believe I can't say this. I never have a problem with words. They always come easy to me, they're always just there. They usually come out before I've even had a chance to think about them.

And then I hear Dad's car pulling into the driveway.

Mum turns and looks out of the window at the drive. 'Speak of the devil.'

I get up. There's no way I can tell her now. I run up the stairs and shut my door just as I hear the front door open and Dad come in.

THURSDAY

Joe

I slept OK last night. I didn't think I was going to. I felt on edge all evening, even though we got rid of the money. It was like there was too much adrenalin in my body. I was jumpy as hell. I couldn't stop thinking. I was expecting the guy who wanted the bag to turn up at any minute and come crashing through my door. I kept thinking about the text message. But I guess I tired myself out thinking about it all cos when my head hit the pillow I must've gone straight to sleep.

The first thing I do after I've woken up is go and switch my computer on and check the news. Cos I have to set my mind at rest, I have to know that no one's taken the bag to the police or anything like that.

I try the local news first. And there's nothing there about the bag, or the car, or the body. Just the story from yesterday morning. I try a couple of other sites as well – a couple of national newspapers. But there's no mention of it at all.

I switch my computer off and sigh. I feel better in a way. I mean, at least there isn't a story saying that the bag's been handed in and they're running forensic tests on it or anything. But I still have a weird feeling. I still don't feel at ease. I feel edgy, nervous. But I'm sure it won't last. The last couple of days have scared me.

After breakfast, I get my bag and stuff together and go downstairs. Out the front door and up the road. The sun's out, though it's not that warm. I'm the first one at the bus stop. I stand at the edge of the pavement and look down, at the gravel that's come off someone's drive. I kick it over the edge of the pavement into a drain. Each stone disappears with a tiny *plop*.

Gradually more and more people turn up at the bus stop. No sign of Ash, though. To be honest, I'm not that bothered after yesterday. I'd quite happily not see him today. But just before the bus is due to arrive, he comes walking slowly down the road. His school shirt is untucked and he's got a big pair of white trainers on. His hair's all over the place, like mine usually is. He looks at me as he gets near to the stop and nods his head in greeting. He doesn't smile. He barges a couple of Year Eights out of the way instead of walking around them.

'You all right, Ash?' I say.

He nods his head. 'Yeah,' he says kind of defensively. 'Why shouldn't I be all right?'

It takes me sort of by surprise. What's he got to be angry about? 'I didn't mean it like that,' I start, but I don't bother finishing my sentence. He's already looking away. Besides, surely he should be the one apologising to me.

The bus pulls up at the stop a few metres from where me and Ash are standing. He barges straight through the queue. 'Get out the way, munchkins,' he says. 'Year Elevens coming through.'

I follow behind him. We're on first. We go right to the back of the bus and sit down.

'You got a note for yesterday?' I say, as all the other kids get on the bus.

He looks at me like I'm being a div, like, *Why on earth would you need a sick note for missing a day of school?* He shakes his head.

'Suit yourself, then,' I say. 'I typed one on the computer and forged my mum's signature.'

Ash just shrugs. 'Who cares?' he says. 'We're leaving

school tomorrow anyway. What can they do?' He looks out of the window and ignores me the rest of the way to school. Which is fine by me.

Ash

The sooner I leave this place, the better. I've had enough of people telling me what I can and can't do, had enough of wearing a uniform, doing pointless homework and all that bullshit. I've had enough of all the other plebs at school as well, hanging around, thinking they're cool. The end of this week can't come soon enough, believe me.

The bell has already gone for the start of morning registration. Most people have gone to their tutor rooms. But I'm still in the playground, walking slowly. I'm in no rush. Eventually I go in through the doors, look left and right along the corridor. There's no one about. All the good little boys and girls are in their classrooms, listening to what their teachers have to say, doing what they're told, so their mummies and daddies will be proud of them. Suckers.

I look across towards the main school door and size it up. I could just go. The door has an alarm on it. I've seen visitors and stuff go through it before, but no one ever pays any attention to the alarm. And even if they did, I'd be gone by the time anyone noticed. They wouldn't catch up with me. And it's not like I'm gonna be missing much – what are they gonna teach us in the last two days of school that we don't already know? If they had anything decent to teach me they would have done it by now.

'Shouldn't you be in your tutor group?'

I look round. It's Mr Coupland. The deputy head. He's got an eyebrow raised, hands behind his back, standing rocking backwards and forwards on his heels, in his shiny suit. He thinks he's the dog's bollocks.

'The bell went five minutes ago, Ashley.'

'I know,' I say. 'I heard it.' I look at the door again. One barrier between me and freedom. I'd love to make a run for it now. I'd love to see Coupland's face.

'Chop-chop,' Mr Coupland says. Patronising idiot.

I sigh and roll my eyes. 'All right,' I say in my most impatient voice. 'I'm going.' And I walk off towards my tutor room. Except, when I'm a few paces down the corridor, I turn my head. Mr Coupland is walking the other way down the corridor, towards his office. I give his back the middle finger and then carry on walking.

When I get to the tutor room, the door is shut. I stand outside for a second, thinking, before I put my hand on the handle and open it. The classroom is silent. Everybody turns in my direction, including Mr Benson, my form tutor. He gives me an evil look as I walk in. I look away from him and walk to my place next to Joe.

'Excuse me, Ashley,' Mr Benson says, 'but you knock and wait for an answer before you come into a classroom.'

I roll my eyes and shake my head. Why does he have to be such an uptight dickhead? Why can't he let things go? 'This is my form room, sir,' I say, 'and I'm coming in for tutor time. Why do I have to knock?'

I look up at Mr Benson. His eyes are narrowed, staring at me. You can tell he's angry but he's trying to restrain himself. Around the room, a couple of people snigger.

'Ashley, if you are more than five minutes late for tutor time,' Mr Benson says, 'you knock before you come into the classroom. And as you enter, you apologise for being late. It's common courtesy. Good manners. Do you understand?'

I nod. 'I understand, sir,' I say. 'I just don't see the point.'

There are more sniggers around the classroom. Mr Benson tries to ignore them. I can feel loads of eyes staring at me.

'I think it's best if we carry on this conversation at break time, don't you?' Benson says.

I shrug. 'If you say so, sir.'

Mr Benson ignores my comment. He looks down at the register. I look around the room. Next to me, Joe has a shocked look on his face. Most of the other people in the room are staring at me, grinning. I grin back at them. Then I turn to look at Mr Benson. He's still looking at the register.

'Um,' Mr Benson says suddenly. He looks up at me. 'Ashley, you were away yesterday. Do you have a note?'

I shake my head. 'No, sir.'

Mr Benson keeps staring at me. 'Why were you off school, Ashley?'

I shrug.

'Were you ill?'

'Not really,' I say under my breath, not loud enough for Benson to hear. But a couple of people around me hear it and laugh.

'Pardon, Ashley? I didn't catch that.'

'I had diarrhoea, sir,' I say.

A few people in the class laugh. I smile. Mr Benson looks down at his register again. I heard somewhere

– on the radio, I think it must have been – that if you want to take a sickie, the best thing to say is that you shat yourself, or that you have diarrhoea, cos everyone just believes you. I mean, what kind of idiot would make up a lie about shitting themselves? Everyone believes it.

Mr Benson looks up again. He smiles. 'Actually, Ashley,' he says, all high and mighty, 'you shouldn't come into school for forty-eight hours after a bout of diarrhoea. Those are the official guidelines.'

A couple more people laugh. I smile again. 'Seriously, sir?' I say. 'So I should go home then . . .'

More laughs. Benson looks so angry at the front of the class. 'Come and see me at break time, Ashley,' he says.

The bell goes and we all go off to lessons.

The bell goes for the end of Maths. Break time. Me and Dylan walk out of the classroom and into the corridor. It's noisy as hell in the school. And it's the Year Elevens making all the noise. I guess everyone else feels like I do. Why play by the rules when you've only got a couple of days of school left? Like I said, they're hardly gonna chuck you out just before you're about to do your GCSEs. Last year Tony Davies actually hit a teacher in his last week of school. It was Mr Box, the DT teacher. Mr Box is a sarcastic bastard. Everyone says that he said something to Tony about how in a week's time he'd be working on the bin lorries, where he belonged. So Tony thought, *Fuck it*, and lamped him one. Mr Box had a black eye after that. And to be honest, I think he deserved it. Tony got an exclusion for the rest of the week, which basically meant he got three days' extra study leave. But he still sat his GCSEs.

'You coming for a smoke?' Dylan asks.

I look at him. I'm dying for a smoke, as it happens. But I also have a date with Mr Benson. I weigh it up in my mind: fifteen minutes with Mr Benson or fifteen minutes with Mr Benson and Mr Hedges. No contest really, is there? I smile. 'Yeah,' I say. 'Why not?'

So we walk through the corridors, knocking Year Eights out of the way, out into the playground and then on to the field. We walk straight over to the edge of the field where the mobile classrooms are, where all the smokers hang out at break time. Two more days and I won't have to go through with this stupid bloody charade. I'll be free to make my own decisions. I'll be able to smoke if I want, when I want. I won't have to hide away like some leper.

A couple of people are already behind the mobile classrooms when we get there. Year Ten girls. Chavs. One of them, Suzie, is known as the school bike. I'd want her pedals cleaning before I had a ride, though, if you know what I mean. You don't know who else has had a ride or what they've stepped in. I get my fags out of my pocket and light one. Dylan takes a fag packet out of his blazer, looks inside and then sighs. He stares at me.

'What?' I say, even though I know exactly what he's up to.

'You couldn't give us one, could you?' he says. 'I've run out.'

I stare back at him. Cheeky bastard. 'You taking the mickey?' I say. 'You asked me if I wanted to come and have a smoke and all the time you didn't have any yourself?'

He shrugs, smiles nervously and nods. 'Sorry, I forgot,' he says. 'So can I have one? Otherwise you'll be stood here like a Billy No Mates.'

I give him the fag that I've already lit and then take another one out of the pack for myself.

'Cheers,' he says. And he takes a puff. 'Hey, you going to Rabbit's house tomorrow?'

I nod, take a drag, breathe the smoke out. 'Yeah. Definitely,' I say. I turn to Suzie and her mate, whose name I can never remember. 'Hey, girls, you going to Rabbit's house tomorrow?'

They shake their heads. 'Why?' Suzie says. 'Is there a party?'

I look at Dylan. We both smirk. I'm not sure that Suzie and her mates are the kind of guests that Rabbit

239

has in mind for tomorrow. 'Yeah,' I say. 'Tell your mates. Only the fit ones, though.'

Suzie and her friend giggle and smile.

Dylan winks at me. We both turn away from the girls and smirk. Rabbit'll kill us.

'Tell you what,' Dylan says. He takes another drag of his fag. 'I'm dreading the Maths exam. I didn't have a bloody clue what Perkins was talking about today, did you?'

I shake my head. 'You'll be all right, Dylan,' I say. 'Who cares if you scrape through with a C anyway?'

Dylan laughs. 'My parents'd go mad.'

I nod. My dad'd go mad as well. But to be honest, right now I couldn't give a flying fuck what he thinks. His opinion is worth nothing.

All of a sudden, out of the corner of my eye I see Suzie throw her fag down and stamp it out in a hurry. 'Shit,' she hisses. 'Quick. It's Benson.'

I drop my cigarette to the ground and stamp it out. Dylan does the same. Then we walk away from the mobiles, back on to the field, trying to look innocent, trying not to catch Benson's eye. But even as I'm trying to ignore him, I can sense that he's heading straight for me. It's useless. I sigh and turn to face him. He marches towards me, his stupid tweed jacket flapping and his paisley tie over his shoulder. He has a grin on his face. He's gonna bloody love this.

'Ashley,' he says. 'Caught red-handed. Not having a good day, are you?'

I let my shoulders sag and look away from him, shake my head, like this is so unfair.

He stops marching and stands right in front of me. He's got one hand on his hip. 'You are supposed to be in detention with me right this very instant,' he says. 'Can you explain to me why you're out here?'

I look across the field at kids playing football. I sigh. 'Forgot,' I mumble.

Benson takes his hand off his hip and tries to move so he's in my line of vision. I look the other way.

'You decided not to come to detention but to have a smoke instead,' he says. 'Ashley, look at me when I'm speaking to you.'

I look at him and smile. I can tell from the look on his face that it winds him up. 'I wasn't smoking, sir,' I say. 'It's a filthy habit. It causes cancer.'

Benson takes a deep breath. 'I can smell it on you, Ashley.'

'That's cos I was standing next to the smokers, sir,' I say. 'Passive smoking, Mr Benson. There's not a rule against that, is there, sir?'

Benson's eyes narrow. He's trying really hard not to get angry, not to shout. 'Empty your pockets,' he says. 'Now.'

I shake my head. But I slowly do as he says. I hold my fags and lighter in front of him, as well as a tissue and my mobile.

'I knew it,' he says. 'Right, we're going to see Mr Watts this very minute.'

My shoulders sag again. Mr Watts is the head teacher. 'Do we have to?' I say.

'Yes,' Mr Benson says. 'Follow me.'

And he starts walking back towards the school building. I walk behind him, taking my time.

Joe

I got away with the note. Benson just took it, read it and put it in the register. He didn't say a thing, didn't even look up at me. Which is just as well cos I was shitting it. I was dreading that he was gonna call me up to the front and ask me about it. And then I wouldn't have been able to lie to him cos I'm rubbish at things like that. I just crack straight away. I can't lie to save my life.

Then Ash came in and started acting like a weirdo anyway. God knows what's got into him. He's acting like he's got a real attitude. Maybe it's cos of the bag. Maybe he scared himself with all this. Or maybe he's just pissed off that we lost the money.

It's his problem, though. He can deal with it. I've got enough to deal with on my own. I still feel freaked out by everything that happened, and everything that could have happened to us. And I haven't even started thinking about my exams. I can't even figure out what's going on inside my own head at the moment, let alone Ash's.

Since I've been home from school, I've checked the internet twice to make sure that there's nothing on the news about the bag. There's no mention of it. I feel relieved but I still feel kind of weird.

Ash

As soon as I get home, I go up to my room and chuck my school bag down on the floor. I put on some music, lie on my bed and close my eyes. And I start thinking about what a shitty day I've just had.

I mean, what is it about teachers that make them think they can tell you how to live your life? It's not as if they're the most successful people in the world. They couldn't do anything else very well, so they ended up being teachers. And they think that gives them the right to tell you what to do.

Earlier today, when I got sent to Mr Watts, he started spouting off about smoking, like he was my bloody dad or something.

'I was a smoker once, you know,' he said. 'I smoked for ten years. Six of those years I was trying to give it up.'

Like I care whether he smoked.

'It's very damaging for your health, not to mention expensive and antisocial,' he said.

I didn't even bother to think of a reply. Did he think I'd never heard that stuff before? He can't seriously believe I care what he thinks.

He looked at me for a bit then got out of his chair. It was quiet. All I could hear was the ticking of his clock. And I remember thinking that every tick of that clock brought the time closer when I would be free and didn't have to stick to school rules.

'You know, Ashley, there are at least half a dozen Year Eleven boys like you that end up here in my office in the last week of school every single year,' he said. 'You could almost set your watch by it.'

I shrugged. So what?

'I don't know what it is,' he said. 'Maybe it's because they're so close to freedom.' And then he went quiet for a bit.

I sighed and shifted in my seat, wishing he'd just cut the crap and get to the punishment. Why do teachers always have to give you all their bloody wise words bullshit?

'I'm going to have to phone your mother,' he said eventually.

I tutted. I told him that I wasn't the only one smoking, but Mr Watts didn't listen. He told me to write Mr Benson a letter to apologise for missing detention.

Just before he let me go, he said, 'You're a good lad, Ashley. You can make something of your life, but don't waste your opportunities.'

I wrote Mr Benson the most sarcastic letter I could manage. I watched him read it. You could see him getting wound up as he read it. But he didn't say anything and didn't do anything. He just kind of seethed a bit. And then, when he'd finished, he screwed the letter up into a ball and threw it at the bin.

'Missed,' I said, just loud enough so that he could hear.

Benson looked at me. He had hatred in his eyes. He didn't say anything right away. But eventually he opened his mouth and said, 'I dread to think what will become of you, Ashley. With an attitude like yours, you'll be lucky to hold down a job in a supermarket on the minimum wage.'

I didn't know what to say to that. I wasn't expecting it. So I just smirked. Then, as I thought about what he'd just said, I felt like telling him that I'll make more money per month than he does per year when I start working. But I kept my mouth shut.

Benson shook his head. 'It's all wasted on you, isn't it?'

I didn't move, didn't answer.

'Get out of my sight,' he said, turning his back on me.

So I did.

Do you know what? Fuck them all. I don't care what they have to say to me. They don't know me. And I don't have to listen to their bullshit.

I get up off my bed and grab my drumsticks. I go over to the drum stool and start to pound away to the music. I'm not as good as Casey Camper, the Porn Dwarves drummer, but I'm OK. We always used to talk about starting a band: me on drums, Joe on guitar, Dylan on bass and Rabbit as the singer and frontman. Joe reckons that he even wrote some songs. He's never let anyone hear them, though.

Usually when I play the drums, everything else seems to disappear. It's like the rest of the world stops existing. Not today, though. I can't let myself go. There's too much on my mind. I'm totally off the beat. Hitting the drums too hard. It sounds rubbish.

So I stop and rest my head in my hands, let the music wash over me, so I hardly even notice it's there. I keep thinking about Benson and Watts, about all the stuff they said to me earlier – all that patronising bollocks. And it really pisses me off that I was the one they picked out for that treatment. I mean, how can they bring me in for smoking – just me – when plenty of others were there too? Dylan was there for a start, standing right next to me, and Benson completely ignored him and just brought me in.

The reason is obvious, though – Benson likes Dylan and he hates me. Dylan's a good boy in class – always does his homework, doesn't answer back, wears the right school uniform. And me? Well, I don't. I'm myself. An individual, not a sheep. And teachers don't like that. They want some pleb who's gonna behave like a sheep or a robot and make their life easier.

One song finishes and the next one starts. *American Apocalypse*, the track's called. I pick my sticks up and start playing again. This time I really concentrate on following the beat. But after a while I start hitting the drums harder and harder and harder with each stroke. Before long I'm not following the beat any more, I'm just whacking the skins as hard as I can, the drumsticks splintering as they hit the rims. And I know that I shouldn't. I'll break something in a minute. But I can't stop. A part of me doesn't want to. A part of me just wants to hit them harder – as hard as it's possible to hit them, to split them and break them and tear the skins. Fuck the consequences. *Bang-bang-bang-bang-bang-bang!* One of the sticks comes apart, splits right down the middle. But I keep hitting the drums. And then I catch my hand on the outside of the snare, on my knuckles. I don't feel any pain, but I see red. Blood. So I stop and look at it. There's a rough bloody edge all across my knuckles where I've bruised them and then cut them. And now that I've stopped, the cut stings. Blood's starting to well up and drip from my hand on to the snare drum.

I get up from the stool and go through to the bathroom, put the cold tap on and shove my hand in the basin. The water hits the cut and immediately it stings. Blood and water mix together and start to swirl around the bowl. There's a kind of psychedelic pattern to start with, but then it just turns pink. I stare at it. And I feel like a total dick. What kind of idiot smacks their own hand against the metal rim of a drum? Didn't I realise I'd cut myself? After a minute I take my hand out of the basin and turn the tap off. My hand feels kind of numb now from the cold water. And it's pulsing. I wrap it in a wet flannel to stop it bleeding everywhere and then walk over to the medicine cabinet and look for something I can use, like a bandage or something. Only there isn't anything. Just a box of plasters that's been there for years. Some of them have got a cartoon of a cowboy and Indian on and the words *Little Brave*. We've had them for years.

I take the box out and fumble around trying to open it. I grab one of the big plasters, a plain pink one. No little kid's pictures of Indians. I take the flannel off and dry my hand carefully on a towel. The edge of the cut has swollen up and gone blue. I take the back off the plaster and stick it over my cut. It doesn't go on smoothly; there's a kind of rut in the middle. But it'll have to do.

As I leave the bathroom, I hear a key in the lock downstairs. And all of a sudden I feel nervous. Whoever it is, Mum or Dad, I don't want to see them.

Joe

There are cooking smells coming from downstairs. Curry. My favourite thing that Mum cooks, without a doubt. It smells delicious from here. And it's making concentrating on my revision almost impossible. Not that I was finding it easy to concentrate on Geography anyway.

After staring at the same page of my textbook for ages I give up on revision and go downstairs instead. I go into the lounge, where Kate's already sitting – or I should say, lying – across the sofa. She's watching crap music videos on the TV, as usual. I budge her up and she tuts and sighs. And then we sit in silence, gawping at *100 Alternative Anthems*. As we're sitting there vegging, the front door opens and Dad and Granny come in. Granny perches on the sofa and asks a million embarrassing questions about each music video, like, 'How can you tell what the words are when he's shouting like that?' Me and Kate sit and smile.

After a bit, Dad steps into the lounge. 'Curry's ready,' he says in a pretend Indian accent. He puts his hands together like some dodgy stereotype of an Indian waiter.

Granny laughs. I cringe. Kate tuts. But we all go through to the dining room.

Ash

'Ashley!' Mum calls from downstairs.

I think about ignoring her. I even look at my bedroom window and think about making a jump for it. But then there's a clomping sound as she starts to walk up the stairs and I know it's too late. I go and lie on my bed, turn my music down low.

'Ashley?' Mum says as she pops her head round the door. 'There you are.'

I look up at her and pretend I've only just noticed she's there. 'Hi, Mum.'

Her face screws up as she looks at me and spots the plaster on my hand. 'Are you OK?' she says. 'What's wrong with your hand?'

I look at the plaster and then without thinking about it, hide it behind my back. 'Nothing,' I say. 'I cut it.'

'Do you want me to have a look at it for you?'

I shake my head. 'It's fine.'

And then it's silent. Mum stares into space. After nearly a minute, I feel like asking her if she actually wants anything.

But then the expression on her face turns from concern to serious and annoyed. 'Um,' she says. And then she pauses. 'I got a phone call at work today.'

I nod.

'It was Mr Watts.'

I don't say anything.

'He said that you'd been caught smoking in the school grounds.' Mum raises her eyebrows, like, *'How dare you!'*

'I know.' I look down again. 'Sorry, Mum.'

Mum sighs. Out of the corner of my eye, I can see her folding her arms. I imagine the cross look on her face, but I don't look at her. 'I'm very disappointed, Ashley. I thought you knew better than that.'

'It's not fair, though. I wasn't the only one smoking.'

'It makes no difference if there were hundreds of you,' Mum says. 'You shouldn't have done it. Smoking's bad for you.'

I roll my eyes. I can sense the lecture coming. I've

already had enough of that today. 'Benson just had it in for me,' I say. 'There were at least three other people standing behind the mobile and the only one he picked out was me.'

Mum just stares at me. She doesn't look impressed.

'And he didn't even catch me smoking. He just assumed that's what I was doing.'

'Were you smoking?'

I nod. 'Yeah. That's not the point, though –'

'It is the point,' Mum says, and she sounds angry. 'And what's more, I got pulled off the shop floor to go and take that call. It was very embarrassing. I had to explain to my manager.'

'Oh, what, I'm in trouble because you got embarrassed? Oh, now I understand.'

Mum looks at me like she's about to go mad at me. She's trying to hold it back, trying not to lose it.

'Anyway, Dad smokes,' I say. 'I don't hear you going on at him. And you both drink like fish.'

Mum just stands there for a second with her mouth open. Maybe I shouldn't have said that.

'How dare you talk to me like that!' she says.

And I don't say anything back. I don't apologise cos I'm not sorry. I'm angry.

'Sometimes, Ashley, you make me feel so ashamed. I can't believe you're the same little boy that I brought up when you say things like that.'

I look down at the bed again. I can feel my face starting to tense up. I want to get up and shout at her. I want to tell her that I'm exactly the same kid she brought up. She made me like this. Her and Dad.

'Say you're sorry,' Mum says. She stares at me.

I ignore her. I cross my arms. No way am I saying sorry to her.

'Ashley, I want to hear you take that back. Say you're sorry.'

I shake my head.

'Ashley,' she says, her voice raised now, 'say sorry.'

'No!' I shout back. 'I won't. And you know what? When you act like this, it's no surprise that Dad's seeing some –' I stop myself short. I can't believe those words came out of my mouth. I want to take them back, to suck them back in.

I look up at Mum. She's staring back at me, looking shocked. A tear forms in the corner of her eye. It falls down her cheek and then to the carpet. And I feel guilty. I feel like a shit. I get up from my bed and go over to her, put my arms round her. She just stands there with her arms still folded. She doesn't move at all. We stand there for ages, saying nothing, Mum crying silently, me wishing that the earth would open up and swallow me.

After a while, Mum moves away. She goes and sits on my bed.

'I'm sorry, Mum,' I say. 'I'm really sorry. I shouldn't have said that.'

Mum sighs. She doesn't look up at me. 'It's not your fault, Ashley,' she says. Her voice sounds strange – empty and distant. 'It's not like I didn't know already. It's just a shock to hear you say it.'

'You knew? You knew that Dad is . . . that he's been . . . screwing someone?'

'Ashley,' Mum says. 'Don't say it like that.'

'Then why didn't you do anything about it?'

Mum hangs her head.

I can't believe I'm hearing this. I can't believe she actually knew this was happening and she's just stood by and let him. 'Cut his bloody clothes up,' I say. 'Shout at him. Throw him out. Bloody stab him. Anything. You can't just let him get away with it and then cook dinner for him when he gets home.'

Mum shakes her head.

I don't know what else to say. I don't know how to feel about this. I feel so sorry for her. But at the same time I feel angry at her, like this is her fault somehow.

I hear a car slowing down outside. The engine sounds like Dad's car. Sure enough, a few seconds later I hear a key in the front door. I look over at Mum. She doesn't look up at me. She looks like a little kid, sitting there on my bed. Why can't she take control? She's a bloody grown-up, for God's sake.

'Right,' I say. 'We're going downstairs. Come on. We're gonna do something about this.'

Mum looks up at me, her eyes pleading with me. 'No,' she says. 'No, Ashley. Not now.'

I shake my head at her and go downstairs. Dad's in the kitchen, getting a drink of water.

'I hope you're happy,' I shout at him from the bottom of the stairs, 'now you've ruined everyone's lives. I hope the bitch you're screwing is worth it.'

Dad turns and stares at me. He looks surprised and angry. I go to the front door and open it. I have to get out of here.

'Come back here!' he shouts at me.

I turn and stare at him.

'Ashley!'

I turn away from him and slam the door shut behind me.

Joe

It's all quiet in the dining room. Everyone's tucking into their curry, crunching their way through poppadoms. I lean over and take the chilli chutney jar from the middle of the table, spoon some on to my plate.

'I see they still don't have a clue who committed the murder in town,' Granny says.

I look up at her. I'm taken straight back to yesterday with a jolt. To the Old House. To the common. To that horrible sick, guilty feeling in my throat and my stomach.

'The sooner they're locked away, the better,' Dad says.

'You're right,' Granny says. 'I don't feel safe with them still on the streets.' She shudders. 'Let's change the subject, shall we? It makes me feel all uneasy.'

The subject is changed, cos no one says a thing. Everybody eats, apart from me. I keep having visions of yesterday, of throwing the bag in the pit and covering it over. I wish Granny hadn't said anything.

'Hey, Granny,' Mum says, 'this time tomorrow, young Joe here will have officially left school!'

I look up at Mum. She's smiling at me sort of proudly. I can feel Granny looking at me as well. So I turn and I look at her.

'I hadn't thought of that,' Granny says. 'Ooh, fancy that, Joe! The next time I see you, you'll be a free man.'

I can't help but smile at the thought of being free of school. 'I can't wait for study leave,' I say. 'But I'll be back there in September doing my A levels.' And then I pop a small bit of poppadom in my mouth.

'Are you ready for your exams, then?' Granny says.

I shrug. 'S'pose so,' I say. Though, to be honest, they've been the furthest thing from my mind these last couple of days.

'He'll be fine. Won't you, Joe?' Dad says. He winks at me. 'He's a Wainwright. A chip off the old block.'

'However you do, we'll be proud,' Granny says.

Over the other side of the table I see Kate stick two

fingers down her throat, pretending to make herself sick. I snigger.

Mum shakes her head and smiles. 'Oh, you two,' she says. 'Behave.'

My phone beeps in my pocket. I take it out. It's a text from Ash. **Meet me at the rec.**

I put my fork down and look across the table at Mum and Dad. 'Um, is it OK if I go out later?'

Dad makes a face. 'It's a school night,' he says. 'I don't think so.'

I make a disappointed face. 'Please.'

Mum looks at me and then at Dad, but she doesn't say anything.

'Your granny's here,' Dad says. 'No.'

'Let him go out,' Granny says. 'Don't mind me. He's only got one day of school left anyway – it won't do him any harm.'

Mum and Dad look at each other.

'He's earned his chance to relax,' Granny says.

Dad sighs. 'All right,' he says. 'But you have to be back before ten, understand?'

I smile. 'OK!' I text Ash straight back.

Ash

I'm walking back along the main road, pushing a trolley that I liberated from the supermarket, sipping a can of beer. I keep getting looks off people. Their faces are a picture as they look down their noses at me and tut. Just cos they're stuck-up and don't know how to enjoy themselves they get snotty when they see someone else having fun. I stare right back at them till they look away.

As I get close to the rec, I see a hoodie up ahead. It's Joe. He spots me and walks over, nods as we get close.

'Why've you got a shopping trolley?'

I grin at him. 'Why not?'

'How'd you get it out of the supermarket?' he says.

'Don't they have those grid things so you can't get them out of the car park?'

I smile again. 'Lifted it over the top.'

Joe shakes his head and laughs. 'Idiot.'

'What? I need it. This box of beers is heavy.' I point at the trolley, where the beers are wrapped in a carrier bag.

'How did you get them?' Joe asks.

We start walking towards the rec. 'I got someone to buy them for me,' I say. 'Nobby.'

Joe sniggers. 'What, *the* Nobby? Nobby the Knob?'

I nod. 'The one and only.'

Joe laughs.

We get up close to the rec. The wall gang are all there, sitting on the wall.

'All right,' Manky Mark calls down from the wall. He's smoking a fag, holding it between his thumb and first finger like the complete chav that he is.

I nod at him. 'All right, Mark.'

'You got beers?' Suzie asks, nodding at the trolley.

I stop walking and nod back.

'Give us one.'

I shake my head. 'Get your own.'

I start walking again, to the gate. I push it open and wheel the trolley through.

Joe

It's nearly ten. I have to be home soon. The beers are nearly gone. I've had two. I think Dylan and Rabbit have had a couple each as well. But Ash has had loads. And it's really starting to show cos he's starting to act like a knobhead. He's talking shit, being nasty.

I sit on the top of the bench next to Rabbit, resting my feet on the seat. And I watch as Dylan pushes Ash round the field in the shopping trolley, racing along, tipping it up from side to side, zigzagging around. All the while Ash has a mad grin on his face, like he's on a fairground ride or something. He's shouting and screaming like a madman. I can't make out half of what he's shouting. I don't want to, either. He's being a dick.

'You watch,' I say to Rabbit. 'Ash'll throw up in a minute.'

Rabbit laughs. 'He's lost it tonight.'

I nod. 'You got that right.'

We watch as Dylan lets go of the trolley with an almighty final push. Ash and the trolley roll on for a bit, before slowing and stopping in the middle of the field.

'It was weird yesterday, wasn't it?' Rabbit says. He says it quietly, almost whispering, like someone might be listening in.

I nod. I stare out across the field as Ash jumps out of the trolley, runs after Dylan and rugby-tackles him to the ground.

'D'you think that's it?' Rabbit says. 'D'you reckon we won't hear any more about it?'

I shrug. 'I bloody hope so,' I say. 'Whoever's got the bag now never even saw us. And they won't care, will they? Not now they've got the money back.'

Rabbit nods. 'Yeah. S'pose.'

But the truth is, I still feel weird about it. I mean, I haven't been spending all day thinking about what happened and biting my fingernails, but every now and then, when I'm not expecting it, it pops up unexpectedly in my mind. And every time that happens, my heart starts racing and I feel nervous and paranoid and sick. Right now is one of those moments. So I try and think about something else instead.

Over in the middle of the field, Dylan climbs unsteadily up into the trolley. As soon as he's in, Ash starts pushing him, weaving in and out and round and round, turning sharply so the trolley tips up and nearly dumps Dylan out on to the grass. Dylan holds tightly to the sides of the trolley. Me and Rabbit watch, not saying a word.

I think of what Dad said earlier and look at my watch.

Rabbit notices. 'What time have you got to be back?'

'Ten,' I say.

'Same here,' he says. 'We should go in a second.'

I nod. But neither of us gets up to go. We both just sit there and stare as Ash runs, pushing the trolley straight towards a hedge.

'For fuck's sake, Ash,' Dylan shouts. 'Stop!'

But Ash doesn't listen. He keeps pushing as fast as he can. At the last moment, just as the trolley looks like it's gonna be swallowed up by the hedge, he tips it up and Dylan falls out, straight into the hedge.

'Jesus!' Dylan shouts. 'What was that for? You dick.'

Ash just collapses to the ground, laughing like an idiot, rolling around in the dewy grass.

Dylan comes across to the bench, rubbing his arm. 'That bloody hurt.'

I jump down from the bench, look across at Ash. He's sitting on the field now, staring into the darkness.

'Let's get him home,' I say.

Rabbit and Dylan nod and we all walk across the field. Ash looks round as we get near him.

'Come on, Ash,' Rabbit says. 'We're going home now. Gotta be back by ten.'

Ash doesn't say anything. He just stares, first at Rabbit, then at me and finally at Dylan. 'Don't be so gay,' he says. He stumbles over his words. He sounds pissed. 'The night's still young. We can get some more beers . . .'

I shake my head. 'School in the morning,' I say. 'I'll get in trouble if I'm not back by ten.'

Ash focuses on me. '*I'll get in trouble if I'm not back by ten,*' he says, imitating me in a prim-sounding voice.

'Stop being a dick, Ash,' I say.

But I don't think he even hears me. He tries to spring to his feet, but stumbles a bit and laughs. 'What about you two gays?' he says to Dylan and Rabbit.

They both shake their heads. 'Going home,' Rabbit says.

'Me too,' says Dylan. 'I think you've broken my arm or something.'

'For fuck's sake,' Ash says, staring at us all. And instead of smiling, he looks angry. 'That's the problem with all of you. You three, you're all mummy's boys. Gotta run home to your lovely parents in your lovely homes . . .'

Rabbit steps towards him. 'Shut up, Ash,' he says. 'You're being a dick.'

But Ash doesn't. He steps towards Rabbit and stares at him, angry. 'Don't tell me to shut up,' he says, 'mummy's boy!'

Rabbit stays still for a moment. You can see him taking deep breaths, trying to stay cool. And I think maybe I should step in and try to calm things down. God knows why Ash said that. He knows as well as anyone else that Rabbit lives with his dad, that he doesn't see his mum. What's he trying to prove? I don't do anything, though. I stand and watch as Rabbit pushes Ash in the chest and then turns and walks away. Ash stumbles back, nearly falls over and laughs. He stares after Rabbit for a bit. Then he looks at me and Dylan.

'Anyone else gonna have a go?' he says.

I look away from him. I've seen him like this before and it's kind of scary. Unpredictable. I just want to get away from here. 'I'm going now,' I say.

Dylan nods. 'Me too.' He goes back over to the bench to his bike. I watch him for a second as he gets on, waves and then cycles off.

I turn to Ash. 'You coming?'

Ash shakes his head in a really exaggerated way, like a toddler. 'Come on, J,' he says. 'Let's stay out and get some more booze.'

I shake my head. 'Nah, I've gotta get home.'

Ash sighs. He sits back down on the grass. And I don't know what to do. Should I just leave him here? I look at my watch. It's after ten now. I have to get home. I can't wait around here all night. Mum and Dad will give me grief. So I start walking across the rec towards the gates. When I'm halfway across I turn and look. Ash is still in the same position, sitting on the grass. For a second, I think about going back for him. But I don't. I'm not his mum. He can look after himself. I keep walking, towards the gate and then out on to the main road.

I walk along the main road. It's pretty much empty, just the odd car cruising past. The sky above is totally clear. I can see thousands of stars. After a bit, I hear something behind me. A clattering sound. I turn round to see Ash running along the pavement, pushing the trolley in front of him. I stop walking and wait for him.

'Wait up,' he shouts as he gets close.

So I stand and wait.

'Give us a push, will you?' he says when he gets to me. He tries to climb up into the trolley. It tips to the side, nearly overbalances as he gets in.

I sigh. I don't want to push him, but maybe it's the easiest way. If I do this, we'll be back in five minutes. If I stand and argue with him, we could be ages. 'All right,' I say. And I start pushing. Fortunately, there's no one around to see.

But pushing the trolley straight isn't easy, not with Ash in it. It keeps sliding across the pavement towards the road. And getting it up and down the curb every time we cross a side road is a nightmare.

'Can you get out?' I say after a while. 'I can't push it straight on the pavement.'

Ash doesn't say anything and doesn't budge. So I just keep pushing. Until I see a car up ahead, in the distance. I push the trolley into the side of the pavement and let go.

'Get out,' I hiss at Ash. 'There's a car.'

Ash jumps out of the trolley, stumbles a bit. And then we walk along the pavement, try and get as far away from the trolley as possible. As the car gets nearer I can see it's a police car, cruising slowly towards us. My heart starts to race. I try not to look.

The car slows down as it reaches us and the passenger window lowers. I feel like I might have a heart attack.

'All right, lads,' the policeman says.

Me and Ash stop walking. 'Yeah, fine,' I say. 'Just going home.'

Ash doesn't say anything.

The policemen sit and look at Ash. He's finding it difficult to balance.

'Has he been drinking?' the officer says to me. 'How old is he?'

I don't say anything cos I don't know what to say.

Ash steps forward unsteadily. 'I'm twenty-one,' he says. 'At least.' And he laughs.

The policeman just stares at him. 'Don't be cheeky, son,' he says. Then he turns to me. 'Get him home now. If we see you out here again tonight, we'll put you in the car. Understand?'

I nod my head. I start walking, nudge Ash in the side to get him moving. The police car sits by the side of the road, watching us till we're on our way. Then I hear the engine rev as it moves off.

We walk most of the way in silence. A couple of cars go by, but that's about it. We turn off the main road and get to the top of Ash's road. He stops and stares down it.

'See you, Ash.'

He doesn't say anything. He doesn't move. He just stands there, staring towards his house.

'Ash?'

He's wordless, motionless. Maybe I'm gonna have to walk him right to his door.

'What's up, Ash?'

He turns round slowly. He has a really weird look on his face. 'Can I sleep at yours?'

I look at him, confused. 'What? Why?'

He looks down at the ground. 'I don't want to go home.'

Mum and Dad'll go mad if I bring him back now, at ten past ten. Ten minutes after I'm meant to be back.

'What do you mean, you don't want to go home?'

Ash shrugs. 'Don't want to talk about it.'

I sigh. He looks desperate. But I can't take him to mine. 'You can't,' I say. 'My mum and dad wouldn't let me.'

Ash spins round on his heels. He kicks out at the pavement and a load of little stones scatter across the tarmac. 'Fuck!' he shouts.

'Sorry, Ash.'

He looks at me. It looks like there's a tear in the corner of his eye. I've never seen Ash cry before. Not even when he was little.

'If I go home now, I'll . . .' he says. He's all hunched up and mad as hell.

'What?'

Ash breathes out really slowly. He doesn't look at me, doesn't answer.

'What's the matter, Ash?'

In a fraction of a second he turns to me, a frightening look in his eyes. 'Right now, I want to kill my dad,' he says. 'If I get home and see him now, I'll do it, I swear.'

I stare back at him, expecting his face to break into a smile, a laugh. But it doesn't. He looks serious. He looks like he means it.

'Look, Ash, I'm going home now,' I say. 'I'm s'posed to be home already.'

Ash sighs. He looks at me, his eyes pleading. 'Please,' he says. 'I can't go home.'

And I don't know what to do. I know Mum and Dad will just take him back to his place if they see him, but I don't want to leave him here. 'Come on,' I say.

Ash smiles for a millisecond. And then the smile is gone.

'I'm not promising anything,' I say.

The lights are on at my house. I can see the glow through the drawn curtains. I stop on the pavement outside and turn to Ash.

'Don't say anything,' I say. 'Let me see if the coast is clear, all right?'

He nods.

I walk up the drive, trying to work out what I'm gonna say, wondering if they'll smell the beer on me and go mad. I put my hand in my pocket and take out my keys, open the door just a crack and stick my head round it. I can hear the TV in the lounge. I look straight ahead through the hall and into the kitchen. The light's on, but no one's in there. I turn to Ash. He looks at me blankly.

'You sneak upstairs,' I whisper. 'Don't make a sound. Go straight to my room.'

He nods and sways slightly. I turn back and step into the house, usher Ash in behind me and up the stairs. And as soon as I can see him going up, I close the front door loudly and go to the lounge, open the door. Mum and Dad are in there, watching the news on TV.

'Sorry I'm a bit late,' I say.

They look up at me and smile.

'Good night?' Mum says.

I shrug. 'OK, I s'pose.'

I stand there in the doorway for a bit longer, expecting a grilling. But no one says anything. Upstairs I hear my bedroom door shut. 'Anyway,' I say, 'I'd better go to bed. School in the morning.'

Dad nods. 'Last day!' he says.

I nod. 'Night.'

'Goodnight, love,' Mum says.

I turn, shut the lounge door and get upstairs quickly.

FRIDAY

Ash

The alarm goes off at 7.30 a.m. and wakes me up. I slowly open my eyes. I'm in Joe's room, lying on the floor. It's not exactly comfortable. I sit up and rub my face with my hands. I feel rubbish. I'm not sure if I'm still pissed or hungover or what. But I know I don't want to be awake. I start asking myself questions, like, what the bloody hell am I doing here? What happened last night? And everything kind of slowly seeps back into my brain. Everything that happened yesterday. And it doesn't take a genius to work out that everything is a mess.

Sitting up in his bed on the other side of the room, Joe yawns. He looks over. 'All right, Ash?' he says in a quiet voice.

I nod, even though I don't feel all right. I've got a nagging feeling that there are bits of last night I don't remember – things I said and did. I put my hand in my pocket and get out my phone. I press the green button and look at 'All calls'. There are two missed calls from home. **10:12**, it says underneath them. I don't even remember my phone ringing.

'How d'you feel this morning?' Joe says. 'You got a hangover?'

I nod my head without looking up. 'I feel rough,' I say. My voice sounds croaky.

I open up the text inbox on my phone. There's one from Dad: **I'm sorry, Ash. Let's talk so I can explain.** It makes me angry just looking at it. How can he even write that? There's no way he could ever begin to explain this to me. I'll never forgive him. Never. I close the message and look down the list again. There are two texts from Mum. I remember reading the first one: **Where have you gone?** I open the other one up, the one I don't remember. **Ashley, come home so we can talk this through. X.** I shake my head as I read it. Like hell I'm going home. I don't want to talk about this. Not with them.

'I'll go downstairs and get some breakfast,' Joe says to me. Out of the corner of my eye, I see him get out of bed and put his dressing gown on. 'You feel like eating?'

I shake my head. My stomach and my throat feel disgusting. I feel like I could be sick.

'How about a drink? Tea, coffee, water, juice?'

I nod. 'Water.'

Joe opens the door and leaves the room.

I open the sent text messages to check if I sent any to Mum or Dad last night. I scan through them. Right away my heart sinks. There's one I sent to Dad. I open it. **How cld u do this to us? I hate u.** I put my phone down. Shit. I lie down and close my eyes.

A few minutes later, the door opens again. I prop myself up on my elbow as Joe comes in with a glass of water and some toast. He shuts the door with his foot and brings the glass over to me. I grab it off him and gulp it down. But it doesn't make me feel any better. It just makes my stomach feel like it has water swishing around inside it.

'I got you some toast too,' Joe says. He puts the plate down on the floor. 'In case you change your mind.'

I feel too sick for that, though. 'Thanks,' I say. 'Hey, Joe, I really need the toilet. Can you check the coast is clear?'

He nods his head. 'Everyone else is downstairs,' he says. 'Go quickly. If anyone comes up the stairs, I'll talk to them loudly so you can hear. Just stay in the bathroom if I'm talking, right?'

I nod. And I get up from the floor, stumble a bit. I

head straight for the door and then across the landing to the toilet, shut the door and lock it behind me. And then I start to pee. It feels good. And it goes on for ever and ever. Or at least it feels that way. When I'm finally done, I go over to the basin and run the cold tap, splash water over my face, cup some in my hands and drink it down. Then I go and stand by the door. I can't hear Joe talking. The coast must be clear. I unlock the door, open it and hurry across to his room. By the time I get there, he's dressed in his school uniform.

'You better go home and get your uniform,' he says to me.

I hadn't even thought about school. 'I'm not going,' I say. 'I'm done with all that bullshit. What are they gonna teach us today?'

Joe shrugs. 'It'll be a laugh,' he says. 'You can get your shirt signed and stuff. I heard there was gonna be a flour and egg fight too.'

I shake my head. 'Nah,' I say. 'I'm gonna take it easy today.'

'Are you gonna go home?'

I shake my head. 'Not right now. My mum and dad'll be there. I don't want to see them.'

Joe sits down on the edge of his bed. 'What happened? What's the matter?'

I don't answer. I weigh it up in my mind whether I

want to explain it all to him or not. If I'm honest, I want to. I want it to be out in the open. Except I can't. I feel kind of embarrassed about it. Why is it that my family have to be the fuck-ups when everyone else has a normal family? I sigh. 'Ah, it's just . . . stuff.'

'You should let them know where you are,' Joe says. 'They'll be worried. They might even have called the police.'

I sit up as soon as he says the word police. He's right. I nod. I get my phone out of my pocket. 'I'll send them a text,' I say. 'Just to let them know I'm OK.'

Joe nods. And he starts getting all his stuff together ready for school.

I sit down on the edge of his bed and write a message: **I'm safe. Going to school now.** I send it to Mum.

I sit and stare into space, not wanting to think but unable to stop the million thoughts going round my head. Questions that have no answers.

My phone starts ringing. *Mum mobile calling*, it says. I stare at it as it rings. Before I can change my mind, I press Answer and put the phone to my ear.

'Ashley,' Mum says. She sounds relieved. Upset.

'Hi, Mum,' I say.

'Where are you, Ashley?' she says. 'I've been up all night, worried sick.'

I don't answer. I feel guilty, like a coward. I confronted Mum with all this shit, stirred it all up, and then I just left her to it. 'Sorry, Mum,' I say. 'I slept at Joe's last night.'

It's quiet at the other end of the phone. I can hear Mum breathing. 'Are you coming home soon?'

'I've got to go to school, Mum,' I say. 'Last day.'

'Right,' she says. Then she pauses. 'I'm sorry about last night, Ashley.'

As soon as I hear her say that, I feel like a total, ungrateful little shit. 'It's not your fault, Mum.'

There's another pause. 'I'll see you after school, though, won't I?'

I don't answer right away. But deep inside, I know I'm gonna be there. 'Yeah,' I say eventually, quietly. 'I'll be back.' And then I hang up.

I slip out of the house with Joe. After he's gone to the bus stop I walk aimlessly, without really knowing where I'm going or what I'm gonna do when I get there. One thing's for sure, though – I'm not going home. Mum doesn't start work till eleven on a Friday and I can't go back when she's still at home. Especially seeing as I'm meant to be at school. I've got myself in enough trouble this week as it is.

So I end up walking the back way into town, through all the executive housing estates. And before I've even realised that I'm doing it, I've walked to the supermarket. I feel in my pocket and take out my money. I have some change and a ten pound note. I head straight for the sandwich bit just inside the doors, take an energy drink down and then look at the sandwiches. Prawn mayonnaise, cheese and onion, beef salad, ham and cheese, et cetera, et cetera. Just the thought of all the flavours makes me want to vom. So I go and grab a big pack of crisps instead and take them up to the tobacco kiosk.

The lady behind the counter takes the can and crisps and scans them.

'Two pounds thirty-five, my love,' she says.

I put my hand in my pocket, take out the tenner and casually ask for a packet of my usual smokes too.

The lady turns round and picks up a packet from the shelves behind her and scans that as well. And I can't believe my luck. She didn't even ask for ID.

'That's eight pounds and four pence,' she says.

I pay, grab my stuff and my change and go.

I walk back to the rec, smoking a cigarette and swigging from my can. There's no one there. No one sitting on the wall. No one in the little kids' playpark. No one walking their dog. Just me. I open the gate and walk straight across the field over to the bench, sit down and try and work out what I'm gonna do. With the day. With my life.

Around ten o'clock, I decide it's safe to go home. Mum'll be on her way to work by now. So I walk back along the main road. And as I do, I pass the flats where they found the body. There aren't any cops outside any more. They must have got all the evidence that they think they're gonna get. But it makes me think of the bag. And of the gun, still buried in the woods. It makes me shiver to think about it. We were lucky. Things could have turned out much worse for us. We could have been tracked down by the guys who wanted the bag back, or by the cops. God knows where we'd be by now if they had. It's not worth thinking about.

I walk on. I still feel really rough. I need to get back to the house, have a shower, change my clothes and eat something. Maybe even have a sleep. Cos I don't wanna be feeling like this. Especially not if I'm gonna be home when Mum and Dad get home. I wanna be fresh, thinking straight.

Joe

I am now a free man. School is officially out and all I have left is exams. It feels really good. And tonight it's Rabbit's party. After the weird week I've had, I think I deserve a good night.

School today was a bit of an anticlimax, to be honest. Everyone was going on about how all this stuff was gonna happen, like a water fight, and an egg and flour fight. And none of it happened. Everyone just signed each other's school shirts, we had a leavers' assembly, and loads of girls started crying. Then that was it. We were free to go.

Right now, I'm upstairs in my room. I've been here since I got home. First thing I did was check the news on the internet to see if there was any mention of the bag or anything. But there was nothing.

Since then, I've been rereading the messages people wrote on my school shirt and then messing around on my guitar. But now I'm bored of playing guitar. So I put it down on the bed, get up and go over to my wardrobe. I'm gonna choose what to wear tonight to the party, though looking for clothes in my wardrobe is always depressing. My clothes are all . . . what's the word? Lame? Unfashionable? Shit? All of the above, really. Apart from my new trainers. And every time I look at them, I feel a little pang of guilt. There's nothing I can do about it now, though.

After standing in front of my wardrobe for ages, I choose a band T-shirt – a black one that really could do with a wash – a zip-up hooded top, a pair of dark blue jeans and my trainers.

Ash

I slept most of the day. I feel a little better for it – not hungover, at least. Right now, I'm sitting on the sofa in the lounge. I see Mum walk up the drive. I feel nervous. My hands are sweaty. I don't know what's about to happen. I don't know how I'm gonna react, or how Mum's gonna react. I don't even know what I want to happen here. I don't know what would be worse – Mum and Dad splitting up, or Mum and Dad trying to make things right.

The front door opens and then shuts with a plasticky *clunk*.

'Ashley? Are you home?'

'In here, Mum,' I say.

A few seconds later, Mum pokes her head round the door. She smiles. At least, she tries to. Only, when she looks at me, I can see a tear appear in the corner of her eye. She walks over to me with her arms outstretched. I stand up and we hug.

'Are you all right, Ashley?' she says into my back.

I nod. 'Yeah.'

We both sit on the sofa. I still feel nervous as hell. This is strange and horrible. I look at Mum. Her make-up has run. She wipes a tear away and smudges her mascara even more.

'I'm sorry, Ashley,' she says. 'I'm really sorry.'

'Don't say sorry, Mum. It's not your fault.'

Mum shakes her head. 'It's . . .' she starts. But then she falls silent and stares across the room.

I close my eyes and put my head in my hands. I take a couple of deep breaths. I feel like I wanna cry. I feel hopeless. But I don't wanna cry in front of my mum. Someone's got to be strong. Someone has to be the grown-up here. I look up. 'What happened last night?' I say. 'After I left?'

Mum doesn't answer right away. I can see her thinking. What's she thinking about? Maybe she's trying to work out whether to tell me the truth or not. Maybe she's trying to think what I want to hear, so she can say it. 'We had an argument,' she says after a while.

'Yeah?' I look at her. She doesn't look back at me.

She nods. 'I called him all the names under the sun.'

'Good,' I say. My voice sounds flat. 'And what did he do?'

Mum stiffens a little. 'He cried, he begged me to forgive him. He said he'd made a mistake. He said he'd already ended the affair.'

I nod. 'Did you believe him?'

Mum shrugs. 'I don't know,' she says. Then there's a pause and all I can hear is the sound of birds singing outside. 'I think so.'

I sigh. I can't believe she bought his lies, that she's gonna give him another chance. I mean, I want to believe that what Dad told her is true. It would make everything easier. But why should I believe him after what he's done?

We sit in silence.

'How was your last day of school?' Mum says eventually.

It shocks me. My stomach turns. Guilt. I make sure I look her right in the eye as I answer. 'OK,' I say. 'It wasn't easy to concentrate, though. I was just thinking about you and Dad.'

Mum nods. She sighs again. 'Sorry.'

I shake my head.

'And you stayed out of trouble?'

I nod. 'Of course.'

I wonder whether this is a trap, whether she knows that I didn't go to school today. But then she doesn't say anything. She looks sad and small and not really like my mum at all.

'Your dad should be home after seven,' she says.

I nod my head.

'Maybe we should all sit down and talk things through. Iron all the problems out.'

I snort with laughter. And then I wish I hadn't. It's just that it's stupid, what Mum said. How on earth can you iron out a problem like this? I shake my head. 'I'm going out tonight.'

Mum looks back at me, disappointed. 'Oh. Where?'

'Rabbit's house.'

'Do you have to? Can't you go out another night?'

I shrug. 'I want to go,' I say. 'It's my last day of school. Why should I sit here while my mum and dad split up and my life falls to pieces? I wanna be out with my friends.'

Mum just sits there. And I feel guilty, like I shouldn't have said that. But, you know what? I mean it. I don't wanna be here when Dad gets home. It's up to them to sort this out. I wanna be anywhere but here. I get up from the sofa.

'I'm gonna get ready,' I say.

Joe

I have a bag from the off-licence balancing on my handlebars as I ride through the woods to Rabbit's. A few cans of cider, that's all. Ash has a half bottle of vodka in his pocket and a bag with a big bottle of Coke in it resting on his handlebars. He has some weed as well.

It's overcast and windy tonight, though it isn't really cold. Feels like it should rain at any moment, but it hasn't so far. The woods smell earthy and damp. And I feel kind of weird and scared riding through them.

We cycle past the part of the woods where we found the car last week. It's gone. Taken away by the police, I s'pose. You wouldn't know that anything had happened there now, except that the tree which had been knocked into the other trees has been chopped down. There are still some tyre tracks, but they're not fresh any more and they blend in with all the others. You'd only notice them if you knew what you were looking for.

We don't say anything to each other for a while after we've gone past the spot where the car was. I don't know about Ash, but I'm thinking about what's happened in the last week and feeling paranoid, like we're still gonna get found out by someone. Even though I know in my head that I'm being stupid. Because the facts are:

1. No one saw me and Ash pick the bag up.
2. There's nothing left to link us to the bag except a gun that's buried in the woods. Finding the gun would be like finding a needle in a haystack.
3. Whoever it is that the bag belongs to has it back now. They're not gonna take it to the police and complain that there's a couple of hundred quid missing.
4. We dropped the bag off before we told them where it would be. So there's no way that they can know who we are – they won't have seen us.

But, you know, even as I think about all the reasons why we're not gonna get found out, I can find little loopholes in them, like:

1. We *think* no one saw us pick up the bag, but we don't know for sure. Anyone could have seen us last Friday. We were both half cut. Who knows who else was in the woods that night?

2. It's possible someone could find the buried gun, even if it's unlikely. And if they handed it in to the police – like we should have done with the bag – the police might link it to us. I mean, they have forensics. All they would need to do is find one fibre of clothing and they could link it to Ash or Rabbit.

3. We don't know for sure who took the bag after we left it on the common. For all we know, someone walking their dog picked it up and took it to the police. And if they did, the police could get my fingerprints and Ash's and all sorts off the bag, couldn't they?

4. We went back to make sure the bag had been taken from the common, and we could have been seen then.

I know I'm being paranoid, but I can't help it. I wish I could be more like Ash and just treat everything like it's a joke. But I can't.

Ash

There are a lot of people at Rabbit's. More than he expected, I think. But he's cool with it. Anyway, it's not as if he has any neighbours who can get pissed off at the noise or anything, seeing as he lives in the woods. And so far tonight no one's being a dick. Everyone's behaving themselves, just having a nice time – having a little drink, having a smoke, having a dance and a kiss and a cuddle to celebrate the end of school.

Not me, though, not yet. I mean, I've had a little drink. Quite a big drink, actually. But I haven't done anything else. No dancing, no kissing or cuddling. But I'm on the case. It's all in hand. It will happen soon.

Right now I'm sitting in Rabbit's garden with a couple

of people from school. We're about to have a little smoke cos I brought some of the weed with me. I light the joint and have a puff on it, take the smoke deep down into my lungs and keep it there for as long as I can manage. After about twenty seconds, I blow it out slowly and break into a massive grin. I feel good. I take another drag and then pass it on to Dylan, who's sitting next to me. He does the same as me, takes two drags from it and passes it round the circle.

I kind of drift away as I watch the joint go round the circle. My mind feels empty for the first time in ages. The joint gets round to Joe, who takes a puff on it and coughs. Trust Joe. He couldn't be cool if he tried. He makes me laugh.

As I sit there, my phone starts to ring. I take it out of my pocket. It's Manky Mark calling. I bet he's after another smoke.

I put the phone to my ear and answer the call. 'All right, Mark?'

'Ash,' he says. He sounds serious.

'What's up, Mark?'

'Listen, man,' he says, 'it might be nothing, right, but . . .'

'What?'

There's a pause at the other end of the phone. 'Some geezers was at the rec looking for you earlier,' he says.

The joint comes back round to me. I take it off Joe

and have a drag. 'Yeah?' I say. 'Probably my dad. Was he stupid-looking?'

'Nah, it weren't your old man,' Mark says. 'Big geezers. There were two of them. They was driving a BMW. Pulled up at the wall.'

I break off in mid-drag and choke a little. I don't like the sound of this. 'You what? In a BMW? Who were they? What did they want?'

'One of them said he wanted to buy some skunk,' Mark says.

I pass the joint on and stand up. I need to talk in private so I walk over to the pond, away from everyone else, to a rickety bench that overlooks it. I sit down. 'Who was this man?' I say. 'What did he say? Was it a cop?'

There's a pause. 'I told you what I know.'

'Did he say my name?'

Mark shakes his head. 'Not exactly,' he says.

'What do you mean, not exactly? Either he did or he didn't.'

'They pulled up by the wall, got out the car and said that they heard there was some kid selling skunk in Fayrewood and they wanted to buy some. Said he might go by the name of Layzee Eyez. No one said anything. I just shook my head, said I didn't know nothing about any skunk or Layzee Eyez. But then one of them got his wallet out, pulled out a wodge of twenty-pound notes. And Suzie jumped down off the wall and went and talked to him.'

'Fuck!' I say. 'Didn't you stop her?'

'I shouted at her,' Mark says, 'but I couldn't do nothing else. They was big geezers, man. Gold chains and all that. I didn't wanna get messed up in their business, you know what I'm saying?'

I close my eyes. This is bad. 'What did Suzie tell them?'

'Dunno,' Mark says. 'She went off and talked to them and she ain't come back to the rec. I called you as soon as I could.'

I run my hand through my hair. I don't say anything. I'm in shock, I think. I can't quite take this in. Who would have known that I had the weed? 'Where are they now?' I say.

'Who?'

'Suzie. The men in the BMW.'

'I don't know where Suzie went,' Mark says, 'but the geezers in the BMW went off somewhere. Revved the engine and did a wheel spin and they was gone.'

I stare at the reeds in the pond. 'Shit!' I say.

'Sorry, man.'

But I hardly hear him. I'm too busy thinking. About who could be looking for me. About whether Suzie gave them my name. About what they might have done to her. About whether they'll be able to track me down. I hang up and put my phone in my pocket.

I get up from the bench, walk back over to where everyone's still sitting smoking. Joe's looking spaced out, waiting for the joint to come back round to him.

Joe

I'm feeling nicely spaced out when there's a tap on my shoulder. I look up. It's Ash. He looks worried. I think about telling him to cheer up a bit, but before I can, he grabs my arm and almost hauls me to my feet. I stumble a bit. My head rushes.

'Come with me,' he says. 'We need to talk.'

I stare back at him, confused. 'What? Why?'

He sighs. 'We need to talk,' he says. 'Now.'

And I start to think. What could he need to talk to me about so urgently? What would make him look so pissed off? My mind immediately fills with a whole host of horrible possibilities.

Ash leads the way towards the house. 'We need to

find Rabbit,' he says. 'He needs to hear this as well. He's involved in this too.'

I nod. And in that moment I know we're in trouble. Something's happened. The realisation makes me feel sick.

We go inside Rabbit's dark, low-ceilinged cottage. The music's blaring out and it's rammed full of people. But I don't look at them. They blur into the background.

Ash goes in and out of rooms – the kitchen, the dining room, the hall – looking for Rabbit. We find him in the front room, talking to some girl that he's fancied for ages.

'Rabbit,' Ash says.

But Rabbit doesn't hear him over the music.

'Rabbit,' Ash says, louder this time.

Rabbit looks over, gives us the kind of look that says, 'Not now.'

'We need to talk,' Ash says.

Rabbit stares right back at Ash, giving him daggers. He does the same to me. But then when he sees that Ash isn't taking no for an answer, he rolls his eyes and says something to the girl. She nods. And then Rabbit gets up and we all go back out of the lounge, through the hall and into the garden. We find somewhere quiet – the bench next to the pond.

'This better be important,' Rabbit says. 'I was in there.'

Ash looks at me and takes a breath before he speaks. 'Manky Mark called me. He says some big blokes in a BMW were asking after me earlier,' he says.

Me and Rabbit look at each other.

'Apparently he even knew my tag – Layzee Eyez. And he knew I had some skunk.'

The cogs in my head start to turn slowly, trying to work out what that could mean. Is it the police? I breathe in and hold the breath, then blow it out slowly.

'Oh my God,' Rabbit says. 'Who would know that?'

Ash raises an eyebrow. 'It must be whoever wanted the bag back,' he says. 'Who else would it be?'

'The police?' I say. But even as I say it, I start to doubt myself.

We're silent for a second, each of us panicking, thinking, staring at each other.

'Why would it be the guys who wanted the bag back?' Rabbit says. 'What would they want? We gave the money back.'

'Not all of it, though,' I say.

Ash chews his thumbnail. He nods. 'Fuck!' he says.

And then we're silent again, staring. I can hear music and laughter and voices coming from the house and the garden, but it might as well be happening in another dimension. I feel like I'm not really here any more. I feel high. I can't deal with this.

'Why don't we just call the police?' Rabbit says.

Ash lets out a nervous kind of laugh. 'Don't be stupid!' he says. 'We can't go to the police. No way.'

'Why not?' Rabbit says.

'Because we're in too fucking deep,' Ash says. 'We've done too much. We spent some of the money. I smoked some of the weed. We buried a gun in the bloody forest! How are we gonna explain that lot away?'

Rabbit nods. And I have to agree. We couldn't explain this to the police. They'd have us in a cell in minutes. But what can we do? There isn't anyone we can turn to.

In the distance there's the sound of an engine and the scrunch of tyres on gravel. 'What's that?' I say.

Rabbit shakes his head. 'Dunno. My dad's not meant to be back till tomorrow evening.'

Ash stands up on the bench and looks over the hedge. 'Oh, Jesus!' he says. 'It's a BMW. They're here.'

I get up on the bench and look too. I watch as the car door opens and a massive guy dressed in black with a shaved head and shades and gold chains steps out of the car. Someone else gets out of the passenger door, dressed almost identically. He's taller and thinner but still big, and has longer hair. They sure as hell

304

don't look like policemen. They look like . . . God, I don't even want to think about it. I duck my head down. I don't want them to see me.

'We need to get out of here,' Ash says. '*Now*.'

I stare back at Ash.

'Right,' Rabbit says. 'Follow me.'

So we follow, running back to the house, through the hall and into the kitchen. Rabbit grabs a set of keys from the top of the fridge. As we stand in the kitchen doorway, waiting, I hear a commotion at the front door. The two men from the BMW are trying to get inside. Rabbit thinks for a second and then runs back out of the house, with me and Ash following, into the back garden, right round the outside of the house to the garage. He puts a key in the lock and then, with a creaking noise, he pulls the garage doors open.

He hurries to his car and tries to put his keys in the door. But as he does so, he fumbles. The keys fall to the ground. Me and Ash stand, willing him to pick them up and get on with it, looking anxiously behind us in case the two men come out of the house. I wish Rabbit would give me the bloody keys so I could do it. He picks them up. This time he manages to unlock the car and opens the door. He gets in, leans over and unlocks the passenger door. I open the door, pull the passenger seat forward and jump in the back. Ash puts the seat down and gets in after me. He pulls the car door shut and locks it right away. Rabbit starts the car. It doesn't exactly roar into life, more splutters. He puts the car in first and floors it. The engine squeals, the wheels spin and the Fiesta rushes out of the garage and on to the gravel drive.

As we speed away into the woods, I turn and look through the back window at the house, at the front door. The two big guys turn at the noise of Rabbit's car. There's a split second before they realise what's happened. And then they both run for their car.

'They're following us!' I say to Rabbit, leaning through the gap in the front seats. I almost have to shout it above the noise of the engine and the squeaks as the car gets thrown around on the bumpy path.

Rabbit doesn't answer – he just nods and changes up a gear. If anyone knows the tracks around the forest, it's Rabbit. He's been driving round it in this car with his dad for about a year.

I turn to look out of the back window. We're throwing up a cloud of dust from the track behind us, but through the dust I can see the BMW. It's maybe 50 metres away. Judging by the state of it and the state of Rabbit's old banger, they'll catch us in no time. There's no way we can outrun them. And besides, there's nowhere for us to go. I try and take deep breaths, but it doesn't help. This feels like a desperate situation.

I look out of the front windscreen. Rabbit speeds towards a tight left bend in the path. He doesn't brake, doesn't slow down, but seems to accelerate into it and then turn the steering wheel at the last possible moment. As we go round the bend, it feels like the car's gonna turn over. I get thrown to the side. My head slams against the window. I put my hand up to my head and give it a rub as Rabbit straightens the car and really guns the accelerator. The trees on either side of the path are just a blur now.

'Where are we gonna go?' I say.

Rabbit doesn't answer straight away. He's staring out of the windscreen, not taking his eyes off the path ahead, concentrating. 'Dunno,' he says. 'I'll try and lose them.'

I close my eyes. I put my hands together as though I'm gonna say a prayer. Which is ridiculous. I haven't said a prayer since I was about seven. I don't believe in God. And besides, even if there was a God, what would he do about this? Does he help people like us, who find a bag full of money and keep it for themselves?

I open my eyes.

In the passenger seat, Ash turns round, looks at the BMW catching up with us with every passing second. He shakes his head. 'This isn't gonna work,' he says. 'They're in a BMW and we're in a clapped-out Fiesta.'

I turn in my seat and look out of the rear window again. Ash is right. The BMW is only a few metres behind us now. I can see the faces of the two guys. They're staring at me, saying something that I can't manage to lip-read.

'You need to do something, Rabbit,' I say. 'They're right on our tail.'

Rabbit looks in his rear-view mirror. 'I know that,' he says. 'I'm trying.'

I look up. The track forks up ahead.

'You can lose them here,' Ash shouts. 'Sell them a dummy. Pretend to go one way and then turn the other way.'

Rabbit doesn't take his eyes off the track, but just nods. He slows down ever so slightly, so that the BMW catches right up. And then, as he gets to the fork, he turns the steering wheel like he's going left. But at the last moment, he turns the wheel back sharply to the right. We come off the path and the car skids a little. I get thrown to the side again. But Rabbit manages to control the skid and get us back on the path, on to the right-hand track. I look out of the back window again.

'You did it,' I say. 'They went the other way.'

Up in the front mirror, I can see Rabbit smiling.

'Yeah. Nice driving,' Ash says, slapping him on the arm. 'That was wicked. Now floor it and let's lose them.'

So Rabbit does just that and we fly along the track. The trees on either side flash past. And I start thinking about what we do next. I mean, even though we've lost them now, we can't just drive for ever. If they've found us once, they'll do it again. And they know where Rabbit lives now. They know what we look like.

'Oh shit!' Rabbit says all of a sudden, looking in the rear-view mirror. 'They're back.'

I turn. They're quite a way behind, but gaining with every passing second.

Rabbit steps on the accelerator and the Fiesta's little engine starts to scream, as though in protest. Stones and dust get thrown up on either side of the car and in our wake as we race along. But still the BMW gets closer.

'They're gaining on us!' I say.

'I know!' Rabbit shouts back. 'I'm going as fast as I can. I don't know what else to do.'

Then a few seconds later, there's a sudden crash and Rabbit's car bumps forward and to the side. I jerk forward in my seat.

'Shit! What was that?' Ash shouts.

I look behind us.

'It was the BMW,' Rabbit says. 'They're trying to push us off the road.'

I watch out of the back window as the BMW surges

forward, towards us. It rams into the back of Rabbit's car, and the back of the car skids sideways. I get thrown sideways too.

'Jesus!' Rabbit says.

I look ahead through the windscreen. There's a kind of crossroads coming up.

'Hold on tight,' Rabbit shouts. 'I'm gonna turn right.'

I grab the handle on the roof of the car and brace myself, watching as Rabbit speeds up to the crossroads and then skids round to the right. I have to hold on tight as the force of the turn throws my weight across the back of the car.

As soon as the car's going straight again, I look behind us. The BMW's made the turn as well.

'They're still behind us,' I say.

No one says anything. There's nothing to say any more. I'm starting to think, this is how it ends. This is how we're gonna die. Either crashed off the road or, if we survive that, beaten to a pulp by the guys in the BMW. Or maybe even shot. Or burned. Like the guy in the flat. I keep looking out of the back window. They're nearly on us again. They'll start trying to crash into us in a second, ramming us off the road.

'I've got an idea,' Rabbit says suddenly. 'Put your seatbelts on.'

We scrabble around and do as he says. My seatbelt gets stuck when I pull it. I let go and try again. This time it comes out and I click in.

'Ready,' I say.

'Brace yourselves,' Rabbit says.

And then he slams down hard on the brakes and steers into the side of the track. The car skids and bumps as we come off the path and on to the long grass. Even with my seatbelt on I get thrown around in the back like a crash-test dummy. Over on the left-hand side, I see the BMW fly past us along the track.

Rabbit's car bumps to a stop.

'Get out and run!' he shouts.

I claw desperately at my seatbelt, trying to undo it. In the front of the car, Ash and Rabbit already have their belts off. They throw their doors open and start running from the car as fast as they can. I fumble for the release on the passenger seat. It takes a couple of seconds to find it and then push the seat up. As soon as I'm free, I jump out of the car and start running for all I'm worth across the bumpy ground, over the divots and lumps that are hidden by the long grass. But as I run, I feel my right foot hit one wrong and I lose my balance. I crash to the ground, head first, get a mouthful of dirt and grass. I scrabble straight back to my feet.

Up ahead, I see Ash and Rabbit as they run desperately into the trees and then disappear among them. A little way up the track, I hear car doors open and feet hit the gravel track. I instinctively look behind me in their direction. And I see the shorter man lift a gun and aim it at me. My heart skips a beat. I bend low and run as fast as I can.

BANG!

The bullet misses me.

BANG!

The second one does as well.

And before he can fire again, I'm in the cover of the trees, running faster than I've ever run before. My feet get caught in brambles and bushes as I run, and bits of the soft forest floor give way beneath my feet in some places, but nothing is gonna stop me. I focus on the forest ahead of me and nothing else. I don't see the trees as I pass them. I can hear nothing but my own breath and the soft hollow thud of my feet on the ground. I have no idea where Ash and Rabbit have gone. All I can sense is me running and the guys behind me aiming guns at me. We're the only things that exist in my world now, the only things that matter.

BANG!

Another shot. Another that misses me. This time it sounds further away, like I'm getting away from them.

I want to look behind me to see where they are, but I resist. I have to focus on what's ahead. I need to keep going. I can't lose time looking behind me. I could stumble and fall. So I concentrate on running, sprinting, eating up the ground with each stride. From what I've seen of the two guys, they don't look like they could manage much of a chase. They're too big and fat. If I can just manage to keep going, they'll have to slow down. I'll be safe. For now.

BANG! BANG!

Two more shots. Two more misses. They definitely sound much further away now. Maybe they're giving up. Maybe that's it. Maybe I've done it. But still I don't look round. I just keep pumping my legs and my arms.

After a couple more minutes, I sense that I'm alone. I don't know what it is. The silence, maybe. The stillness of the forest. Whatever it is, I'm sure they've stopped following. So I turn my head to look. There's no sign of the two guys from the BMW. I can't see them anywhere. I slow right down and then stop. I turn and look the way I've just come from. All I can see is trees and undergrowth. No other humans. No movement. I stand and listen and I can't hear anything. Just my own blood pumping around my body, the sound of me trying to catch my own breath and some birds in the trees.

And I wonder if they're out there right now, hiding,

watching, aiming their gun at me. I shudder. I feel exposed here. I move over to the left and hide behind a tree, wait till I get my breath back.

Ash

I just ran for my life. And I kept running till I was sure that I wasn't being followed. I have no idea where the others are. One second I was running with Rabbit, the next I was on my own. I never even saw Joe. I got out of the car and just made a run for it. I didn't even stop to let him out of the back of the car. Fuck. I hope he got out.

And now I'm here, crouching down behind a tree, catching my breath, wondering what the fuck I do next, praying that the others are safe. Cos when I was running I heard shots. I didn't stop to see what was happening. I just kept running, trying to get as far away from there as I could. I seriously hope they didn't hit Rabbit or Joe.

315

I close my eyes for a second and try and compose myself. There's so much fucking adrenalin running through my body. I'm jumpy as hell. And I feel paranoid, like the blokes from the BMW could be anywhere right now. They could be right on me and I wouldn't know.

I need to get out of the woods. And I need to find out what happened to Joe and Rabbit. I need to know they're all right. I mean, I didn't hear any screams or anything. And I would have done if they'd been hit, right? But maybe you don't scream if you get hit by a bullet. Maybe you just fall over. And die. And that's it. The end.

I get my phone out of my pocket and write a text: **R u safe? Where r u?** I send it to Joe and Rabbit. And as soon as I've sent it, I realise that I could've just made a big mistake. What if they're hiding? What if the two blokes from the BMW hear Joe and Rabbit's phones beep and find them?

I put my phone on silent straight away and I sit and wait for a reply. I look at the time on my phone. 20:01. And I make a promise to myself: if I don't get a message by 20:05, I'm gonna try and get out of the woods on my own. And I'm gonna call the police.

The time ticks by slowly. All around me, up in the trees, I can hear the birds calling. Innocently flitting about, roosting, getting ready for bed. I look at the time again. 20:03. I stare at my phone, willing a message to come through, to bring me news that Joe and Rabbit are both OK. But nothing happens. The seconds continue to tick slowly past. And I start to get really scared. 20:04. It's been three minutes. Why haven't they replied? They must have been caught. Or worse . . .

I look out from behind the tree. The light's starting to dim. It'll be dark soon. I strain to hear anything, see anything. But it feels like I'm all alone. No one else is here. I get the urge to break the silence and solitude – to shout, to scream. I even open my mouth. But I don't make a sound. I'm not stupid. I'm not suicidal.

I look at my watch. Ten seconds to go before I make the call. Where the fuck are they? And then my phone vibrates in my hand. It gives me a shock. I look at it and hurriedly open the message. It's from Joe. **I'm OK. They shot at me & missed. Think I'm near the Old House. Meet u there. U seen Rabbit?**

I breathe a sigh of relief. Joe's safe. I'd convinced myself he was lying in a pool of blood somewhere. And it would have been my fault. Right away my phone goes again. A message from Rabbit. **I'm safe. Where shall I meet u? U with Joe?**

I smile to myself. But in a second the smile is gone. I send messages back to Joe and Rabbit, let them know we're all safe and tell them we'll meet in the Old House.

I get to my feet and look around me once more. And then I start walking in the direction of the Old House, using the trees as cover. With every step, I look all around me, my ears tuned in to even the slightest of noises. If I hear anything, if I see anything, I'll be down on the floor in a split second. I have to be careful.

Joe

I'm going in the direction of the Old House when I hear something. I freeze then hide behind a tree. I'm sure it was a voice. I stare all around me, trying to find what made the noise, but all I can see is trees. Nothing moving. Nothing human. Everything is still.

But then I hear it again. And this time I'm sure – it's two voices. They've got London accents. I stay absolutely still. I even hold my breath. They're not far away. I can't quite make out what they're saying, but their voices are loud enough for me to know they're close and getting closer.

I keep staring out from my hiding place, and then I see the two guys from the BMW come out from behind a tree, walking in my direction. Heading straight for where I'm standing. I start to panic. They haven't seen me, but if they keep walking this way they're gonna be where I'm hiding in about twenty seconds. They'll find me and kill me.

I need to think straight. I need to do something. I have to save myself.

The two guys keep walking. They're not talking any more. One of them has a branch in his hand. As he walks, he's using it to beat the undergrowth out of the way. And every time he rips the bushes apart with a swipe, I imagine what he could do to me. He'd rip me apart in seconds.

I have to make a decision right now. I have to do something before it's too late. They're heading right for me. They're so close I can smell their horrible aftershave. They'll be here in five seconds.

I take a breath. I make my decision.

I stay absolutely still and wait, watch every heavy step that they take. As they get closer, I see that they're gonna pass by a couple of metres to the left of the tree I'm hiding behind. I wait and watch, wait and watch as they step closer, closer, closer. And when they're level, I lift my right leg and move around the tree to the right, trying to stay out of their sight.

Crack.

I step on a twig and it breaks.

And their footsteps stop.

'What was that?' one of them says.

'What?'

'I just heard something move.'

I stay motionless. I can't see them from where I am, and they can't see me. If I don't make another noise, maybe they'll just assume it was a bird or something and keep on walking.

I hear the great thumping footsteps again, coming my way. And inside my jeans pocket my phone starts to vibrate. My God. I feel like I'm having a heart attack here. The footsteps get closer and closer. And I know what I have to do. I turn and start running as fast as I can, away from the tree, away from the two guys.

Ash

I keep low, moving from tree to tree. My eyes and ears are on stalks, looking and listening for any movement or sound. I don't want to walk into a trap. The guys from the BMW are bound to be here somewhere, looking for us. And if they are, I have to see them before they see me.

But as I make my stop-start way through the woods, it's almost completely silent. The only movement is the breeze through the trees, making the branches rustle.

Even though I'm stopping behind trees with every three or four steps, taking time to listen, I manage to get through the woods quite quickly. And before too long, I know for sure where I am. Up ahead there's a track. And over on the other side, hidden a little way back, is the Old House. The gun is near too, buried in the soil. I stop behind a tree for a second and think. But it doesn't take me long to make up my mind. I want the gun. Just in case. I'd be stupid not to get it.

I creep through the trees and the undergrowth as carefully as I can. Across the track. On the other side of the track, I take a couple of seconds to get my bearings and then start walking in the direction of where the gun is hidden. I scan the ground, looking out for where we buried it. And then I see the tree, the one with my tag on it. And a few metres away, a patch of soil that looks different from the rest. This is it. This is where the gun is. I drop to my hands and knees and start digging.

A couple of minutes later, with the gun in my pocket, I creep through the trees and the undergrowth, my eyes fixed on the Old House up ahead. When I'm no more than ten metres away, I stop still. I watch and listen for about thirty seconds, making sure no one's here already, my hand on the gun as a precaution. I look over at the door, at the bit of boarding. There's no sign of anyone about. Though I guess they'd hardly be making it that obvious if they were here, would they?

I creep through the undergrowth, bent double. I wonder whether I should call something out before I try and go in, but I decide not to. I carefully pull the boarding away from the doorway. I don't go inside right away, though. I look at the dingy interior of the Old House till my eyes adjust and I'm sure that no one else is here. When I'm sure it's safe, I slip inside and carefully close the boarded-up door behind me.

I walk through to the room on the left, straight over to the chair, and sit down, take my fags out of my pocket. I light one and take a drag. It's only now, now that I'm sitting down, that I realise how nervous and jumpy I am. I take drag after drag after drag from my cigarette. And as soon as I've taken my last drag and stubbed the fag out, I think about lighting another. But I don't. Instead, I get up from the chair and go over to the boarded-up window. I peek through a small crack in it. There's no sign of anyone else. It's nearly dark out there now.

As I look out at the darkening forest, I sigh and think about what we're gonna do next. Cos whatever we do is wrong. Call the police and we'll be in massive trouble for what we've done. Don't call them and we've got two psychos who've already killed someone looking for us. Two psychos who know who we are. I look down at my phone. I write a text to Joe and Rabbit. **Where r u?**

As I send the message, I hear a noise and look out of the cracks in the window. It's Rabbit. He pulls the board away from the doorway and then a few seconds later he comes through.

'What the fuck!' he says as he sits down on a wooden box. 'What the fuck is happening?'

I shrug and shake my head.

'Those guys had a gun!' he says. 'They were shooting. I thought I was gonna die.'

Neither of us says anything for a bit. Rabbit takes out his phone, probably checking the message I just sent him.

'You know where Joe is?' Rabbit says.

I shake my head. 'No. He said they shot at him, but he's safe. Haven't heard from him since.'

Rabbit doesn't say anything for a while. He sighs, rubs his eyes, gets up and goes over to the window and then sits back down again. He's twitchy. Like I feel. He rubs his chin, thinking. 'What d'you think we should do?'

I shrug. 'I don't know.'

'I think we should call the police,' Rabbit says. He stands up again.

'No,' I say. 'We call the police and we're in trouble. We took the bag. We kept it. We spent the money. Sold the drugs. We handled the gun – a murder weapon. And we tried to hide it. I've got it in my pocket right now. They're not exactly just going to slap us on the wrists and let us go, are they? We could go to prison.'

'You dug up the gun?' Rabbit gets up. He kicks at the chair he's been sitting on. 'Argghh!' he shouts, frustrated. 'How the fuck did I end up in this situation?'

'Shh,' I say.

Rabbit leans in really close to my face. His face is full of fear and anger. 'You know what'll happen if we don't call the cops?' he whispers. 'We'll get killed. Those guys know where I live, for fuck's sake!'

I put my head in my hands. He's right.

Joe

Behind me I hear the two guys shout to each other, but I can't work out what they're saying. All I can concentrate on is getting as far away from them as I can. I keep my legs and arms pumping, literally willing myself forward.

BANG!

A gunshot. It makes me jump, but it misses me. I keep running, thinking about whether I should hide behind a tree or just keep going. If I try and hide, they'll find me sooner or later. I need to keep going. So I keep running. I have no idea where I am any more. I'm completely disorientated. But that's not important right now. Survival is the only thing I care about.

BANG!

My leg buckles underneath me. I fall to the ground. I'm hit. It feels like my foot has just exploded. I close my eyes and scream in pain. My hands automatically go down to my foot. It's warm and wet. I take my hands away and open my eyes, look at my hands. They're covered in blood. My blood. I shut my eyes and groan.

When I open them again, the world feels like it's swimming in front of me, like someone's got a big spoon and stirred up all the colours and sounds. I feel sick. I hear footsteps approach, but I can't tell where from. And then I see four legs standing in front of me. I look up. It's the two guys. They stand over me, angry. And I notice that the bald one has a gun in his hand, pointed at the ground. I stare at it, waiting for him to lift it and put me out of my misery. And as I do, tears start to form in my eyes and fall down my face.

'Not so fucking smart now, huh?' the bald guy says.

I shake my head. I don't want to do anything to provoke him. As I look at him, I notice a wound on the top of his head, a straight line going across that's dark red, like it's just starting to heal.

'Where's the rest of my fucking money and my skunk?' he says.

I shrug my shoulders. I open my mouth to reply, but

the words just stick in my throat. In my pocket, I feel my phone start to vibrate again.

'Where's your friends, kid?' the taller guy says.

'I don't know,' I say. It comes out shaky, full of tears.

'Course you do,' the shorter guy – the one with the gun – says. 'And if you want to live, you're gonna tell me where they are and where my money is, understand?'

I nod my head. In my pocket my mobile stops vibrating. There's a surge of pain in my foot. I wince and scream. I'm gonna bleed to death like this. My jeans are covered in blood. My trainer is saturated.

'Let's get him up,' the short guy says.

The taller guy bends down and picks me up, throws me over his shoulder and carries me back through the trees to the path, to Rabbit's car. They open the passenger door, pull the front seat forward and throw me in the back.

Ash

I take my phone out of my pocket. 'Joe still hasn't answered my bloody text,' I say.

Rabbit makes a noise, like he's sucking his lip. 'Why not?'

I make a face at Rabbit. 'How am I s'posed to know? What d'you think I am? Psychic?'

Rabbit tuts, but he doesn't say anything. He goes over to the window and peers out through the cracks. Then he takes his mobile out of his pocket. He looks at it and shakes his head.

'Come on, Joe . . .' I mutter under my breath. 'Come on.'

Rabbit walks back towards me. It's almost pitch

black in here now, but I can guess what his expression is. Worried and scared, like mine. Why won't Joe just let us know he's OK? I mean, it could be something as simple as his battery died, cos he's crap for that. Nearly as bad as me. Always forgets to charge his phone. And he's always saying he can't get a signal.

Rabbit looks at his phone. 'I think we should phone the cops,' he says. 'Joe might be in danger.'

I stare back at him.

'Forget about getting in trouble for the money and the gun and whatever. Joe could be in danger right now and there's fuck all we can do to help him. We need the police.'

I sigh. I'm scared. I'm fucked. I'm going to prison. And Joe needs us. 'Give it another minute,' I say. 'He'll probably come in through that door any second.'

Rabbit sighs and starts pacing around the room.

I put my elbows on my knees and my head in my hands and try and think. Only I can't think straight – there's too much going on in my head. Around me, I can hear Rabbit pacing, I can feel the air moving as he walks around the room, sighing and kicking at the floor, frustrated and angry and scared. And I still can't work out what it is I'm trying to think.

Rabbit stops pacing. 'Fuck it,' he says. 'I'm gonna do it. I'm gonna phone the cops.'

I sit up and look at him. I want to tell him not to,

that he'll land us all in the shit. But I can't. So I just sit there and watch as he taps 999 into his phone and then looks back at me. He presses Dial and holds the phone to his ear.

As he's waiting for an answer, my phone starts vibrating. I take it out of my pocket and look at the display. It's Joe.

I wave my hand at Rabbit and point to my phone. 'Rabbit!' I shout. 'Hang up! It's Joe!'

Rabbit stares back at me, the look of shock on his face lit up by his phone's display. He presses Cancel on his phone and slowly lowers his arm.

I press Answer and hold my phone to my ear. 'Joe! Where are you, man? Why didn't you answer my text?'

There's no answer at the other end, just background noise.

'Joe?'

'Hello?' It's not Joe's voice. It's gruffer, deeper. It's the voice I spoke to the other day, the one that I told where to look for the bag. They must have found Joe's phone. Shit.

'Where's Joe?'

There's no answer right away, just more background noise. Car doors shutting, mumbled voices, a moan. 'He's right here,' the voice says.

'What have you done with him?'

There's more noise in the background, another

moan. It sounds like Joe, like he's in pain or something. I look across the room at Rabbit. He's just staring back at me.

'Now it's time for you to listen to me,' the voice says. 'It's time to stop fucking about. Time to stop playing your stupid little games. Someone's already been hurt. And if I don't get the rest of my money and my skunk back soon, someone might just die. Do you understand?'

I take a deep breath. 'What do you mean, someone's already been hurt?'

'Your friend. Joe.'

'What have you done to him? Is he all right?'

'He's alive. He'll survive. As long as I get what's mine.'

'Let me speak to him,' I say. 'Please.'

There's just background noise at the other end of the phone again. Two muffled voices, not Joe's, though. The gruff voice comes back on. 'All right,' he says. 'You got ten seconds.'

More background noise.

'Ash?' says Joe. He sounds distant. Terrified. Like he's crying.

'Joe,' I say, 'are you all right? What have they done to you?'

Joe doesn't answer right away. He breathes shallow breaths, like he's in pain. 'They shot me.'

'What? They shot you? Where?'

'My foot,' he says. 'Listen, Ash. Do what they say, please. Whatever they say –'

And then there's a *clunk* and Joe's voice is gone.

'Joe?'

'You've had your chance to listen to your boyfriend,' says the voice. 'Now it's time for you to listen to me. If you want to see him again, you better do exactly what I say.'

'OK. What do you want us to do?'

Rabbit sits down on a box, still staring at me. He cups his face in his hands.

'First thing, kid,' the voice says. 'No cops. If you even think about calling the cops, your friend, little Joe, dies. Do you understand me?'

'OK. No police.'

'Good. Now, when you gave me my bag back, there was nearly three grand and a big bag of skunk missing. I want them back.'

'Right,' I say. 'Where d'you want us to bring it?'

There's no answer. I can't hear anything at the other end. Not even Joe moaning. The guy must have his hand over the phone or something. 'Right,' he says. 'I'll give you half an hour to go and find the rest of my money. And then you deliver it to me at nine thirty p.m. There's an industrial estate in Fayrewood. I want you to go right to the end of it. There's an empty unit. Number twelve. I'll be parked outside it in your friend's shitty brown car. You bring the money in a shopping bag and I'll give you your friend back.'

'OK. We'll be there.'

'You better be,' the voice says. 'And you better have every penny of my money. Your friend's life depends on it.'

And then the phone goes dead.

I put my phone back in my pocket. Rabbit stares at me, waiting for me to say something. How do I tell him what I've just heard?

'What is it? Is Joe all right?'

'No, they've got him. He's shot.'

Rabbit looks at me, wordless, shocked. He runs his hand through his hair. 'Let's call the police.' He takes his phone back out of his pocket.

I shake my head. 'Put your phone away,' I say. 'They said they'd kill him if we call the cops.'

Rabbit slowly puts his phone in his pocket. 'What do we do, then?'

I shrug. I feel useless. I feel like crying. 'They want the money. All of it.'

'We gave them the money already, though,' Rabbit says. 'Didn't we?'

I shake my head. 'Not exactly.'

'What the fuck?'

I take a deep breath. 'Me and Joe spent some of it,' I say.

Rabbit kind of stamps his foot and turns round on the spot, like he can't even look at me. After a second he turns back. 'How much?'

'Nearly a grand,' I say. 'Plus the money I gave my mum.'

'But . . . you said there was five hundred in the bag?'

'I lied.'

'Jesus,' Rabbit says. 'I don't believe this. So how short are we?'

I shrug. 'Nearly three grand.'

'For fuck's sake. What do we do?'

I shake my head, say nothing and think. 'We'll have to bluff them,' I say. 'Get together what we can and meet them. We'll take the gun, just in case. What else can we do?'

Rabbit doesn't answer. He just stands there, terrified, and nods his head.

Joe

The taller guy gets out of the passenger seat. He leans in and pulls it forward. 'Get out,' he says to me.

I look at him, trying to see if he's serious. My foot's pretty much hanging off – how the fuck am I meant to get out of the car? But he just looks back at me. He's expressionless, emotionless, as though he's doing something mundane like waiting for the kettle to boil, rather than kidnapping someone with a gunshot wound.

I swing my legs forward, so my feet are hanging out of the car door. I grab hold of the door frame and the seat, pull my weight forward and then put my left foot – my good foot – on the ground. As soon as I do, pain shoots from my right foot up through my leg. I wince and nearly lose my balance.

'I'll tell you what, son,' the bald guy says, getting out of the driver's seat. 'I hope you didn't get any blood on your mate's car seats.'

The tall one laughs. 'Yeah. Take it from me, son, blood's a bastard of a stain to get out!'

They both laugh while I stand there in agony, wishing I could die right now so I don't have to be here any more. What are they going to do to me? The shorter guy goes round to the boot and opens it.

'Get in here,' he says to me.

I don't move immediately. I keep hoping this is some kind of joke, that in a second they'll crack into a big smile and everything will be all right.

'Get a move on,' the bald guy barks at me.

I hold on to the car and hop round to the boot. With each hop and each landing, my right leg cries out in pain. I grit my teeth so tightly that I'm sure I can taste blood in my mouth. But I make it round to the back of the car. I can feel my right foot pulsing in pain. I close my eyes and bite my lip for a second. Then I look in the boot. It's tiny. And filthy. They can't really want me to get in there. I look at them.

'Please,' I say, and my voice shakes like I'm gonna cry, 'don't do this. There must be another way to do this.'

The bald guy shakes his head. He holds his gun up so I can see it. 'The only other way to end this is with one of these,' he says. 'The choice is yours.'

Then they both stare impatiently at me. I close my eyes and feel like crying. I wonder if I'm the first person they've ever put in a boot, even though I'm sure I already know the answer. And I wonder what happened to the others who they put in the boots of cars. I'm guessing that they're not around to tell the tale.

The taller guy puts his hands on my shoulders and half lifts, half shoves me over into the boot. I land on my shoulder. The two of them pick up my legs and push them into the car, almost fold me into the space. The boot slams shut.

It's pitch black and it smells kind of mouldy. My legs and arms are all squashed up. I try not to think about what this is doing to my foot. Outside, I hear muffled voices and then footsteps on the gravel as they walk to the front of the car. The suspension makes the car wobble as they get in and slam their doors shut. The engine starts with a whine and a splutter. A second later, the car lurches forward and I get thrown against the back of the boot. My foot smacks against the inside of the boot, sending another wave of excruciating pain through my body.

I feel sick. I think it's the pain that's doing it. Or maybe it's cos I must be losing blood. I mean, my trainer feels absolutely soaked through. I wonder how long it will take before I just bleed to death if I don't get to a hospital. And I start to panic. I think back to the first aid we did back when I was in the Scouts. They said you have to put pressure on a wound to try and stop it from bleeding, to slow it down. I guess my trainer is kind of doing that already, though it's already saturated with blood. I rack my brains for something else that I can use. My hoodie. It was my favourite, but that hardly matters now. It's gonna get covered in blood, but it might save my life. For a bit, anyway. Until Ash and Rabbit turn up without the money and the two guys kill us all for wasting their time.

I struggle to get my hoodie off. It's not easy cramped up in the boot of a car. I have to bend my arms into all kinds of painful positions behind my head. But eventually I manage. And then I reach right down to my foot. I put the body of the hoodie underneath and wrap the sleeves round and round, pulling it as tight as I can. And when I've done that, I tie the sleeves in a double knot on the top of my foot. Straight away it feels better, like I still have a foot. I could be just imagining it, being hopeful, but I'm sure it feels like it's bleeding less.

I should try and think about something else apart from the pain. That way I might be able to fool my body that this isn't happening, that there is no pain. I think about how I could get out of this situation. If there is a way out. The two guys took my phone and didn't give it back. They're not stupid. Anyway, even if I did have my phone, I wouldn't know where they're taking me. Which makes me think. If I concentrate on the movement of the car, I might be able to work out where the car is taking me. Right now we're still in the forest, I'm sure of it. It feels bumpy. And the wheels sound like they're crushing stones underneath them. Every now and then the car turns right or left and I try and picture where we are. After a couple of minutes, it stops. Just for a second or two. When it starts moving again, it wheel-spins and turns sharply to the left. I get thrown around the boot again and knock my foot. I wince.

But instead of focussing on the pain, I focus on the movement of the car. The engine of Rabbit's car whines as it accelerates, but the ride is much smoother now. We must be on tarmac. On the main road, I reckon. We must be on our way to the industrial estate, like the bald guy told Ash.

I wonder what'll be waiting for us there. Whether Ash and Rabbit have phoned the police. They could be there right now, waiting to ambush us. I kind of hope they are. It's got to be the best chance we have. The police'll know what to do in a situation like this. Whereas me and Ash and Rabbit . . . well, we're just kids. We're rabbits in the headlights. We can't handle this. We'll get ourselves killed.

And I start thinking about what they said, about the missing money – three grand. I start to work it out in my head, how much I spent and how much Ash spent. And at the absolute most, I reckon it works out at five or six hundred pounds. And I don't know what to think. Are they trying to get more money out of us? Cos if they are, none of us are gonna have that sort of money lying around. Or maybe there's something that Ash hasn't told me. It wouldn't be the first time.

I feel the car go round a bend in the road. Another surge of pain in my foot as it gets bashed against the inside of the boot. I try and imagine where we are. Maybe the bend in the road near the petrol station, going out of town. Or maybe the mini roundabout. It's hard to tell. I've completely lost my bearings. It's hard to concentrate on anything when your foot feels the way mine does.

I start thinking again, to keep my mind from the pain. And I wonder what would happen if Rabbit and Ash called the police – whether we'd get into trouble for what we've done. We did some stuff we shouldn't have, sure. Illegal stuff. But nothing that bad, really. It's not like we killed anyone. All we did was find a bag and make some bad decisions. Everything the two guys have done surely outweighs all the bad stuff we've done. They take that sort of thing into account when they decide whether to press charges against you. Or at least, they do on TV.

But the more I think about it, the more I think that Ash wouldn't call the police. Calling the police, asking for help isn't the kind of thing he does. Even in a situation like this. A situation where we might all die.

The car goes round another bend. I manage to brace myself just in time to stop myself from getting thrown against the side of the boot. That one *must* be the mini roundabout. Which means that we'll be at the industrial estate any minute now. There's a knot in my stomach. I feel like I might throw up. Is this how everyone feels before they die? I thought you were supposed to see angels, or find the answers to all life's questions, or something. But not me. I just feel like curling up in a ball and crying. I want my mum and dad. Even my sister.

I start to think about what they'll think when they find out what happened, the secrets that I've kept from them. They'll be disappointed in me. And they are gonna find out now, aren't they? One way or another. Everything's gonna come out now. There's no way I can hide this – the fact that I have a bullet hole in my foot – if I even get out alive.

The car turns another corner. Another jolt of pain

343

sears through my foot, my leg. And then another turn almost straight after. And another. The car reverses, turns again. And then it stops and the engine is switched off. And then nothing. The car just sits there.

Ash

We come out the other side of the woods and on to the main road. A car goes past with its lights on as me and Rabbit run along the side of the road.

'I need to stop at my place,' I say to Rabbit. 'I should be able to find most of the money and I've still got a lot of the skunk.'

'All right,' he says. He looks at his watch. 'We have to be quick, though. We don't have much time.'

A minute later and we're outside my house. There's no car in the drive. The curtains are all drawn and through them I can see the glow of the downstairs lights.

I turn to Rabbit. 'Wait out here,' I say. 'Won't be a minute.'

I take a deep breath, step up to the front door and unlock it. As soon as I get inside, I walk straight through to the kitchen to the bag for life where Mum keeps all the carrier bags. I grab one and turn, and suddenly Dad's there in front of me, coming through from the lounge, gripping a half-full tumbler of whisky. The side of his face is red and scratched.

'Ashley,' he says. He sounds surprised.

'I haven't got time,' I say. 'Where's Mum?'

Dad shrugs. He's pissed. 'I was gonna ask you the same question.'

'What?'

'I don't know where she is,' Dad says. 'Crazy bitch hit me, packed a bag and then took off with my bloody car. She's not answering her phone.'

I stand there for a second and stare at him. Fuck.

'I need to talk to her, Ashley,' Dad says. 'Why don't you call her on your phone? She'd answer your call.'

I shake my head, barge past him and run upstairs.

'Ashley, come down here this instant!' Dad shouts.

I ignore him and go into his and Mum's room. I stand and stare for a second. It's a mess in here. Mum's clothes are all over the floor. I try and work out where she would have put the money I sent her. She would have hidden it somewhere, I'm sure. I go over to the chest of drawers near the window. Most of the drawers are already open. I search through them, but there's nothing there, just Mum's clothes. So I go over to her bedside table and rummage around. Still nothing. I try the built-in wardrobe, look among the shoe boxes stacked at the bottom.

'What are you doing?' Dad says.

I get up and turn round. 'Nothing,' I say. 'Leave me alone.'

Dad stands there, staring at me. 'Get out of my wardrobe!' he says.

I sigh. 'Have you seen an envelope?'

'An envelope?'

I nod. 'Yeah. Mum got it in the post the other day.'

Dad shrugs. 'What kind of envelope?'

'Forget it,' I say. I'm not gonna find the money now. I don't have time to search everywhere. Maybe Mum's taken it with her anyway.

Dad moves unsteadily out of my way as I leave his and Mum's room. I hear him follow me out along the landing. I go into my room and slam the door closed. I swing a kick at my drum stool. It falls over, smacks into the bass drum. For a split second I look at the snare drum, sizing it up for a kick as well. But I manage to stop myself. I don't have time to waste.

I go over to my desk and grab an A4 pad of paper, tear it into quarters and then stuff it into the carrier bag. When I'm done, I open the drawer of my bedside cabinet and take out the money that I kept aside. Four hundred pounds in fifties, twenties and tens. I pile it on top of the ripped-up notepad paper. I frown. It's not gonna fool them. Not for long anyway. But maybe it'll buy us some time. Maybe.

I grab the rest of the skunk and put it in the carrier bag. Then I roll up the bag so it's just like a small package, hide it in my hoodie and go back out of my door, along the landing and on to the stairs. And below me on the stairs is Dad. He's looking straight at me. I stop where I am.

'Come downstairs and talk to me,' Dad says. 'At least let me explain, Ashley.'

I shake my head. 'I'm going out,' I say. And I start walking down the stairs again.

Dad moves into the centre of the stairs, blocking my way. 'Ashley, please,' he says. 'This is more important than going out with your mates. This is your family.'

I snort with laughter. 'Like you'd know about family,' I say. 'Like you give a shit. Get out of my way.'

I step down. Dad still doesn't budge. He spreads his arms across from the banisters to the wall. I try and stay calm.

'Ashley?'

I look down at the stairs for a second, then close my eyes and take a deep breath. But it doesn't help. Instead, anger surges through my body into my chest and then my throat. And before I can think about what

I'm doing, I push Dad in the chest. He falls down the stairs – four or five of them – and lands at the bottom in a heap, still clutching his glass, his face wet with spilled whisky and blood from the scratch on his face.

And all I can do is stare at him as he lies there pathetically in a heap. He's not hurt, he's just drunk. And I hate him.

I rush down the rest of the steps, stopping at the bottom where Dad's still lying. He pushes himself up on his hands and looks at me. I get an overwhelming urge to kick him in the ribs or spit on him or something. But I don't.

I leave the house, slam the stupid bloody plastic door behind me. It doesn't shut and flies back open.

'You OK?' Rabbit says. 'What happened?'

'Let's go,' I say. We go and grab a couple of bikes from the shed – me on my dad's and Rabbit on my old bike.

Joe

I've been lying here squashed up in this boot, trying to take my mind off the pain and what's about to happen. I've been thinking about everything that led up to this, to me being here in the boot of Rabbit's car with a hole in my bloody foot. Thinking right back to last Friday night, when we found the car and the money. Cos that's what it all boils down to, isn't it? That moment. The moment we picked up the bag, we sealed our fate. That's what led us here.

But what if we hadn't? What if we'd made different decisions? Like last Friday. If I'd decided not to go out, down the rec, none of this would have happened. I would never have gone back home through the woods, never have found the car, never have found the bag. All that would have happened is that I'd have seen the stuff on telly about the dead body in the flats and thought it was weird, that stuff like that doesn't normally happen in places like this. But it would have had nothing to do with me. Nothing at all.

Someone else would have found the car and the bag, someone walking their dog the next morning. And I bet they'd have got straight on the phone to the police, like my gut instinct told me to. If only I'd listened to it. If only I'd had a signal on my phone.

But instead I'm here, feeling sick, scared that I might die. I'd give anything to go back in time, to change the decisions I made, to have stayed at home last Friday, to not have seen the bag, to not be here now. Anything.

I don't know if we can make this right now. Well, I mean, I know we can't. I've got a bullet hole in my foot. If I don't die first, I've got to get to a hospital. And then they'll ask all sorts of questions. We won't be able to hide it. The best we can hope to do is to escape with our lives. And the only way we're gonna do that is by making the right decisions from now on.

I press the button on the side of my watch and the digital screen lights up. The car's been stopped for more than ten minutes now. And the doors have all stayed shut. They must be waiting for Ash and Rabbit.

Ash

We cycle along the main road without a single word or even a look at each other. What is there to say now?

We pass the wall where all the chavs usually hang out. Only they're not there tonight. For a second, I wonder why not – they're always there – but then I remember the party. It'll still be going at Rabbit's house. It'll probably have gone crazy there by now. Everyone will have trashed the place. Not that it matters. Nothing does really. Only what's about to happen.

We go straight over the mini roundabout, past the turning to the supermarket on the left and keep going out of town on the main road. A little way up the road we see the sign pointing off to the right: Fernside Industrial Estate. I stop by the side of the road and turn to look at Rabbit. He looks as nervous as I feel. He's white as a sheet.

Without a word, we check the traffic and pedal across the road into the industrial estate. As soon as we're in, we stop by a big brown sign that has all the units listed on it – unit number and name of the business. Next to number twelve there's a blank space where the company name should be.

My brain kind of freezes. All I can think is that I don't want to do this. I want to turn round before they even see me and cycle as far away from here as possible. I want to escape from everything. To start running and never stop.

But Joe's with them and he's been shot. I can't leave him. I got him into this mess. If it wasn't for me he'd be at Rabbit's party right now, off his head on half a cider and a couple of tokes off a spliff. But he's not.

I put my hood up as we start pedalling again along the empty road that runs through the industrial estate. All the units are shut up. There are street lamps on, bathing the pavement in a dim orange light. There's no one around. I look at the numbers on the signs outside the units as we pass them. 2 . . . 4 . . . 6 . . . 8 . . . 10 . . . And then number 12.

Rabbit's crappy car is parked on the forecourt outside the unit. As I cycle across the road towards it, I feel the gun in my pocket. It makes me feel weird, makes me realise how serious this situation is. But it's reassuring that it's there. Just in case.

I stare at Rabbit's car as we approach it. The two guys are squashed up in the front seats like the car's too small for them. They watch us as we get closer, their faces set in stony stares. I can't see Joe, though, and it's difficult to tell whether he's in the back of the car or not cos the two guys are blocking my view.

I put my foot down on the ground to brake when I'm just a few metres away. A couple of seconds later, Rabbit pulls up alongside me. We let the bikes fall to the ground. And then we stand and stare at the guys in the car, who just stare straight back at us. You can tell from their eyes that they mean business. They're cold and emotionless. But still, I stare back at them. I don't back down and neither do they. Nobody gives an inch.

Inside the car, the bald guy says something and then both guys move to open their doors. They get out slowly, stretching, adjusting their belts, dusting the arms of their coats, like they're stopping at a service station for a toilet break rather than holding a hostage. The bald guy coughs then spits on to the ground in front of him. I look at them both, at their hands, expecting to see a gun. But their hands are empty. Their guns must be hidden. In their waistbands, probably. I wonder if they know I'm armed. I put my hand in my pocket, feel the pistol, put my finger on the safety catch. I pause for a second, feel the catch between my fingers. For a second I think of flicking the safety off, but then the thought goes through my mind that the gun could go off as I walk and blow my leg off. I take my hand out of my pocket.

The bald guy steps towards Rabbit and me. He smiles. A false smile. 'So, which one of you is Mr Lazy Eyes?' he says. He laughs to himself.

I nod ever so slightly. I say nothing. I stare back at him, trying not to let on that I'm shitting myself here.

Slightly behind the bald guy, the other one just stands there. He folds his arms. The expression on his face is the kind that says he'd snap our limbs into tiny pieces in a second if we were to try anything.

'You know, you're lucky I'm a patient sort of man,' the bald one says. 'You're lucky I haven't killed you after the runaround you boys have given me.'

I still don't say anything. I just breathe deeply. I shift my feet slightly and the gun rubs against my leg. I could pull it out right now and finish this in a second.

Two shots. But I don't move. I keep my hands by my sides, the rolled-up carrier bag full of torn-up paper and banknotes and weed in my left hand.

'So,' says the bald one, 'is that my money or what?' He isn't smiling any more. He has the same deadly serious look on his face as the other guy.

I nod. 'Yeah,' I say. My voice chooses this precise moment to make me sound like I'm a thirteen-year-old with a breaking voice. I clear my throat. 'What have you done with our friend?'

The bald one smiles again. 'He's safe.'

'Where is he? I want to see him.'

The taller guy shakes his head. 'Nah,' he says. 'You give us the money then you see your friend. Understand?'

I don't answer. I turn and look at Rabbit. He stares back at me, frozen in fear. I look at the two guys again, trying to work out whether I believe them or not. Whether this is a trick. Whether they even still have Joe.

No one says anything for what feels like hours. The wind gusts across the industrial estate, blowing leaves and litter around. From the main road I hear a souped-up engine accelerate and then slow back down again with a roar and a splutter.

'Right, stop fucking around. I want my money,' the bald guy says. 'Then we can all go home. Give it here.'

I shake my head. 'Not till I see my friend is safe,' I say. 'I don't believe you've got him.'

'For fuck's sake,' the bald one says. 'Who do you think you are? Some kind of gangster?'

He beckons for us to walk round to the back of the car. Me and Rabbit follow. The bald guy opens the boot slowly. It's dark and I can't see a thing in there to begin with. But as the dim orange light makes its way in, I see a body lying curled up, and I feel like vomiting. It's Joe. For a second I think he's dead, but then he tries to sit up. He looks out at us all. He looks awful. His face is pale and drained. And then I notice his foot. He's wrapped it in a jumper, but the blood is soaking through it.

'Fuck, Joe! Are you all right?'

He nods and grimaces. 'Have you brought everything?'

'Yeah,' I say.

Joe looks at me with a confused expression. And I know what he must be thinking: *how have you got their money when we spent it?* But then he closes his eyes and grimaces again and his hand shoots down to his foot.

'Are you OK, Joe?'

He nods and opens his eyes again. He looks kind of vacant, as though he's gonna lose consciousness. And I know that what he needs is a hospital. Fuck the rest of this. The most important thing is that he could bleed to death if he doesn't go to a hospital soon.

I look at the bald guy, who's still holding the boot open.

'Can we get him out of there?' I say.

The bald guy shakes his head. He pushes Joe back down and shuts the boot.

We walk round to the front of the car. And as we do, I put my hand in my pocket again. I put my hand on the gun and flick the safety catch. Off.

'He needs to go to hospital,' I say. 'He's gonna die if he doesn't.'

'Well then, maybe you should hurry up and give me my fucking money before it's too late for your friend.'

I take a deep breath. It sounds stupid to even say it, but I suddenly realise that we've been so naive. All this time we've been trusting some gangsters who have already killed someone to give us back our friend, to let us go safely. And there's no way that's gonna happen, is there? They'll kill us all. They know that if we take Joe to the hospital with a gunshot wound, the police will be on to them. They're gonna make sure we don't speak to anyone. They're gonna stop us the only way they know. With a gunshot. The only way out of this situation is in a coffin. Full stop.

I turn and look at Rabbit for a fraction of a second.

He still looks terrified, like he can't deal with this.

The bald guy makes a movement, which I see out of the corner of my eye. I turn to see him pointing a gun at me.

'Let's stop playing now, kids,' he says. 'Give me my money and we can all be on our way. You can get your friend to a doctor, and I can get out of your lives for ever. No one else gets hurt.'

I nod my head. In my pocket I feel my phone start to vibrate. I try to ignore it, take a couple of deep breaths, take a second to think. I hold up the carrier bag for them to see.

The two gangsters follow it with their eyes. 'Give it to me,' the bald one says. He still has the gun pointed at my head. Only now his eyes are looking at the bag and not at me.

I toss the bag at them, throwing it high so they have to look up to follow it. And as they're watching it fly through the air I pull the gun from my pocket and aim at the bald guy. Without stopping to think I pull the trigger.

BANG!

I judder backwards with the force of the shot. And I can't believe what I've just done.

The bald guy collapses to the ground, a bullet hole ripped through his leg. The gun drops from his hand

and clatters as it hits the ground. And in that same second – as he watches his partner collapse to the floor – the taller guy reacts and reaches for his own gun. I aim again and pull the trigger.

BANG!

The bullet hits him in the side, in the stomach. He falls to the ground next to the bald guy.

I stand and stare for a fraction of a second, not believing what I've just done, wishing I could suck the bullets back out of them. But then something in my head snaps me out of it. I run straight over to the two guys, kick their guns away from them, behind me, towards where Rabbit is. They fly across the concrete, making a metallic scraping noise.

I take a step back, keeping the gun aimed at them all the time. They lie there, slumped, bleeding. I concentrate on moving my gun through the air, pointing it at one of them and then the other. They stare straight back at me, their eyes cold, like they're storing the image of my face away for future use.

'Put the gun down, kid,' the bald guy says in a croaky voice.

I sense something behind me. I turn my head. It's Rabbit. He's got his head in his hands. He looks like he's ready to pull his hair out. 'Fuck,' he says, staring at the bodies on the ground. 'What did you do that for? You shot them.'

I look back at the two of them, slumped against each other, leaking blood over the concrete forecourt.

'Phone the police,' I say to Rabbit. 'And an ambulance too. Do it now.'

Joe

As the boot slowly opens, I can't bear to look. I close my eyes, say a prayer in my head that this will be quick, that I won't feel anything.

Then I hear a voice. 'Joe, come on, let's get you out of there.'

I open my eyes and see Rabbit standing over the boot. A wave of utter relief washes over me. 'You're alive,' I say.

Rabbit doesn't say anything. He doesn't smile or nod or anything. He just moves round to the side of the boot, grabs me under the arms and pulls me up. I scream as pain surges through my leg. Rabbit stops for a second and looks at me, still saying nothing, before he pulls me again. I grind my teeth, close my eyes as he drags me out. I try and put the weight on my good leg, put my foot down on the ground.

In a couple of seconds I'm out. Straight away I lie down on the concrete, eyes closed, biting my lip so I don't scream. I wait a few seconds for the worst of the pain to pass. I sit up.

'What happened?' I say. 'Are you OK? I heard shots.'

Rabbit nods. He looks at my foot, at the jumper covering it. He undoes the knot and examines it. I look away. I don't want to see what my foot looks like. It feels like it's pretty messed up. 'We're OK,' he says.

I look around. We're on a forecourt in the industrial estate, by the look of it. It's dark. There are street lamps on, casting a kind of dim glow around the place. And then I see Ash, standing a couple of metres from the car, pointing a gun at the two guys who were in the BMW. They're both lying kind of slumped against each other and Rabbit's car. There's blood leaking from them both, forming into glossy pools on the concrete. One of them is saying something to Ash. I can't hear what, but he looks angry and he keeps grimacing in pain.

Rabbit ties the jumper back around my foot and then stands up. He stares across at Ash, at the two guys, like he can't believe it either. He looks scared.

'What happened?'

Rabbit looks at me. His eyes look weird, like he's not really there. He rubs his face with his hands and gets a smear of my blood on his forehead. 'Ash did it,' he says. 'He shot them.' Rabbit shakes his head. He paces around for a few seconds. He looks like he doesn't want to believe what's happened. 'Fuck, man. They pulled a gun. They were going to shoot us. He had to shoot them first.'

And we sit on the concrete in silence, in the orange light of the street lamps. The whole time, Rabbit doesn't look up. I look at Ash pointing the gun at the two guys, ignoring what they're saying. And I can't work out whether I feel grateful that he shot the guys or not. Maybe he saved our lives, but maybe he just screwed the rest of our lives up. After a few seconds, though, I have to lie down again. I feel weird, like I'm gonna pass out or something.

'Rabbit,' Ash shouts over, 'you should go. This had nothing to do with you.'

There's a long pause before Rabbit says, 'No way. I'm staying till the ambulance gets here.'

And then no one says anything for ages. I close my eyes and try not to think about the pain, about the state of my foot. Nothing happens till I hear a siren out on the main road. It sounds like it's heading in this direction. I think about sitting up to watch for it. Except when I try to sit up, I physically can't do it. So

I just lie down propped up on my elbow and wait. And in about twenty seconds, the siren gets really close. It sounds like it must be on the industrial estate by now. I open my eyes, look across at Ash. He's slowly stepping backwards, towards us, keeping the gun trained on the two guys. As he gets over to us, he holds the gun out for Rabbit.

'I have to go,' he says. 'I have to find my mum.'

'What?' Rabbit says. He sounds angry. He doesn't take the gun.

'I have to.'

'What about us?' Rabbit says. 'You can't leave us to explain this!'

I think of things that I want to say to Ash, but I can't open my mouth to say them.

'Blame it all on me. Tell the police it was all my fault,' Ash says. 'Say you didn't know anything about it.'

Flashing blue light starts to bounce off the walls and pavements of the industrial estate. The sirens are almost deafening now.

Ash drops the gun and runs past the two guys and the car and away towards the wire-mesh fence at the end of the industrial estate. I watch as he climbs over the fence and falls into the field on the other side. He gets up and starts running again.

Seconds later I hear the roar of an engine and then the screech of tyres. I hear a car door open and footsteps on the forecourt. Over in the field, I watch Ash's back disappear into the darkness. I lie back down, take a deep breath and close my eyes.

My Inspiration for IN THE BAG

The idea for *In the Bag* came to me as I was walking home one day and a police car screeched to a halt on some wasteground nearby. I turned to see the police chasing a man. The guy on the run had a holdall, which he threw away as he was chased. The police ignored the bag and continued chasing him. And I started to wonder whether the police had even noticed the bag and what would happen to it. What if someone found it? What would be inside? And if, as I assumed, it was money, would whoever found the bag keep it or hand it over to the police? I wondered whether anybody would be able to keep a secret that big, or whether it would slowly eat away at them.

The idea of stumbling across something so life changing has always appealed to me. In fact, many of my favourite books and films are based on that very idea – *Millions*, *Fargo*, *Shallow Grave* and *A Simple Plan*, to name but a few. I couldn't resist writing my own story about a bag of money and the dangers that are associated with it.

I hope you enjoy reading it.

Jim Carrington

Check out the **Jim Carrington Fan Page** on **Facebook**

Read on for a taster of
Inside My Head
also by Jim Carrington . . .

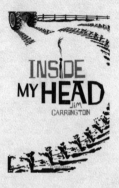

PAUL KNAGGS looks forward to school.
Because at school he can rip Gary Wood to shreds.

And GARY just takes it – usually.

DAVID is Knaggs's friend.
He does what Knaggs says – usually.

ZOË has moved from London to the middle of nowhere.
As far as she's concerned, life is over.
And then she meets the school loner, Gary.

GARY – KNAGGS – DAVID – ZOË.

When their stories collide, things get messy.

David

I'm already on question four as the bell goes.

'Hand in your books when you've finished,' Mr H calls over the noise. 'Then you can leave.'

Mills and me hand our books in and walk out of the lab, to the cloakroom.

About thirty seconds later, Knaggs joins us. 'D'you see Wood?' he says. 'I thought he was gonna start blubbing!'

I nod my head. 'Yeah, I know,' I say. 'He looked like he was gonna explode.'

'Leave it now, though,' Mills says. 'You know what he's like.'

I nod.

Knaggs shrugs. 'He won't do anything. He's a pussy!'

No one answers him. I avoid Knaggs's eyes.

We all set about looking for our blazers and bags on the floor of the cloakroom. I find my blazer, brush the dust off it and start looking for my bag.

Then there's a noise. *SMACK!* Loud and shocking.

The whole place goes silent and we all turn to look. Knaggs is lying on the floor of the cloakroom, holding the side of his face. His mouth is open. He looks stunned. For a second, I'm confused. But then my brain starts to fill in the missing parts and I look around for Wood. But he's not there. The door out of the cloakroom swings shut.

We all crowd round Knaggs.

Mr Moore comes and gets me out of literacy, next lesson. He doesn't say what it's about. He just walks me through the empty corridors in silence. But it's obvious what he wants me for.

When we get to his office, I expect to see Knaggs sitting there. But he isn't. Neither's Wood.

'Take a seat, David,' Mr Moore says. He points at a comfy green chair.

I sit down in it and sink back. But I feel awkward, so I sit up straight instead. My hands are sweaty. My heart's pounding.

Mr Moore starts off, going on about how I'm a responsible boy and that he trusts me to tell the truth and all that stuff. I just sit there feeling weird. See, I know what he's gonna ask me to do. He wants me to point the finger. He wants me to grass someone up. Knaggs or Wood. It's what teachers always want – some mug like me to make their job easier. I have a decision to make, I know. I can tell him the truth and keep the teachers' rules. But the thing is, then I'd be breaking the kid rules. I'd be breaking the biggest kid rule of all: grassing up my best mate. Or I can lie. It's the kind of choice where I have no choice.

'Tell me what happened in the science lab, David,' Mr Moore says.

I sit and think for a moment. The truth's easy. I know exactly what happened. We were messing about all lesson, like normal, and Knaggs started taking the mick out of Wood. The rest of us just encouraged him to do it. But Knaggs pushed it too far. Anyone could see how angry Wood was getting – he was about to explode. And then Wood went mental. But I can't say any of that, not the stuff that actually happened. Knaggs would get into trouble. I'm gonna have to lie, bend the truth a little. Otherwise my life won't be worth living. I shift uncomfortably in my seat. I've got a nervous guilty feeling in my stomach and I haven't even started lying yet.

'Was there an argument, David?' Mr Moore says. 'Tell me what you remember . . .'

I look up at him. He's looking straight at me, almost smiling but not quite. I take a deep breath. 'It started when Gary came into science late, sir,' I say. No lies yet but my heart's still beating like crazy. 'Gary and Knaggs – I mean, Paul Knaggs – well, they were having a laugh, taking the mickey out of each other, just winding each other up.' My voice is shaking slightly. It doesn't sound like me talking.

Mr Moore picks a notebook up off his desk and then a pen. He writes something down. And then he stops and looks up at me again. He smiles. 'It was both of them, you say?'

I nod.

Mr Moore makes more notes. Then he looks up at me. 'OK. How were they winding each other up, David?'

I look down at my feet. 'Don't know. Just the usual, really. They always do it. Just calling each other names and that. It was nothing serious, sir. It was just a bit of give and take.'

I look up. Mr Moore's writing more things in his notebook and nodding his head. Over his shoulder I can see a signed cricket bat and an old photo of the school team. I stare at them. God, I wish I was outside playing cricket instead of sitting here.

'Go on,' Mr Moore says.

I look back at him with a start. I must look guilty as hell. So I look at my shoes again. See, I'm a rubbish liar. People can see it in my eyes straight away. I can't hide it. 'Well, then we all got on with our work. Tried to get it all finished before the end of the lesson. Except Gary. He just sort of sat there and stared at the desk. He looked angry. And then he tried to start it all up again,' I say. And I hate myself for saying it. I think of Wood sitting there in the lab, with that angry face, taking it all. I should be telling Mr Moore about that. But I can't. I can't grass on Knaggs. That's the rules. The kid rules. He's my mate. I have to stick up for him. 'Gary kept trying to start it all off again, calling Paul short and that. And so Paul took the mickey back a bit. And that's when Gary started to look *really* angry, like he couldn't handle it any more.'

Mr Moore raises his eyebrows. 'I see,' he says. 'Can you remember exactly what was said?'

I stare back at him. The 'sort of' smile has gone from his face. He looks serious now. I feel like he's about to rumble me. I shake my head. 'Not exactly, sir,' I say. I look up at the cricket bat again, to avoid looking in his eyes. 'Gary was taking the mickey out of Paul for being short. And Paul was taking the mickey back, saying Gary's head looks like a cheese puff. And then Gary just got really angry. He said he was gonna kill Paul – that sort of stuff.'

Mr Moore raises his eyebrows again and notes something else down in his book. He underlines it three times, then looks back at me. 'You're sure that's what he said, David . . . ?'

I nod. 'Yeah.' My heart's thumping so hard I can hear it in my ears. I feel sick. I want to be out of this room.

'Absolutely sure . . . ?'

I take a breath. 'Yes.'

'Thank you, David,' Mr Moore says. And then he shows me to the door.

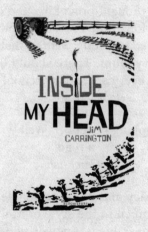

AVAILABLE NOW

Praise for **Inside My Head** by Jim Carrington:

'I loved it and you should go read it'
Bloggers Heart Books

'A thought-provoking read'
Bliss

'Witty and hard-hitting dialogue and a compellingly
written storyline'
Irish Post

'Claustrophobic and unbearably tense, it's extremely
compelling and gives a good deal of pause for thought'
The Bookbag

'One of the most thought-provoking and compelling books
I have read for a long time . . . This book is utterly believable . . . and it is so perfectly written that you actually feel
the sting of every taunt. There should be a copy of this
book in every secondary school library'
Book Zone 4 Boys

'A thought-provoking novel . . . Well written and worth
a read'
Chicklish

'A very, very pacy and unputdownable contemporary
novel . . . Very much in the style of Melvin Burgess and
Kevin Brooks, this is a powerful debut novel'
Love Reading 4 Kids

'Easy to relate to and impossible to put down'
Armadillo